4-13

RIT.
h e

MADSELIN

Also by Norah Lofts

THE CLAW
THE OLD PRIORY
THE WAYSIDE TAVERN
THE DAY OF THE
   BUTTERFLY
THE HAUNTING OF GAD'S HALL
GAD'S HALL
DOMESTIC LIFE IN ENGLAND
QUEENS OF ENGLAND
THE HOMECOMING
HAUNTINGS—IS THERE
   ANYBODY THERE?
KNIGHT'S ACRE
CROWN OF ALOES
NETHERGATE
OUT OF THE DARK
A ROSE FOR VIRTUE
LOVERS ALL UNTRUE
THE KING'S PLEASURE
THE LOST QUEEN
HOW FAR TO BETHLEHEM?
THE CONCUBINE
THE HOUSE AT SUNSET

THE HOUSE AT OLD VINE
THE TOWN HOUSE
HEAVEN IN YOUR HAND
SCENT OF CLOVES
AFTERNOON OF AN AUTOCRAT
WINTER HARVEST
ELEANOR THE QUEEN
BLESS THIS HOUSE
THE LUTE PLAYER
A CALF FOR VENUS
SILVER NUTMEG
TO SEE A FINE LADY
JASSY
I MET A GYPSY
HERE WAS A MAN
WHITE HELL OF PITY
REQUIEM FOR IDOLS
  and YOU'RE BEST ALONE
COLIN LOWRIE
BLOSSOM LIKE THE ROSE
HESTER ROOM
THE BRITTLE GLASS
THE GOLDEN FLEECE

With Margery Weiner

ETERNAL FRANCE

madselin

NORAH LOFTS

DOUBLEDAY & COMPANY, INC.
GARDEN CITY, NEW YORK
1983

Library of Congress Cataloging in Publication Data
Lofts, Norah, 1904–
  Madselin.

    1. Great Britain—History—Norman period, 1066–
1154—Fiction. I. Title.
PR6023.O35M3 1983   823'.912
ISBN 0-385-18103-5
Library of Congress Catalog Card Number 81-43769

MADSELIN

CHAPTER ONE

"The Abbess herself is against your going," Hild said at last. She had exhausted all her own arguments and hoped that this reference to accredited authority would do what she had failed to do.

"I know that, not being an idiot or blind," Madselin said. "But I am not yet under her rule." She looked about her and thought—And I hope never to be.

This, the better of the convent's two guest chambers, was about nine feet square, with a floor of bare earth and walls of undressed flint; it had a doorway but no door and the window opening was at the moment covered by the stiff hide of a young calf, into which, at the shoulders, two holes had been burned so that it could be suspended from wooden pegs driven into the wall. Every so often a gust of wind struck this make-shift shutter so that it swung inwards with a creak and a groan; each time some snow whispered in, it lay on the floor and it did not melt. The room held two beds, wooden frames set on roughly hewn legs, with rope lashed from top to bottom and from side to side and mattresses which were merely sacks stuffed with mouldy straw. There was also a stool and in a niche in the wall a candlestick, holding a thin, crooked candle made of fat so inferior, so ill-prepared, that there was still some salt in it; when the flame touched a grain it spat and flickered, burned blue, threatened to fail altogether. Everything in the house was equally poor and mean and comfortless. Imagine spending the rest of one's life here! The rest of one's life. A jolting thought. The rest of one's life might mean a day, or two or three. In the last sixteen months so many horrible things had happened: people killed or maimed, for no apparent reason; homes set on fire and people, even professed religious, turned into the roads and the woods to fare as best they could. How long could one live, out of doors, in this weather? If the new man at Bradwald for spite, or in a moment of sportive drunkenness, demolished this little house, how long would the rest of one's life be?

It was difficult, even now, to realize that the future—that vague tract of time, stretching ahead checkered with predictability, uncertainty, hope, activity, the future that one spoke of when one said, "Next year," or even, very occasionally, "When I am old"—had suddenly ceased to exist.

Religious people, of course, had always said that the brevity of life and the imminence of death must be remembered and each day ordered as though it were one's last. Yet now, with disaster and possible death threatening, the Abbess and those she ruled seemed no less fearful than ordinary people, no more resigned. They still hoped that by lying low they might escape.

And that, until Monday, two days ago, had been a hope shared by the whole of the Rinland.

Hild said, "Then if you are still set, I'll brush your hair. Though with this wind blowing . . ."

"I shall wear my hood."

"And nothing will move you?"

"Nothing. Talk is wasted, Hild. And I have thinking to do."

She thought of the Rinland, her home, that little isolated area enclosed by the bend of the river, sharp as an elbow, and the forest. It had four settlements, one the small, unvisited, unpatronized religious house at Wyck, where she now sat, and the three communities which, in the old fashion, were still called "towns." Scartoke, where she had been born, Bradwald, where, as a married woman, she had been mistress, and Ing. But for a single winding road, in bad weather almost impassable, the Rinland had no link with the mainland. It had been

occupied, long ago, by Angles coming in from the river who
had found it a good place to settle. Dense forest to north and
east sheltered it and gave it a climate unusually mild; it was a
rare year when vines set out on the south-facing slopes failed
to give a crop; the soil was fertile; except for salt and a few
other luxuries, the Rinland was self-sufficient. Once a year the
wool buyers came with their donkeys and pack ponies, and
every now and then, intent upon finding a new market, a
pedlar would plod in. But the place had been so cut off, so
remote, that Madselin's father, in his late fifties when she was
born, had heard from his father an account of the arrival of the
first missionary, sent by the Bishop of Dunwich to bring this
little corner of paganism into the fold, the great fold of Christendom. The most obvious result of his labours, apart from the
baptisms, had been the ban on marriage between people
closely related. God—the Christian God—so much disapproved
of the marriage of first cousins that only the Pope in Rome
could make such a marriage permissible and legal. The missionary—Madselin's father had even remembered his name—
Angus—had been so gentle and yet so inflexible on this, as upon
every other point of doctrine, that men from the Rinland had
gone inland, to Cressacre and Bemid, even to Colchester, to
find wives for themselves and husbands for their daughters.
But the Rinlanders still spoke of Cressacre and Bemid and
Colchester as "abroad." From the Rinland, in fact, you could
go abroad, any morning, any afternoon, provided you had a
good horse, in order to buy something, hear what was going on
in the outer world, or fix up a marriage. But there were many
Rinlanders who lived and died without ever travelling even so
far as Bemid and confined their traffic with the outer world to
paying their taxes, selling their wool and welcoming the priest
and the pedlars. When, in the April of 1066, a great comet
flared for seven nights in the sky, it predicted, for the people of
the Rinland, some domestic disaster, murrain in the cattle,
blight on the corn, or the sweating sickness; and when, three

months later, plague broke out it was generally believed that this was the disaster which the sinister star had foretold.

By late September those who survived knew differently. The comet had warned of invasion from north and from south, of the death of Harold, last of the English, and the victory of William the Norman on Senlac's bloody field.

Yet for the Rinland even this world-shaking event had seemed remote. When, in the late summer of 1066, the fyrd was called out to march with Harold to Stamford Bridge to repel the invasion of his own brother, Tostig, and of Harold Hardrada, there was hardly an able-bodied man to be spared. Madselin's husband, Eitel, lay in his bed, talking wild, fever talk; Britt Four Ox, still pallid and shaky, Uffa the miller and four or five others, aided by women and children, were working from the moment the dew dried to the time when it fell again, to get in the harvest for them all. It had irked Madselin to be obliged to stop them in their labours for so long as it took to hold a consultation about what to do, but Eitel was the elderman of the Rinland and she was his wife and the call to the fyrd was not one to be lightly disregarded. On the other hand, what of the corn, already overripe?

Britt Four Ox had solved the problem for her; it was understood, he said, that all able-bodied free men—and in the Rinland all men were free—were liable to be called up for military service, but only half at a time and turn and turn about. More than half the able-bodied men here were either dead, or sick, or still too weak to do more than milk a cow; therefore it was reasonable that the few who could work in the field should stay and work. Uffa said that he had so far escaped the sickness, but was about, he thought, to succumb. "And who would thank me to go out, taking it with me, as the pedlar brought it here?" The others had all nodded and said, "Aye" and "So it is with me," or "Britt is right."

But two boys, not yet come to full strength, tired of doing three men's work every day from dawn to dark, said they would go. They wanted to go. Madselin armed them from the motley collection of weapons that hung on the south wall in the hall and saw them off, saying, "God go with you, Gurth, and with you, Eric; and bring you safe home." But as they trotted away, to fight in a place they did not know, for a cause they did not understand, she had thought, "Two less! The corn will stand in the field until Michaelmas!" And but for the fact that she had so much on her hands, Eitel so sick, Hild over the worst but weak as a kitten, old Bertha in her own house but all alone and likely to die, she'd have taken a scythe and gone out and swung it herself.

At Scartoke the situation had been much the same except that the plague, having begun its ravages there, was nearer its end, and Madselin's mother, the Lady Edith, found six men fit to go; she loaded them with arms for twelve. Eric of Ing went himself, with another six, but the plague had already fastened on him and he died before the muster left Colchester.

In this manner the Rinland escaped the first of the Conqueror's punitive laws—that every man who fought at Senlac should forfeit his possessions. At the end of the narrow, twisting road, both Bemid and Cressacre changed hands, but the Rinland went on as before, merely paying heavier taxes into different hands and with everybody working harder to fill the place of the men the plague and the fyrd had taken. Everyone except Eitel—always prone to melancholy and doubly so since his illness—had begun to hope that the Rinland might be spared this disaster as it had been spared so many others. And then, at noon on Monday, after sixteen months, the blow had fallen.

Hild, who had been brushing Madselin's hair with a coarse-textured, borrowed brush, began to divide it for plaiting. Madselin jerked her head aside.

"Leave it. Loose it will help to keep the wind out."

"So!" Hild said, and the one word was eloquent of disapproval and disappointment. Madselin had sat silent for so long that Hild had begun to hope that she was thinking the matter over and realizing the madness of the action she proposed. Hild now saw why the Lady Edith had made so free with the stick. When reason and coaxing failed, what else was there to do? She wished she were in a position to use force. To take a stick and batter and bruise . . . She was a little astonished by the violence and pleasure of the thought. But, such action being impossible, she reverted to fear and anxiety and, under their prod, became cunning.

"This is Wednesday," she said. "You have been away from home two nights; but you have not hungered, nor lain in the thicket, nor been bitten by the cold. Where have you been? That is the first thing they will ask. So they will find this house and we shall all be turned into the woods to starve."

"And that is all you can think of," Madselin said with spite; knowing that she, too, had brooded on the sorry prospect, and dreaded it, and was now being unjust. "You and the Abbess. Loyal as pigs, both of you. While he lived my lord was good to you; presents four times in a year and never a rough word. As for this house, did he ever cull flock or herd, or go hunting without remembering them? Now he lies out in the wind and the snow and when I say I will go and ask leave to bury him, what do I hear? From you, 'This is a dangerous errand!'" She mimicked Hild's pleading voice. "And from the Abbess, 'Do not, I pray you, draw attention to this house.'" Her imitation of the Abbess' voice was more vicious. "To my mind *she* was the one who should have done the asking: and would have if she had a pinch of spirit in her fat carcass. Her veil protects her, and behind her asking there would have been the Church and all . . ." she made a wide movement with her hand, "Christendom."

Hild said quickly, "That power stood the old priest in poor stead. He asked. And he was mocked and jostled."

"He is a foolish old man," Madselin said savagely. "There are times when I could mock and jostle him myself."

None the less Hild's reminder of how Father Alfleg had been treated made her stomach lurch and she laid one hand to her body, just above the girdle. Hild noticed and pressed her advantage.

"Father Alfleg said that these are the dregs of the Norman barrel; not one well-born man amongst them. Ruffians, he said, my lady, *ruffians*."

"They are all ruffians; led by a bastard. And because they are ruffians and leave good men to rot on the midden, I must go and ask for Eitel's body. Nobody else will go, so I must."

And why? Hild asked herself. Why and why and why? Never, so far as Hild could remember—and they had grown up together—had Madselin shown any sign of piety, until last evening. Her confessions were always brief and perfunctory and far from complete, her penances grudgingly performed; any excuse was good enough to serve as a reason for not riding to Ing to Mass. This insistence upon proper Christian burial for Eitel was completely out of pattern.

Nor could it be explained as arising from wifely affection. Other people might think so, and in so thinking be deceived, but Hild was not. Hild had been there.

Hild had been there when the Lady Edith had told Madselin that she was to marry Eitel of Bradwald. Hild with her own ears had heard Madselin say, "That old man! With four teeth gone." Madselin had come back from Winchester to Scartoke with a whole new set of airs and graces, but when she was upset she could match her mother for loudness of voice.

"It is all arranged," the Lady Edith said. "And you will do as I say."

"That I will not. Never. Nothing shall make me."

"Nothing it shall be then," Madselin's mother said; and she had taken Madselin by the scruff of the neck and hustled her across to the dovecote, the only place at Scartoke which could be used as a lockfast place without upsetting the whole household. "And there you stay," she said, "until you are ready to be obedient."

A day passed, and another. A gloom fell on Scartoke and everyone walked very warily. On the third morning the Lady

Edith opened the dovecote and all the birds wheeled and winged from the lattices at the top of the tower; and from the stony cage at the base, Madselin was dragged, all soiled with droppings, and pale and already losing substance.

Hild and others had watched; had heard the Lady Edith say, "How now?"; had heard Madselin say, "No." Hild and everyone else had thought it heartless in a mother then to take a stick and beat and beat a daughter so frail and feeble seeming. But she beat her and flung her back; but, coming back into the hall she had grieved and worked her hands together. And once said, "If only she had been like Ethel, a stout girl." And again she had said, "What a cursed thing it is that a poor widow woman, in order to get her heifer to market, must mar it."

Hild had always held two attitudes towards Madselin; one made up of love and admiration, of gratitude and admiration and love; the other darker, envy, hatred, jealousy and envy. In the crisis the former attitude gained the upper hand, love and admiration mingling with pity; so on the evening of that third day, just as dusk was falling, Hild crept out across the garth, carrying what she had saved from her midday dinner and a cup of ale.

It was almost as if the mistress had been watching; for she swooped down on Hild and beat her, too, which was not right, Hild not being a slave, but the lady was past such niceties; she beat Hild so hard that she was limping for two days; and forbade her to go in the garth again, except to fetch water from the well at the other end. All the same, Hild's action had done some good, for a little later, when it was almost dark, the lady had stumped across to the prison with bread and a beaker of milk and thrust them in.

After that Hild contented herself by singing as she drew water, making up the songs as she went along; she sang that the red cow had calved, that the speckled hen, thought to have been taken by a fox, had in fact laid away and was now home with six fluffy chicks behind her. She mingled this homely news with expressions of sympathy and repeated advice to be sensible. She had to pick her time for singing for the lady was never far away. In fact by the sixth day the grass between the hall door and the dovecote showed a little trodden track where her feet had been, coming and going, going and coming, carrying her to scold, to threaten, and finally again to beat her daughter.

On the sixth day Hild, carolling away, had real news to impart; there was to be a wedding at Ing; Stigand of Bemid was to marry Eric's daughter Gundred. All were bidden to the feast. "Wish you to go, no more no no!" Hild sang.

The lady came out and told Hild to spend her strength on drawing water and make less noise. She carried a spitted partridge in her hand, and went to the dovecote and waved it about outside the locked, slatted door. Hild and the others, listening in the hush, heard her tell Madselin that the bird was cooked just as she liked it but it could not be eaten there. She also spoke of the wedding and promised Madselin a new gunna and skirt, yellow and tawny if she wished. "And you may borrow my amber beads." She added, "Clad thus and with some flesh back on your bones, you could outshine the bride."

So then Madselin came out, to be bathed and fed and cossetted. She always denied that the festivity and the dress and the beads had any part in her change of mind. It was the partridge, she said, that weakened her will. Hild and the rest believed her, for she was a girl of good appetite as a rule.

The second wedding came so hard on the heels of the first that no new clothes were thought necessary; but the Lady Edith this time gave the amber necklace instead of lending it. Hild went with Madselin when she moved into Eitel's hall, and in almost two years had never seen Madselin behave in a truly wifelike way; towards Eitel she had behaved as a spoilt daughter would behave to a doting father, never anxious to please, always expecting to be pleased—and that not too easily. Old Eitel bore with her whims, her flashes of temper, her wilfulness, and remained fond, following her about with his gaze and laughing when she teased him, lifted into the seventh heaven of delight by a few kind words, almost weeping with joy if one of his presents chanced to please her.

Why should Madselin care so much about him, dead, when she had cared so little for him, living?

As Hild asked herself this question, Madselin answered it.

"He died bravely," she said, as though speaking to herself.

That was true; in the end Eitel, old, fumbling, kind and doting, by Madselin's unkindly, youthful standards hardly a man at all, had shown his true mettle.

At Bradwald they were about to sit down to dinner when a man arrived from Scartoke, so breathless with hard running that it was some time before he could speak. When he could he told of twenty Normans, all mounted and armed, who had arrived there to take possession. One who spoke a little English had tried to explain what it meant but the Lady Edith had refused to look or listen, and had sat down in her chair, refusing to stir. One of the rabble had run her through with his sword.

There had been no time to imagine that bustling, fearsome woman dead, for the man had gone on to say that the Normans were now near Bradwald. The man who led the group was to take the whole of the Rinland.

Eitel looked at the wall where his weapons—unused for many a year—hung. He said, "Boy, blow the horn. Who wants my hall must take it."

When he said that everything that was wild and fierce in Madselin, all that she had inherited from the brave savage men who had come in from the sea and settled the Rinland, and from the brave free women who had accompanied them, rose to the surface as it had risen in the past to the old tales of courage or recklessness.

"I will take my stand by you," she said. The words were hardly spoken before she knew that she was not as brave as she would like to be. Part of her could feel the joy of splitting the head of an enemy—perhaps her mother's murderer—with a cleaver from the kitchen, a battleaxe being too heavy for her, but at the same time she felt the jar and thrust of the enemy's steel.

"You will *not*," Eitel said. "You will take Hild and get to the ladies at Wyck. If you argue I shall knock you senseless and have you carried there."

He blamed himself for not having sent her long before. If any women in this stricken land could reckon themselves safe, nuns might. England had not been overrun by pagans; Normans were Christians, though bad ones, and would surely respect the black horsehair veil. But he had delayed, hating to deprive himself of her pretty ways and lively company.

The boy called Alfred, tiptoe on a bench, was handing down the weapons from the wall and Eitel's real attention was with him. But he sensed Madselin's hesitancy, seemed even to sense that she was wondering about her chestful of clothes, trinkets and treasures; he said, "Take nothing but your cloaks. Go. And God keep you."

Reaching out his right hand to take the kite-shaped shield from Alfred, he put his left arm round her and kissed her. He had kissed her many times, diffidently, desirously, or, sensing his failure, sadly, and often enough she had turned her head, so that the kiss fell on her cheek, or, failing that, she had taken his kiss with lips that were cold and unresponsive. Now, when she kissed him with fervour, because he had established himself in her esteem, and with gratitude, because he had refused to allow her to put her courage to the test, he kissed her as a man, his mind on other things, might brush away a fly. As she said, "God keep *you*, Eitel," he was pushing her towards Hild, Hild whom no situation seemed to catch unawares and who stood holding two cloaks.

"Go," Eitel said.

As they ran from the hall towards the woods and the path that zigzagged towards Wyck the horn was crying. Not in its ordinary way, calling to dinner or supper, or to talk. The boy who blew it was young, too young ever to have used it before as a call to arms; how did he know? But he did, and as Mad-

selin and Hild fled across the winter-bleached commonland towards the shelter of the leafless woods the sound of the horn
followed them, infinitely sad and final, crying out that the last
corner of the free world was dying.

Dying: because what could Eitel and a few lumbering
farmers do against twenty armed and mounted Normans?

News of what he had done was brought to Wyck on Tuesday, by Osric, the boy who had blown the horn. Eitel and his
handful, the boy said, almost babbling—he'd travelled the five
miles between Bradwald and Wyck with a great gash in his leg
and burns about his face and head—had held the stockade
around the hall until it was fired in two places. Then they had
retreated into the hall itself and taken another stand. One Norman had moved to fire the thatch, another had stopped him,
striking down the brand, and the door had been attacked by a
ram, rooted out from the abandoned stockade. Then there had
been fighting in the hall. Osric had stood, he said, close by
Eitel, and then, slashed in the leg and knocked senseless by a
blow on the head, had fallen, near, too near to the fire trough.
When he came to himself, he was out on the dung heap with
three dead men, Eitel one of them. "All dead except me." He'd
then made his way to Wyck, partly because he had nowhere
else to go, and partly because he remembered that when he
was a little boy his mother had carried him to Wyck and one of
the nuns had cured his racking cough.

That nun was still alive, very old and deaf as stone, and before his tale was fully told, she was plastering his burns with
her mixture of goose grease and honey and another ingredient
known only to herself, the secret of which she intended to pass
on from her deathbed. He yelped at every touch, interrupting
his story, which, though it brought nothing unexpected and
was only the confirmation of fear long felt, yet brought dismay
to those who heard.

The Abbess was the first to recover herself.

"It is to be hoped," she said, "that no others will follow *his* example. I know that this house cannot remain undiscovered forever, but every moment of delay is in our favour. When things have settled a little this new man at Bradwald will see that there is nothing to be gained by sacking a place so poor as this. And what is more, I place some faith in the King's wife. She is a very pious woman who out of her own purse founded an abbey for nuns at Holy Trinity. Her influence will make itself felt. In time. If we can remain unnoticed. . . ."

No other refugee came in from Bradwald, but late in the day the old priest from Bemid jogged up on his decrepit mule. To Madselin, who had known him all her life, he had always seemed very old and because of poor sight was inclined to falter and hesitate and peer, but in the short time since she had seen him last, he seemed to have added twenty years to his age. He had gone to Bradwald to bury the dead and been told never to set foot in the Rinland again.

"The new man at Bradwald is one of the worst sort," he said, in a voice threatened by tears. "Far, far worse than Sir Volfstan." And that was saying something. Bemid, from which Stigand had ridden away to the war, had fallen into the hands of a Norman lord, Lord Bowdegrave, who, because he had been given several better manors, had put in an agent, a kinsman. Sir Volfstan had made many changes at Bemid, all for the worse, but he had not interfered with the old priest who through all these troubled months had gone his rounds, performing his office at Bemid, at Ing and at the convent, and carrying news. Most of what the Norman occupation meant in terms of cruelty and hardship and bondage had reached the Rinlanders' ears by way of Father Alfleg.

"And now I am to come no more. I have been given my quittance. They jostled and mocked me. They spoke of a *proper* priest. They would not allow me to bury the dead."

The Abbess said, "Was this place mentioned?"

He blinked at her with his milky old eyes and considered.

"No. Not by name. No, I am sure. I did not name it, and they do not know it."

"Did you *say* where you were going?"

"No. The new man told me to get back to Bemid and to stay there. He spoke to me through one who has a little English, but much Latin. Outside the rubric I never had much Latin, nor any need for it. I could not talk to him, except to ask again for permission to bury the dead."

"Did they see you take the path to this house?"

"How should they? Nobody came out with me or helped me to mount. I was mocked and jostled and sent off with a sore heart."

"Good," the Abbess said. "Not your dismissal, Father Alfleg, but that secrecy should be maintained."

"They will search out the last bean," he said. "These are the dregs of the sour Norman barrel. Not one well-born man amongst them. They are ruffians. If they wanted this house and the little chapel for a pigsty they would drive you out and the pigs in—with the same stick. They have driven me out. And until this *proper* priest he spoke of arrives, the Rinland is excommunicated. For no fault; at one man's word. This is the worst of all. In the time of their worst need, to be denied the consolation . . . to have their babies unbaptized, to die unshriven . . ." His voice faltered; and then, as though he had drawn upon some hidden reserve, he said with something like violence, "I know what will happen. Left alone they will go back to the old ways and worship trees! I know! I know! The true faith has always lain very thin in the Rinland. Nobody knows what an uphill task mine has been for nearly fifty years. A lifetime's struggle wiped out at a word." The thought unmanned him; tears gathered in his eyes and two spilled over, and ran very slowly, more like oil than water, into the crevices of his worn face.

The Abbess thought of many things which she might say by way of comfort--that the faith was mighty and must prevail; that despair was sin; that something must be left to God. She said none of them, she asked a practical woman's question.

"When did you eat last?"

It had the desired effect; no more tears spilled.

"Is this a time to think of eating? I cannot remember. Yesterday. Yes, yesterday I think."

"Did you not break your fast?"

"Not today. No, Frieda was out most of the night, tending a sickbed. And I left early, being needed at Scartoke and, I thought, at . . ." He broke off in confusion as he realized that his first duty, upon entering this house, should have been to offer words of comfort to the stricken, stony-faced girl who in a single day had lost both her mother and her husband. He began to repair this omission in a manner very earnest, but confused, explaining that though Eitel and Edith had died unshriven, the mercy of God and the understanding of God were infinite; and breaking into that kind of talk to say, "Maybe the new man at Bradwald had the right of it. Maybe I am past usefulness. No *proper* priest would look upon the bereaved and weep over his own woe. Child, forgive me if you can."

The Abbess disliked to see him abase himself to Madselin, who had not shed a tear nor given any other sign of sorrow, thus proving what the Abbess had always held, that Madselin was a cold, hard creature, with a frivolous nature, incapable of real feeling. So she interrupted, saying, "I think you need food."

After the dismal meal he confessed them all, first warning them that this must be a full and good confession since none knew when the next might be, nor what might happen on the morrow. In the morning he would say Mass—for the last time in their little chapel—and then they must be careful to remain in a state of grace for as long as possible.

The custom of public confession was one which Madselin always secretly deplored; stripping one's soul of its sins was as embarrassing as stripping one's body of its clothes. In addition to this she had a feeling that Father Alfleg was so old and unworldly that only simple failings would reach his understanding. Listening to the nuns, who seemed positively to enjoy confessing and gabbled away naming trivial mis-demeanours—a reluctance to get out of bed, an uncharitable thought, greed over a helping of peas porridge—she wondered what Father Alfleg would say if she confessed to having har-boured rancorous thoughts about her mother, to having been an undutiful child; to having been a lukewarm wife to Eitel. These were the matters now in the forefront of her mind, for now that mother and husband were dead she was experiencing the inevitable remorse and self-accusation. Between them—Ei-tel by wanting her to marry him and her mother by forcing her to do so—they had ruined her life, or so she had chosen to think. The thought had hardened her against them both. But in the clarity of death she knew that she had wronged them; her mother had wanted only the best for her, comfort and plenty and steady affection. Eitel had wanted only to supply these things. It was Stigand of Bemid who had ruined her life, and in trying to hide from this fact she had spoiled, for two people, the last months of their lives.

It was this realization that had held back the tears; tears were for small sorrows, or for things that were no sorrow at all; one shed tears of temper, one shed tears to make sure of hav-ing one's own way. This was a hard grief and one not to be shared with or exposed before anyone, least of all Hild and the Abbess and these women who had been locked away from the world so long that they thought the mere desire to stay in bed was culpable.

When her turn came she said rapidly, in a low voice, "Fa-ther, forgive me. I have been guilty of hatred and of cherishing thoughts of vengeance. . . ."

In the little, low, smoke-filled room everything seemed to come to a jolting halt. Might not, ought not, everyone present have said the same thing? Did not everyone in England hate the Normans and wish to be avenged on them? And that while professing allegiance to Him who had said, "Love your ene-mies."

The old priest thought—I too. And he thought—She was always honest, even as a child.

Two paternosters.

That light penance done with, Madselin, fully dressed, lay down on the comfortless bed and pulled her cloak about her. It was very cold and every time she moved the sour smell of mould from the mattress was disturbed and became stronger. Hild snored in the other bed and Madselin relived, as she had the night before, the whole of her short married life: the evasions, the coldnesses, the exactions, the subtle unkindnesses, the mockery; all met with patience and kindness, sometimes with a sigh, or a sad look. She had held happiness for Eitel within her gift, and failed to bestow it. She'd thought him weak, when he was strong; thought him timorous, when he was brave. And now he lay, that good, kind, misused man, out in the wind and the night, on the dunghill.

Remembering was senseless, remorse useless; she knew that, yet it went on, her mind wheeling. Then the thought came, and, though it was breath-stopping, it was a relief because it stopped the wheel and offered something not of the past, but of the future to think about and plan for. She did the thinking, and the planning, tentatively at first and then with more assurance. And finally she thought—I have nothing to lose. She examined that thought and saw its truth. With her hatred of the cold, her love of comfort, her liking for food, she would be better off dead than living a long drawn-out death-in-life at Wyck, or, on the other hand, living the short, brutal death-in-life of a beggar on the road.

The morning was dark under a louring sky that threatened snow. In the tiny convent chapel the altar candles gave a weak and flickering light, and the old priest, making less attempt than usual to conceal his lack of sight, fumbled and seemed to lack the air of serene authority which had always fallen upon him when he was officiating. His awareness that this was the last time that he would bless and break the bread in this place extended to them all. In something of this atmosphere must that first ceremonial breaking of bread, in the upper room, more than a thousand years ago, have been performed.

Afterwards they breakfasted together, a meagre meal. Madselin knew that in the storeroom there must be bacon and salt beef and smoked mutton hams; she had seen the baskets packed. Sweet russet apples, too, from the trees at the end of the garth beside the hall at Bradwald. But the meal was "tinkers' broth," the poorest food of the very poor; bread soaked in hot water and sprinkled with a little salt.

Even the Abbess felt bound to apologize.

"We must hoard what little we have," she said. "There will now be no gifts coming in from anywhere. We may have a long time on very short commons." She looked at Madselin and at Hild and added, darkly, "With extra mouths to feed."

"Not mine," the old priest said mildly. "I must set out, forthwith, for Bemid."

Madselin said, "Dare you stay here one more day?"

"Dare?" he asked, halting his spoon and giving her a reproachful look for using such a challenging word. "It would be . . . unwise; but if there were good reason, yes."

"To bury Eitel."

"But that I tried to do yesterday and was driven off. How then?"

"I intend," she said, "to go myself, and ask."

"I would not advise . . ." Father Alfleg said, then his voice was drowned; the Abbess, the ladies, even Hild, all talking at once, saying how impossible, how dangerous, how witless, how dangerous and again how dangerous.

She waited, moving her spoon about in the tinkers' broth. Then, when everything had been said at least three times and there was quiet, she said, "Will you lend me your mule?"

It took him a long time to answer. For one thing the old mule was very dear to him and had never been lent to anyone. And if he lent it now, would it not seem that he approved of and was willing to help with this hare-brained scheme? He

thought of the way he had been treated yesterday in Bradwald
hall, and shuddered to think what might happen to one unpro-
tected English girl in such rough company.

Finally he said, "It would be useless, my lady. The mule
would not go. Put my weight in meal on his back and he would
make the round unguided, knowing when to stop and when to
go. From Bradwald he will come to Wyck, but I do not think
that even I could make him go the other way."

She said impatiently, "That is begging the question. Will
you lend me the mule and leave his gait to me?"

"I do not wish him to be beaten. Never since he lived with
me has he felt a blow. Nor must he be hurried, he is old and
stiff-jointed. But he is strong, oh yes, very strong. And my lord
Eitel was a spare man. He could carry him, unhurried. . . .
But, child, I have sampled the temper of this new man and his
riff-raff. I cannot aid and abet . . . Truly I think that it would
amuse him to set you to turn a spit, or make you offer him his
cup, on your knees. Or worse. . . ."

"That I must risk," she said. "Eitel was a good man, and my
husband. Is he to lie where he lies, for lack of asking?"

"But I did ask . . ." Again his voice was lost in the female
clamour, saying the same things over again. Again she waited,
growing, had they but known it, more and more set in her
mind, as was her way when opposed. With the width of the
table between them, Father Alfleg with his long-sighted eyes,
could see her face with reasonable clarity and thought—If she
lives to be old, she will look just like her mother. It occurred to
him that further argument was useless. And yet he *must* argue.

"You have no notion of what these men are like," he said,
raising his voice. "There is not one there who would *know* how
to behave to a woman gently reared as you have been. Your errand would be mocked and you would be insulted. Or
worse. . . ." he added that warning again. "And for what?
The souls of the dead are safe in the hand of God. Christian
burial is a good and desirable thing, but men have been
drowned at sea, torn to pieces by wild beasts, or died in pagan

lands. I will say a Mass for Eitel." In his earnestness he had let his spoon slip, he feared not into the bowl; he fumbled around to recover it and see what mess, if any, he had made. "Think," he said, "how *we* should feel, how we should blame ourselves if we let you go and you did not return. Besides, if you did not return, what of my mule?"

She felt towards him a flash of the impatience that Eitel had so often aroused. She said sharply, "The two who had the right to let or to prevent me doing things are dead, Father." She jerked a ring from her finger. It had been Eitel's gift, a small but very full-coloured ruby in a heavy gold setting, intricately worked.

"If they put me in the kitchen this would not be *proper* wear. Take it and buy yourself a *proper* mule."

Hild recognized in the emphasis and repetition of the hurtful word the sharpness of tongue which had so often made the poor old master wince. The Abbess looked with something like awe at a gem worth so much meat, so much flour. Father Alfleg said, "It would buy a team of mules; but not one of them would know the way from Bemid to Scartoke and from Scartoke to . . ." Then he remembered that never again, on the old mule or a new one, would he ride his rounds. He looked at the trinket, leaning back on the bench, the better to see it, and was about to tell her to put it back on her finger. Then he thought of the company into which she was venturing; she'd be better off without it. Also to be considered was the good that he could do with the money it would fetch; there were hungry mouths in Bemid now.

Suddenly it was all too much for him. He wanted to tell Madselin that if she went to Bradwald it would be against his advice, but with his blessing. He managed to say, "I shall pray . . ." and then he put his head down on the table, oversetting his bowl, and wept unashamedly.

The hide shutter swung and groaned. Hild lifted Madselin's cloak onto her shoulders and then turned to take up her own.

"I am not taking you," Madselin said. She spoke abruptly though she was touched by this evidence of loyalty overcoming fear.

"It would not be seemly for you to go alone," Hild said.

Seemly! If I live and ever feel like laughing again, I will remember that, and laugh.

"If I can go at all, I can go alone. In fact better so."

She meant it. Despite everything, there was still within her, as much a part of her as the beating of her heart, and as little a matter of volition, an awareness of her status. She was a daughter of Scartoke; mistress of Bradwald. Horrible things, in these horrible times, might happen to her, but not quite the same as might happen to a serving wench; especially if the men were as ruffianly as the old priest said. Hild was so plainly terrified, and terror in the weak provoked cruelty in some people. She was terrified herself but no one would ever guess that.

"You stay here, Hild," she said in a softer voice. "This house is as safe as any. It may be as the Abbess says."

The fear in Hild's face eased a little, but her hands wrenched at the stuff of her cloak as though it had been washed and she were wringing it. The shutter cried again and she looked towards it and shivered, thinking of the Lady Edith, that formidable old woman who had reared and shaped her. What would *she* say if she knew that Madselin was about to walk five miles, dragging a balky mule and going into danger, while Hild skulked here in shelter? The Lady Edith had also died unshriven and hers was just the kind of turbulent, restless spirit that would walk and seek revenge. Hild feared many things, but ghosts most of all. The Church recognized only one ghost, the Holy Ghost, dovelike and quite incomprehensible, but Hild knew better; there were other, awful ones; and if she failed in her duty to Madselin, the ghost of her old mistress would haunt her. She could see herself, alone in this little room, and then not alone. . . .

"I would sooner come," she said.

"But this is not your errand, Hild. And you cannot help me."

"With the mule, I could. And with the . . . load."

The words gave Madselin a shock. It was strange how you could plan a thing in your imagination, as clearly as if it were real, and yet overlook something of importance. She had not given a thought to how she would get Eitel's corpse onto the mule's back because when she thought of Bradwald she still thought of it as a place filled with boys ready to perform her bidding, eager even to forestall a wish. She had not realized, but Hild had.

"I shall manage," she said, wondering *how*.

Hild thought of Eitel, too. Kind and gentle as he had been, if *his* ghost walked, as well it might, it would not deal kindly with Hild who had let his cherished darling go unattended.

"I shall come," Hild said. "I have as much right to walk in the woods as anyone."

"Then remember, whatever happens, that it was of your own choosing. You are a free woman."

"May that be true of me, and of you, this time tomorrow." She swung her cloak about her.

"Amen to that," Madselin said. Then she added, almost defiantly, though there was now, alas, nobody to defy, "For myself I would as soon be in the Bradwald kitchen as in this place. At least it is warm; and no spitboy ever went hungry."

"That is true," Hild said. But to work in the kitchen would be a come-down for her who had always been a personal handmaid, almost a companion. And how much more so for Madselin? Still, if that were the worst there was to fear . . . And Madselin spoke as though it were. Hild cheered up a little.

Their send-off was doleful, though in a way ridiculous. Everyone behaved as though Hild and Madselin were going to certain death, but at the same time heaped on warnings and instructions. Father Alfleg, though he no longer owned the mule, was concerned for its well-being and its behaviour. He said in a whisper, close to Madselin's ear, "I never told anyone because it seems a little disrespectful to give a saintly name to a beast; but when we are alone I call him Martin, and to that he responds. Use it if you must. And I beg you, do not hurry him."

"One might think," Madselin said, "that I intended to haul home a Yule log."

The Abbess again implored that no mention of the house at Wyck should be made. "It would do no harm, if you succeed, to turn towards Ing and then turn into the woods at the pool. That would deceive them."

"But that would make a longer journey," the priest protested. "Two miles at least. And *loaded*."

The snow was falling thickly, driven by a squally wind, and within a few minutes Madselin realized that a cloak was not the best wear for a woman walking against the wind and tugging at the bridle of an unwilling mule. Her cloak was warm and fine—another gift from Eitel—made of wool, lined and edged with marten fur; if she could have hugged it to her she would have been snug enough and would not have needed gloves. As it was, her right hand and arm were exposed and soon icy cold, and the cloak, held open by the position of her arm, caught every gust of wind and flapped, offering little protection. But soon the path took a sharp turn and for a short stretch they walked in comparative shelter.

All the way between Wyck and Bradwald the path veered in this manner, and at each turn there stood a massive oak tree. There were two stories concerning the making of this path and the shape it took. One said that it dated back to the very earliest times when oak trees and the mistletoe that grew on them were looked upon as sacred and to cut down an oak tree was to cut down a god. The other told how one of the first missionaries to the area had lost heart and become mad and sought to find a retreat in the forest where he could live and never again look on the face of a fellow man. He had cut a way through the trees with a small hatchet and was obliged to leave standing any sizeable tree. The nun's house at Wyck was supposed to stand at the place where he found a pool of drinking water and enough nuts and berries to sustain him until he could harvest a crop from the seeds he carried with him. To this day the nuns grew peas known as Alwyns, paler and smaller than ordinary ones, and of a specially delicate flavour.

On the first sheltered stretch Madselin stopped, took off her girdle and tied it firmly about her waist. Then she moved to the other side of the mule's head and took the bridle in her left hand, cuddling the other under her armpit. They plodded on.

Another oak, another turn, and the wind was at them again. The mule stopped and turned about, trying to bring his bony hindquarters and scanty tail against the blast. The wet leather slipped from between Madselin's cold-paralysed fingers and for a moment he was free and would have set off briskly on the known track back for Wyck, but for the fact that Hild stood in his path.

"Catch him," Madselin said and Hild did so, without thinking. Almost immediately, she regretted it. Had she let the creature pass, she thought, they would have had no choice but to turn back. Those two or three paces in the wrong direction had shown that the mule could move if he wanted to. He'd have gone back to Wyck and the errand would have been impossible. But she caught him.

"I'll take a turn at his head," Hild said. She had seen how much of their progress, this far, had been the result of Madselin's straining arms. With a less urgent hand on the bridle the slow pace would grow slower; the snow would thicken, in places drift, darkness would fall, even Madselin's stubborn will would weaken. They'd turn back. The brief moment of comfort, inspired by Madselin's words about kitchen work, had passed without trace and Hild felt again that they were walking into a wolf den. The comfortless little room at the convent now seemed a haven of safety and all that Hild wanted was to be back there. *With* Madselin.

Because servants, even when wearing cloaks, must have their hands free to carry or pass things, Hild's cloak had slits in the sides, and, because she had never worn gloves in her life, her hands were hardened to the cold. She suffered less than Madselin had done, and she did not heave on the bridle.

Another oak, another turn, a slightly more sheltered stretch. Two more twists and they would reach the spot which for Madselin was haunted; not by a ghost of the kind that Hild feared, but by a memory which could be very sharp and clear, as though the thing had happened yesterday, or blurred, so silted up by subsequent events and emotions that it lacked all meaning and significance. She never knew which it would be; memory, it seemed, depended upon many outside things—the weather, one's state of mind. On Monday, for example, scurrying past the place she had not thought of it at all. Now, with even more to fear and more to think about, and the weather as wrong as it could be, she was having a remembering day.

It had happened when she was eleven, six long years ago. In the Rinland, where for all practical purposes everybody belonged to one family and the deeply rooted traditions of freedom extended even to females, girls enjoyed a delightful and—as Madselin learned later—an unusual right to come and go and move about as they wished. Madselin and Ethel, her older sister, on their stout, shaggy little ponies, rode about unattended; nobody asked where they had been, or why, so long as they were punctual at the meal table, and washed and brushed.

On that morning of late spring—the most beautiful time of the year—Ethel and Madselin were to ride to Wyck to collect some linen undergarments, destined for Ethel's bridal chest, which the nuns had been stitching and embroidering for some months. That had been arranged on the previous evening, but in the morning Ethel, pallid and rather puffy faced, her hair gone dull and lank and her eyes shadowy, had said that she would rather not ride today. So Madselin had gone alone, riding her pony, who was called Harefoot because he was so swift and the colour of a hare, and accompanied by her hound, whose name was Wolf because he was so like one. His mother was a true hound, smooth-coated and the colour of cream, but he was hairy and grey and everybody said that a wolf had fathered him.

The hawthorns were whitening and the bluebells were opening; the woods were scented and breaking into green. It had been a delightful ride to Wyck, where Madselin had handed over the payment for work done and parried the Abbess' questions, with the well-tried answer, "I do not know." In those days, to Madselin, the Abbess was a woman who always asked questions to which she could give no answer. On this occasion, "When is the wedding to be?" "I do not know." And that was true, for Ethel's betrothed was one of Earl Harold's men and was at the moment fighting with his lord in Wales. Nobody, not even Wynfrith himself, could say exactly when the Welsh would be subdued and he free to take his bride.

"And when do you go to Winchester?" was another question.

"I do not know," Madselin said, scowling because the whole idea of being sent off to Winchester, to live with her aunt Camilla, the sister of her first stepfather, was utterly sickening.

"The discipline of a properly ordered household will be very good for you," the Abbess said, noting the scowl.

Madselin said nothing; she tied the parcel of linen to her saddle, taking good care that it was properly balanced, and said goodbye, escaping from the questions and the convent smell and something that she sensed of disapproval in the Abbess—so different from her mother's rages, but just as nasty and less understandable. Then she scrambled up onto Harefoot and said, "Go." He went; the track twisted and at the fourth or fifth turn, pounding along, he'd suddenly halted and swerved and reared in such a way that Madselin, taken absolutely unawares, had been unseated. She'd slipped down over his hindquarters and found herself, astonished and appalled, face to face with a wolf.

Harefoot, swerving, had deposited her at the base of an oak tree, an oak tree with a low branch that did not, because it pointed back to Wyck, overhang the path. Without thinking, acting on pure instinct, she grabbed at the branch, hauled herself up, steadied herself, advanced to another branch which did overhang the path and, getting astride it, looked down. Harefoot had gone, heading back to Scartoke; Wolf, who had been some twenty paces to the rear, ran up, saw the real wolf, dropped his tail and turned, heading back to Wyck. And there was Madselin, alone, but safe, perched on a bough, well out of the wolf's reach, but stranded, for who knew how long? And why hadn't the wolf gone after Harefoot, who might have outrun her, or Wolf, who could have been a match for her. For the wolf, a female, was in very bad condition. Even through the rough, tufty coat her ribs stood out, ridged like new-ploughed furrows, and below her pinched-in hollow belly hung the drawn-out, tugged-at dugs that offered an explanation of her state. A female, with hungry cubs and no male to hunt for her, for them. It was possible almost to feel sorry for her. It was possible, in the time it took to think two thoughts, to think —She's hungry herself and has at least four to feed! And— You're not going to eat me!

Madselin knew about wolves, which were common enough in the thick woods; they were cowardly, skulking creatures who snatched lambs, or goats, and were in return hunted for their pelts. Only in the depths of winter did they combine into packs that a man must fear; then in numbers, and hungry, they were to be feared, and they were feared. From about four weeks before Christmas to six weeks afterwards men were a little careful how they went about, and in the depths of the forest woodcutters and charcoal burners took to their huts at dusk. But in early spring the wolves mated and separated into couples, and the male of the pair hunted rabbits and hares and young partridges and pheasants, new-born lambs and fawns. A good dog, a fire, a pine torch could easily deter their maraudings. Madselin had never imagined that she would be afraid of a wolf.

But there was, about this wolf, a certain deadly purposefulness. She had not pursued Harefoot, who was swift and had iron-shod hooves, or Wolf, who was swift and strong and had teeth as sharp as her own. She had fastened her attention upon the weaker, more defenceless prey, the girl who, unseated by her pony, deserted by her hound, had only just managed to gain the safety that the oak branch offered.

The she-wolf, without taking her eyes from Madselin, took some short, quick paces to left and to right as though meditating a spring and its chance of success; then she sat down, facing the tree. With her gaunt ribs and flaccid teats less in evidence she looked absurdly like Wolf sitting on the rush-strewn floor behind Madselin's chair at home and waiting for her to throw him scraps of fat and gristle, of meat too charred, or too undercooked for her taste. There was the same air of purposeful waiting, the same certainty that sooner or later the titbit would fall. In the dog this attitude had an appeal; in the wolf it was sinister. For this was the least travelled path in the whole Rinland; it might well be a week before anyone walked or rode along.

It would not be a week before someone came in search of her, of course, but it might well be a night and a part of next day. It all depended upon whether anyone saw Harefoot scampering into the Scartoke stable with an empty saddle. Like all four-legged things he was a creature of habit; he'd go straight to his stable, take his accustomed place amongst the other horses and stand there. The boy Ulf would make his rounds just before dusk, and seeing the pony still wearing harness would simply conclude that Madselin had been too short of time or too idle to see that the saddle and bridle were removed. It would not be the first time. And inside the hall, nobody would worry; the rule about punctuality at table cut two ways; if you were not there when the trenchers were brought in it meant that you were not at Scartoke. Her mother and her stepfather would simply think that on this fine spring day she had ridden on to Ing to visit Gundred and been asked to have supper there and spend the night. Or they'd think that she'd fallen in with old Eitel of Bradwald and gone home with him because he had some supper dish of which she was fond, or some new puppies to show. She'd spent nights, unexpectedly, at both Ing and Bradwald several times, snug amongst the other women and girls on the floor of the hall, where there was always room for extra beds. Hers was not a worrying family and unless Harefoot was seen between the gap in the holly hedge and his stable, or Ulf grumbled to one of the serving boys and so the unsaddled pony and her absence were connected, nobody would even wonder about her until tomorrow at midday dinner. Then they might; but even then it would hardly occur to them that she had been treed by a wolf.

And there was the night to think about. Suppose she fell asleep and slipped from her perch? . . . She was a very prompt sound sleeper. She shared a kind of nook with Ethel who slept less well and was jealous and had once said, hurtfully, "You sleep like a pig!" She very much doubted whether, even in this uncomfortable position, she could stay awake from dark to dawn. But she must, or she would fall and the she-wolf's teeth would meet in her throat, as Wolf's did in a rabbit's.

She looked at the wolf and the wolf looked at her, waiting, prepared, like Wolf, to wait forever. A cloud ran over the sun as clouds often did at this time of the year and a purplish shadow engulfed everything, the almost white hawthorns, the small reddish leaves of the oak tree, the green, the grey-tawny wolf, her own pale hands clenched about the bough. She thought—I must tie myself fast; and put one hand to her waist. But because it was spring and because she had set out for Wyck, where the Abbess, she sensed, had no liking for her and was critical, she had put on not her girdle of stuff but her silver belt, a series of engraved plaques linked together and fastened by a hook, shaped like an S lying on its back. As a tether it was useless, not flexible enough, its length not adjustable. She wondered, almost idly at first, and then with growing purpose, if it might serve as a snare. If she could cast it over the wolf's head, would the wolf behave as Wolf the hound did when he was tethered? He always pawed at the collar in a frenzy of rage. If the wolf did that, and pushed one paw through the belt, it would be a three-legged wolf, easily outdistanced.

She removed the belt, linked the clasp again and began to edge cautiously along the bough. The wolf stood up, watching with even greater intensity. In the purplish gloom its eyes shone like green glass, lighted from behind. It lifted its upper lip and showed a glimpse of white fangs, of moist tongue. Madselin shivered. Then, steadying herself, she leaned out from the bough and dropped the belt. It fell exactly as she had hoped, but the wolf did not behave in doglike fashion; with the shining belt around her neck, dangling low on her shaggy chest, she turned, leaped a clump of young bracken and disappeared into the undergrowth. Madselin sighed; a hidden enemy was worse than one in the open. Now she would have to spend the night in this tree and she would have to stay awake. She had just time to think this when her ear caught the sound which the she-wolf's sharper sense had detected seconds earlier, the creak and jingle of harness, the muffled plod of a horse's hooves on the soft-packed leaves of the track.

He came into sight, a stranger, the most handsome young man she had ever seen, with yellow hair and beard. His tunic was blue and he wore a gold chain.

She said, "Hi! Hullo there!" He checked his horse and looked up.

"Hullo," he said. "And who are you; the Queen of Elfhame?"

"I'm Madselin of Scartoke. I've been treed by a wolf. I'm coming down now." She lowered herself to the first bough, from which she was prepared to jump, but he brought his horse up alongside, reached out his right arm and lifted her and sat her down on the saddle in front of him.

"I am grateful," she said, a trifle breathlessly. "I was afraid I must spend the night there."

"How long were you perched there?"

"A very long time. Hours. At least so it seemed."

6187

For the first time in her life she gave unprompted thought to her appearance; her hands were filthy and scratched by the rough tree bark; her skirt was rumpled and stained with green; bits of bark and leaf clung to her hair.

"Which way were you bound?"

"I was going home to Scartoke. When we met the wolf my pony threw me and my hound ran away. If it hadn't been for that bough . . ."

Now that it was over she knew just how frightened she had been, and felt sick, and thought how awful it would be to be sick in front of this beautiful young man. He seemed to sense her feeling, for he gave her a little hug and said, "You're safe with me. But I think you should have a steadier pony and a more reliable hound."

"Oh, they're both very reliable as a rule," she said, moved by some obscure impulse of pride; privately she was resolved that it would be a long time before Harefoot had another apple, or Wolf any edible scrap. "May I know your name?"

"I am Stigand. Young Stigand. Of Bemid."

"Oh," she said, a little startled; he was nothing but a name to her, but she knew about him: old Stigand's younger, unsatisfactory son. The Black Sheep, she'd heard him called, and she had always imagined him as black of hair and eye, swarthy of skin, with a cruel, secret look. Whereas he was—she twisted herself so that she could see his face again—beautiful, everything about him, beautiful, the skin a mixture of rose-colour and tan, the eyes bright blue. He understood the one startled word, the almost surreptitious glance: she's heard tell of me, he thought to himself, and been given to believe that I have a crook back, and probably horns and a tail as well.

"I'm here to take leave of my mother," he said. "And I was on my way to carry a message to my aunt at Wyck."

"Let me not interrupt you," she said. "Turn about. For me time does not matter." She would have been willing, in fact delighted, to ride with this beautiful young man forever.

"It will do tomorrow," he said. "I do not leave until Thursday."

"For where?"

"Byzantium," he said, as though speaking of Colchester. "The Emperor there is hard pressed by the Turks and needs soldiers."

Purgatory, Hell and Heaven were no farther away than Byzantium; the only difference was that since Byzantium was on this earth a man might possibly go there and return.

"For how long?"

"Until I am dead, or too old to be of service."

So her hope that in three years or four, when the mysterious thing that had happened to Ethel—and to Hild—happened to her, and she was marriageable, this handsome and agreeable man might . . . dwindled and died. It died with an audible sigh, which she excused by saying, "That wolf ran away with my belt, the only one I have."

"How was that?"

She told him, speaking distantly, as though to someone already in Byzantium and out of reach. Even when he laughed and said the idea of hobbling the wolf was clever, and promised that tomorrow when he rode to Wyck he would take six brave hounds and try to track down the wolf and recover the belt, she felt no differently.

That was the meeting that they had.

She remembered it all. Life since then had taken as many twists and turns as this path, along which they dawdled, making slower progress, and the daylight, never really fully born, beginning to die. She slapped the old mule and used his given, secret name, saying "Hup, Martin," again and again. But the real trouble was Hild; she was not moving herself, or dealing with the beast, with any real determination. She had set out, but she had no wish to get there.

"I'll take his head now," Madselin said. "You get behind him and slap him."

"As you say," Hild said. And then her face took on a look of surprise, of something near pleasure.

"Lady! I have just thought of something that was overlooked. These are Normans; how can you talk to them and tell them what you want?"

"One of them has a little English, Father Alfleg said."

"Oh." In the confusion and the gabble Hild had missed that point.

"And the rest speak French. As I do. In my aunt Camilla's house French only was spoken at table. I shall make myself understood."

Hild sighed, relinquishing the bridle. She moved to the rear of the mule and because there now seemed no way out for her and there was nothing else upon which to wreak her troubled temper, hit him hard. With a more determined hand on the bridle and a harder hand behind him, he made better progress. None the less, the short, snow-laden day was fading when they came to the place where the thick forest began to thin into the belt of secondary growth, the part from which the men of Bradwald had taken first the wood for the building of their houses, the making of their ploughs and their furniture, and then, in successive generations, the fuel for their hearths and their forges.

And here disaster could be smelt on the air. While the thin young trees that had sprung up in the place of the old and the thickening snow still veiled Bradwald from them, Hild and Madselin could smell the acrid scent of smouldering timber and thatch. It was quite different from the smell of fresh firewood, heaped on a hearth to warm or to cook and making its way through the roof vents.

Bradwald burned. But why should any man in his right senses, even a Norman, burn Bradwald, the best and biggest hall of them all? Compared with it Ing and Scartoke were nothing, were dog kennels. Bradwald hall was eighty feet long and had two sleeping chambers and a screen between the hall and the door to the kitchen. Eitel's father had enlarged it and brought it up to date. It was a most comfortable and commodious house—as Madselin's mother had pointed out.

But it was possible that a set of ruffians, such as Father Alfleg had described, were incapable of recognizing the worth of that good hall. It took a person of quality to recognize quality in horse or hound or hall, and what was not recognized might be resented and, because resented, destroyed.

"They've burned it," Hild said, "and gone away."

Madselin brushed the snow that now lighted softly and melted slowly from her face, and said, "I fear so," because the idea of Bradwald being burned was horrible, and at the thought of its being destroyed she felt the same pang of remorse as she felt when thinking about Eitel and her mother, for she had not properly appreciated her home, either, until now, when it was too late.

"But if *they* are housed at Ing or at Scartoke, it might be possible to take what we have come for, without asking."

"That is true," Hild said and breathed a little prayer of thankfulness to Holy Mary, Mother of God, who had not been deaf or without pity, after all. Heartened, she brought her hand down in a slap which made the old mule take a few trotting steps. They emerged onto the edge of the commonland.

And there, across the whitened grass, through the veil of falling snow, Bradwald stood, sturdy and sound as ever, deeply thatched, firmly rooted, with its barn and stable and byre clustered about it, like chickens about a mother hen. From the central vent in the roof of the hall, and from the one at the kitchen end, the smoke swirled out and hung, mingling with the snow. The place looked just as it always had, at this time of day, in such weather. The sour smell of burning came from the left of the common, from two houses which had stood unoccupied since their owners died of plague.

"It seems we must ask, after all," Madselin said, and Hild knew that she would have been glad to avoid the ordeal of asking. Then why do it? The answer occurred to her suddenly.

Like herself, Madselin was frightened of night walkers and
was afraid that Eitel, left unburied . . .

"Lady, he never hurt you in his lifetime, he would not
frighten you now. And perhaps he knows that you meant well,
that you came so far. . . . Let us turn back before it is too
late."

"I am going in. But Hild, I have a thought. To take the mule
might be unwise. It would look as though I expected my request to be granted. I shall leave him here, and you with him
to see that he does not wander back."

Hild looked along the path they had just left; under the
trees it was already shadowy; to stay here, alone on the edge of
the forest, would be as bad, was more than she dared do.

"I dare not," she said, almost crying because to choose between two courses, both horrible, was such a wrenching business. "I'll tether him," she said. She twisted the bridle rein
about a stump. The old mule sighed and sagged.

"You chose to come," Madselin reminded her and then her
mind jolted upon another thought, intimately related to Hild's
coming. "And Hild, if it should come to rape . . ." She felt the
need to justify herself for speaking of such an intimate thing,
because though she and Hild had grown up together in
cramped quarters there had always been an invisible barrier,
an area of reticence between them. "They were all thinking of
rape, though no one spoke the word. And it might happen. If it
should, do not struggle or resist. Give way. It will hurt less."

At any other time Hild would have turned away her head or
put up her hand to hide her smile. How innocent they were,
ladies! Hild had been raped—if that were the term for the
deflowering of a mystified girl by a clumsy boy—when she was
twelve, and it had meant as little to her as the breaking of a
nail or the splitting of a lip in cold weather. Since then several
men—Madselin's stepfather amongst them—had used her for
their pleasure. Only once had it meant more to her than the
hope of a present afterwards; and that had been with a young
man who had come in to buy wool. Then it had been wonder-

ful, an experience quite unlike anything her mistress could
ever have known in the master's bed. Three years ago now,
and though Hild had looked for him each June after the shearing, the young man had not come again.

"And don't let them see that you are afraid," Madselin said.
"Try not to look frightened . . . God in Heaven! What . . ."

It was a hump, lying in a little hollow, directly in their path,
a hump mounded with snow.

"It is an ox," Hild said.

It was an ox, or what remained of one, roughly hacked about
by somebody who though not a skilled butcher had known
what he wanted and taken it. The liver, the tongue and part of
the rump had been cut away. What was left was not a pleasant
sight, but neither Madselin nor Hild were squeamish about
such things. It was what lay on the far side of the carcass, half
under it and somewhat sheltered from the snow, that shocked
them: a woman, not immediately identifiable, because her
head had been split like a billet of wood.

"Old Bertha," Madselin said in a small voice. "I gave her
that cloak when I had this." She spared a bitter thought for the
time and attention she had given the old woman in the plague
time, when nobody else had time to spare, being so busy with
their own sick, or with the harvest. I might have spared myself; and she would have died in her bed.

"She was trying to get her ox away," Hild said. "She
cherished that beast beyond . . ." She broke off, for Madselin
had turned away and was being violently sick, in the worst
way, from an empty stomach. Hild went to her, placed her left
arm around the heaving body and her right hand against the
bowed forehead.

"I've got you," she said. "Lean on me. There! There!"

The spasms passed. Madselin, still in Hild's hold,
straightened herself and wiped her wet face on her wet sleeve.

"Thank you, Hild. It was the tinkers' broth. . . ."

"It was the sight of old Bertha's head split like a pig's for smoking," Hild said brutally. "And if we go on we shall see worse."

"Leave me go," Madselin said and moved forward. "At least they died together, Bertha and her ox." It was possible to envy, briefly, those who were dead, who could never be hurt again. It was also possible to think that if that awkward, unfriended old woman had died in the effort to hustle her ox to safety there was nothing so extraordinary in what she herself was doing, claiming the body of the man who had loved her and from whom she had withheld her love.

Osric had spoken of the stockade being fired, and here, ahead of them, was the place; three stout timbers charred, a gap through which, lifting their snow-and-mud-clogged skirts, two women could pass and step into what had been, until Monday, Eitel's private domain. To their left the barn. The high doors closed and the bar dropped. Madselin had never seen it so—who would steal from Eitel? And nobody about, nobody moving or busy at this hour which should have been, in the Rinland always had been, the busiest hour of the winter days.

She had planned the time of her arrival carefully. In the Rinland from March to September, people ate at midday and at dusk; from September to March they worked on what was called "the one-team" or "the one-plough" system, missing the midday meal and making supper, served early, do for both. This was the hour when men, coming in from the fields, would be feeding pigs, milking cows, penning geese and hens against foxes before going in to close doors and shutters, throw logs on the fire, rest, eat and go to bed. It was the hour, Madselin knew, from a lifetime of experience, when men were most open to persuasion.

But Bradwald at this hour, on this day, seemed dead.

Skirting the barn, they came to the byre, which was a clod building, thatched, and with the thatch extended over a little forecourt in which cows could stand and be milked. And here, at least, someone lived and moved. There, tethered to one of the worn shiny posts which upheld the thatch, was the red-and-white cow which never would stand without being tied, but which gave the creamiest milk of all. And sitting on the three-legged stool, with his head pressed against the cow's flank, and his fingers busy, squirting the milk rhythmically into the wooden bucket, was Wat, Eitel's cowherd for many years. A homely and reassuring sight.

She was about to say his name, when, sensing the presence of someone behind him, Wat lifted and turned his head in a way that spoke of fear, the expectation of hurt. Madselin said, "Wat," on an outgoing breath and Hild made a mewing noise, buckled at the knees and fell sideways into the slushy mud churned up by the cow's feet. In the middle of the old man's forehead was a brand, a letter R, puffy and blackened at the edges, red and raw in the centre.

"My lady," Wat said in a voice thin and high with alarm. "We thought you safe. Why are you here? Get gone! Get gone!" He rose from the stool, staggered and leaned against the cow's flank, moving his arms in a driving-off gesture. "These are terrible men. Devils in men's shapes. Escape while you may."

She tried not to look at the red weeping wound, but into Wat's eyes, though they, with their expression of fear and despair, were just as disturbing. On the rim of her mind a thought formed—That is the face of England! The near detachment did not mean lack of pity or concern, it was just that to people of Anglo-Danish blood the fanciful, metaphorical phrase came naturally; and in her the tendency had been fostered by her stay in Winchester where things that would have been offensive in plain speech could be said in stylized phrases and be acceptable.

"I had to come," she said. "I could not leave my lord's body on the dunghill."

"Where a man's body lies does not matter," Wat said earnestly. "It is how he lived and how he died that is reckoned. They will not listen to you; they would not listen to

Christ Himself. I beg you, go while you can. Get back to Wyck and pray. Pray that death delivers us soon."

Because the temptation to flee was sharp she spoke more sturdily.

"It will heal, Wat. You are alive. How many more?"

"All who did not die with my lord. There was no killing after. The men are in the barn."

"And the women?"

"Unharmed; huddled in two houses. But you . . . it could be different for you. Suppose they," he moved his hand a little, indicating the brand, "did this to you?"

In her mind she felt the terror of being held down by rough hands, the heat of the iron approaching, the bite of it meeting flesh.

"What does it mean?"

"That we are his cattle, his slaves."

"What does the shape mean?"

"His name is Rolf. We bear his name now. So may you, unless you make good your going. My lady, I beg you. . . ."

Terror welled up again, but she knew that if she gave way to it she would carry shame with her to the grave. Eitel and her mother had been brave, and if she, who had acted badly towards them both, proved in the end to be less . . . No, she must go on. And at the very back of it all was the feeling that it was unlikely that she, Madselin of Bradwald, had much more than a rebuff to fear.

She said, "Wat, when Hild comes to her senses, tell her to wait here for me, inside the byre in the warm."

"You go in?"

"I must."

"Ill will come of it." The terror that flickered in his eyes leaped. "But I must milk," he said. "They want fresh milk. I must not keep them waiting. God do better for you, my lady, than He did for the rest of us."

He sat down on the stool and lowered his head, careful not

to press against his brand. She saw tears fall, with the milk, into the bucket.

She used the fanciful phrase again.

"Remember, Wat, the brand was set on your brow, not on your heart. God keep you."

Now she knew that what she did must be done quickly before the last spark of courage and determination failed. And what a pity it was, she thought, as she went towards the door of the hall, that Eitel's father, when he made his improvements, had surrounded the garth with a high crinkle-crankle wall, which, running like an unwound ribbon, offered niches in which plum and cherry and pear trees flourished. The only entry to this enclosed space was through the kitchen door, outside which lay the midden. From Scartoke or from Ing with the unwalled garths it would have been possible to steal softly around and take . . .

The main door now stood before her. Osric said it had been rammed, but it was already mended and rehung. To the left of it the line of narrow windows, not yet shuttered, showed pinkish-gold from the fire within. She had seen it thus many times, coming back from a ride or a visit, certain of the welcome within, the heaped fire, the meat on the spit, the warm soft bed. These things she had valued, since her comfort had always been a thing of great concern. What she had not set store by was the smiling face, the outstretched hand, the face that had lighted at her coming.

She had known that Eitel was dead, she had come to claim his body, but he had never seemed so dead, as now, now, with his door closed against her.

The door was fitted with a heavy iron ring which when turned lifted the latch inside; in all her time at Bradwald it had not been necessary for her to open the door for herself and she was surprised to find how stiffly the ring turned. She was obliged to set both hands to it, and even when the latch lifted —she heard it above the sound of men's voices coming from within—the door resisted her. But the wind came to her aid;

the door swung and she swung with it, still clinging to the handle. The draught made the fire flare and throw a lurid light upon startled faces and upon steel as men got to their feet and reached for their arms. The wind, sucking outwards, dragged at the door so that she had to move quickly to avoid being carried out again.

It was, she reflected with regret, far from being the dignified entrance she had planned.

And she wished with all her heart that the alarm in the hall had been justified; if only she could have surprised them like this, with half a dozen stout men behind her. Half a dozen would have sufficed; no guard anywhere, the door unbarred, jerkins thrown open, shoes off and drying by the fire, wine slopping about. But, of course, whom had they to fear, now?

Relief after alarm, the sight of one female, dripping wet, muddied to the knees and with some snow unmelted on her hood and shoulders, roused hilarity in the men. They laughed and called out to her with words which, carelessly spoken and cutting across one another, seemed momentarily unintelligible, far removed from the French she spoke. But their meaning reached her. They were jeering her, and their own unwarranted fear.

The man who sat in Eitel's chair at the raised table that ran crossways at the far end of the hall hammered with his fist and shouted an order. There was silence and when he spoke, in better French, and in a voice of exceptional clarity, she understood him well.

"Who are you?"

"I am Madselin, widow of Eitel of Bradwald."

"What do you want?"

"To ask a favour."

"Who is with you?"

"A serving girl."

He spoke to the man on his left, who jumped down from the low platform on which the table stood, and began calling names, the owners of which rose and took up their arms again.

They clattered towards the door. By the time that the man who had been at the table was level with her he had his sword unsheathed in his hand, and he said, "If that was a lie, God help you!"

There was such hostility in his voice and in his pale, rather bulging eyes that her heart seemed to stop. It was a thing she had never encountered before, a thing impossible to imagine. Hatred, a wish to hurt, as though she had done him some deep, personal wrong. If Hild, coming out of her shock-swoon, met such a look, she would die.

"It is true," Madselin said, backing a step and spreading her arms as though heading off a dangerous animal. "One serving girl, come with me out of loyalty. Do her no harm."

The man at the table said, "Search. Any you find bring here; unharmed—unless they attack." The door opened, the fire and the candles flared; the door thudded. In the hall there remained a few men, most of those at the trestle tables wounded, and the two at the top table.

"And what is this favour?"

It must be done properly. And the order that anyone with her was to be unharmed, gave a little hope. She set out to walk towards him, and her path took her past the fire, extravagantly heaped in the long shallow trough that ran down the centre of the hall. In the heat the snow on her hood melted and began to drip, falling like the tears she had not shed yet. She jerked her head back and the sodden hood slithered off, revealing her hair. Her hair had always been admired because its colour was so rare, a dark amber. In the Rinland, where hair varied between golden and near-white, and in Winchester where Camilla and her French-born ladies were dark-headed, her hair had always attracted attention. Even her mother had once indirectly praised it, saying, "You are fortunate to be desired by any man; with your head-rail on and your hair hidden, you look like a drowned kitten."

At the moment she gave her hair no thought, her feelings too much concerned with fear—here in her own hall, always so safe—and with humiliation—coming as a suppliant to the place where she had always ruled like a queen—and with a consciousness of being amongst enemies—here in the home where she had been loved.

The tables had two cloths, the topmost of white linen, the under one of scarlet cloth thickly embroidered, the work of Eitel's first wife, who had been a notable needlewoman. It fell to the edge of the little platform, concealing the legs of the table, and of those who sat behind it. As she walked she kept her gaze on the intricate pattern, afraid to look higher, lest she should see in the eyes of the new master of Bradwald that same look of hatred, and be deterred. When she was near enough to see each stitch plainly she went down on her knees, put her hands together and bowed her head and said, "I have come to ask leave to take my husband's body and give it burial."

There was a silence long enough to enable her to think—I should have called him lord.

Rolf said, "It is already done."

She looked up, surprised. The new lord of Bradwald looked down at her and his face told nothing. It was a face of bronze, cast in harsh lines. It was the face of the man who sat beside him, a plump, ruddy, fleshy face that informed her that what Rolf had just said was a lie. For as she looked the fleshy human face took on two expressions, running into one another. One was the surprise that she herself had felt, and then, hard after it a look which asked—Now what made you say that?

She said, "If that is so, I have come on a wasted errand and disturbed you for nothing." Taking such a risk; hauling the mule along against the wind. But it was not true and she knew it. Eitel lay on the midden and she was being fobbed off with a lie. Without knowing that she had moved she stood up, facing them both and knowing that, having made the gesture of courage and come here, the best thing now was to withdraw, she narrowed her eyes and said, "What priest committed him to the grave? And where does he lie?"

The fat man answered the first question. "I said the words of the committal. I am not a priest; I never took more than deacon's orders; but I know the words, and since there was no priest . . ."

Rolf said, "Under the apple trees, in the garth." And that again astonished her so much that her disbelief was swallowed up by a sense of wonder that he should have said that. For when Eitel lay very sick of the plague he had said that he wished to be buried under the apple trees. "I shall not be lonely there," he had said, raving. "My wife will sew in the shade on sunny days; and my children will play." His sewing wife had been dead for many years and his only child had died soon after, of the same lung-sickness. And had he died then Madselin would have disregarded this fever talk and buried him at Ing, where the little church was, with his other wife, his child, his father and mother.

And now this stranger said, "Under the apple trees." She knew a moment of complete confusion and that was new to her. In all her seventeen years every issue she had faced had been simple, mainly concerned with what she wanted and could attain, with what she wanted and had failed to get, with what she must or must not do. Nothing so far had prepared her for a situation where she half believed and half doubted what she was told, and was sure of nothing. She did not know what to do, or what to say; and it did not matter; she had accomplished nothing useful. There remained only to get herself and Hild safely away.

While she stood hesitant the fat man spoke into Rolf's ear, and, answered by a nod, got up, jumped from the platform and approached her. He moved with an incongruous buoyancy and nimbleness.

"You could help us," he said, "by answering a few questions."

To help them was the last thing in the world that she wished to do and perhaps this unwillingness showed in her eyes, for he said, softly, "It would make things easier—for all." Then, tak-

ing her assent for granted, he removed her cloak and indicated
that she should take the chair which he had just vacated. *Her*
chair. He spread her cloak over a trestle near the fire, and as he
did so said something which made two of the remaining men
get up and go out, not by the main door, but towards the
kitchen. She knew their errand as well as though she had herself dispatched them. They were to take Eitel's corpse from the
midden, dig a shallow grave and make the lie good—in part.

The fat man hopped back onto the platform and took the
chair on Rolf's left. So now she sat here with two of the enemy,
men capable of deceit over even so trivial a thing. In return
she would lie and mislead them as much as possible. Not that
it would be easy, with two pairs of eyes watching her so
closely; the fat man's with a lively intelligence and Rolf's with
cold intensity.

"This is Giffard," Rolf said. "Words come easy to him."

To the first question there was only one possible answer.

"How many went into hiding with you?" Giffard asked.

"None."

"Then where are the rest?"

"How can I know? When Hild and I fled all the Bradwald
men were here, preparing to fight."

"You are asking me to believe that thirty men—some not full
grown—tilled so much land and did all else that there was to
do?"

"Since the plague, when so many died."

"There *were* empty houses," Rolf said.

"You and your serving girl fled. Where to?"

"A woodcutter's hut in the forest."

"And came back, alone, the two of you, to remove a
corpse?" He asked the question quite gently, his expression
was amiable; his suspicion was plain.

"We borrowed a mule."

"And how—in your woodcutter's hut—did you know that
your husband was dead?"

"By arrangement. If Eitel had not come, or sent for me by the third day, I was to assume him dead."

"I see. You would know that he had not been taken, and held?"

With more force than she would have thought was left in her she said, "Eitel was not one to be *taken!*"

"No," Rolf said. "As he lay dying . . ." He looked down, and she looked too, and saw that his right leg was propped on a stool, wrapped not with a bandage, but in—yes, surely—the bark of a tree. Eitel's last blow! And she had despised him. In order to avoid the weakness to which that thought led she thought quickly—I hope the wound rots and you die of it! Not that that would avail; there were plenty of Normans.

Giffard said, "Well, none of that was of much importance. Thirty men, you tell us, maintained this manor. On what terms? How many were free? How many owed day service, or other dues?"

But for the fact that she had lived for a time in Winchester she would not have understood that question; but as it was she did, and said, "Here, all were free. There was no day labour. There were no dues."

Again the amiable face wore a look of incredulity; and again Rolf intervened.

"As in Lincolnshire, Giffard."

Giffard said, "Yet *here,*" he looked about him, "one wide, high house, the others humble. And if your husband had no dues, he was their lord."

"But that was his birthright. When our people came in from the sea there was always one, stronger or wiser than the rest. The leader." She looked at the south wall. The first Eitel's great battleaxe and round shield which had hung there had been snatched down and used; but high on a peg, beyond the boy's hurried reach in that moment of disaster, was his horned helmet, and lower down the harness that his almost legendary horse had worn. "Eitel's great-grandfather was that man," she said. "So when the place was taken, he had the leader's share and was acknowledged as lord. And his sons after him."

"And who," Giffard asked with the air of a man making his conclusive point, "ploughed and harvested for him?"

"Any man with time or oxen to spare when his own work was done. And then there were the young men, second or third sons. They lived with us here, and were fed and clothed and given a share . . . as were the older men who owned land but had time to spare for ours."

"The young men were serfs," Giffard said.

"No. They were free. They could come and go. . . . It was different here. . . ." And it was all over now, the free men of Bradwald branded and locked in the barn. And she, here, Hild waiting in the byre, the old mule tied to a stump. It was now full night; through darkness and snow they must make their way back. To Wyck. Where the Abbess would regard them as two extra mouths to feed.

I shall not go back there. The old mule is mine, I bought him. I will drag him to Colchester and sell him there and buy a harp. Thanks to Camilla I know many French tunes and Hild— if she wishes to come with me—can learn to sing them; she has a good voice. . . . It would be a form of beggary, but not complete, music is something that should be paid for. . . . But alongside that thought ran another; why should I *buy* a harp, when my own is there, hung on the wall in the sleeping chamber, just above the chest that holds my best clothes, my amber beads and the two gold bracelets that were too big for me. And my belt, she thought, the silver belt which Stigand brought back to me, after that day's hunting. For the belt had done its work after all; it had caught in the thicket and held the she-wolf captive, easily overcome by Stigand's six brave hounds.

Giffard said, "Small wonder then that a place so lacking in order should be so poor."

"We did not lack order. And we had all we needed."

"And where did you keep your treasure?" Giffard's voice

was still gentle, but he asked the question as though it were the one to which all the others had been leading.

"We had none."

"The lord of Bradwald owned only a golden ring; his lady a string of amber beads, a belt of silver and two bracelets of gold?" When he looked disbelieving he raised one eyebrow.

"There were eight silver pennies in the chest, also," she said quickly, pride and anger in her voice.

Giffard nodded, accepting the tone of that remark as proof of honesty, and Rolf said, "Those who said it was a poor place spoke truly."

A poor place! Where everything that was needed was plentiful, and coined money laid by for the taxes. A place virtually self-supporting and which had a surplus to be bartered for such things as salt and needles, dyed stuff and such luxuries. The derogatory word angered her; but the days were gone when in this place her anger, or her mere peevishness, could make them quail. She said, quite meekly, "If all your questions are answered, have I leave to go? My girl will be waiting. And so will the wolves. . . ." She was not aware of it, but when she mentioned the wolves a bedrock honesty lay bare, akin to the mention of the eight silver pennies. Ever since her encounter with the she-wolf on that momentous day she had cherished a secret dread of wolves; and a part of her mind, even as she sat there, thinking about hauling the old mule, and Hild, along the road to Bemid, and beyond, had been concerned with slinking dark shapes in the shadows. . . . But they must be faced, too.

If the mule, and Hild, had moved more willingly; if her request for Eitel's body had been acceded to without delay . . . they would now have been half-way back to Wyck, at least half-way. And her intention to have Eitel properly buried by Father Alfleg would have strengthened her.

"I have one further question," Rolf said. She thought of her harp, hanging there in the inner room. It would save buying one.

"I have answered many," she said. "And the request that brought me here was, alas, too late. If I answer another question, may I make another request? Very small?"

That question was not to be answered immediately. The main door opened; the man with the pale, bulging eyes and those who had gone with him came in, together with a great flurry of snow.

"We found nobody. No sign of any intruder."

"Then where is Hild? Did you look in the byre?" Asking this urgent question, forgetful, acting as she had last week when what she said mattered, Madselin leaned forward across the table top.

"We found no one," the pale-eyed man said again, speaking to Rolf but giving her one fleeting glance—What are you doing there? And how dare you put a question to me? There was a small confusion, a stamping of feet, a shrugging of shoulders against the clinging snow. Giffard bounced out of the chair which when she entered had been occupied by the pale-eyed man and dragged up a stool for himself. And at almost the same moment, behind the screen, the kitchen door opened and a delicious smell of roast pork wafted in, overcoming the odours of wood smoke, candle grease, wet leather and men's sweat.

The fools had killed the little spotted pig! Sheer waste. In three months time he would have more than trebled his weight. Sucklings were eaten at Michaelmas, or Christmas, the runts of the litter, fattened up, sometimes even fed by hand because the sow could be selective, favouring the strong, pushing the weak away. The little spotted pig had been selected to survive, to live out his year, to become a bacon pig, his haunches, well grown, to be hams.

Well, they were ignorant fools; profligate; bandits. Old Bertha, who was able to outwork any man any day, lying out there, dead, beside her ox, a good worker, too. If they went on like this, killing workers, killing bacon pigs, the place would soon be poor: especially with so many unproductive men to be fed.

Into this thought concern for Hild intruded; she could only hope that she had gone home with Wat.

Then Rolf asked his question. "This woodcutter's hut, was it well provisioned?"

She wanted to say that it was, that in England even the woodcutters ate well. But that would provoke their greed and set them searching, which would be hard on the genuine woodcutters. So she said, "No. I have not eaten meat since Sunday." There was honesty in that complaint, too.

"You can eat with us if you wish," he said.

One did not eat with one's enemies. With the men who had killed one's husband.

"No. No. I must find Hild and be on my way."

"If Peter failed to find her she is under cover. There are other things you can tell us. It may be a long time before we find another English person who speaks our tongue."

"I have told you all I know. Allow me to leave now. And I should take it kindly if you would permit me to have my harp." The direct request, the careful civility, had a certain childishness, reinforced by sudden unsureness of manner. She was confused again. The offer of food might be an excuse to detain her for some sinister purpose, there was that to be considered; also to be considered was her now almost overwhelming hunger. She had always liked food, and except for the days in the dovecote had always eaten well. Now, with her world in ruins about her, calamity on every side and fear nibbling away, she was hungrier than she had ever been, even in the dovecote where determination had borne her up. The scent of roast pork . . . and it might be a long time before she had her next proper meal. And at the back of her mind was the knowledge that, if the new lord intended to keep her there, he could, and would, whether she had shared his supper or not.

Hild—assume that she was in Wat's house.

The old mule—tethered where the smell of burning would

keep the wolves away. Abruptly she changed her plans. She would eat, eat her fill; then, if she could, get away, with the harp; go to Wat's house and sleep there and get away at cockcrow.

With another complete change of manner, a reassumption of dignity, she said, "Since I am already late and you have invited me, thank you, I will sup with you."

Peter said, "This is unwise, Rolf. Penalties, you said, for any man who went near one of *their* women and now you invite one to supper."

The insolence of it amazed her. In Bradwald all men had been free and when they met, in this hall, as they often did, to discuss matters of communal interest, each man spoke his mind, and frankly; but Eitel was lord and no man would have dared to speak to him in that tone of voice. The new lord of Bradwald showed no surprise, no sign of being offended. "Here is the meat," he said.

The man who carried the great dish was a stranger to her. Behind him came Alfred and another boy, Child, each with a pile of wooden trenchers. Alfred saw her, looked amazed and frightened and missed a step; Child, with his eyes on what he was carrying, walked into Alfred and propelled him forward so that he bumped into the rear of the dish-bearer, who turned and gave a snarl. Had his hands been free clouts would have accompanied that wordless expression of anger and contempt. Madselin remembered how Father Alfleg, reporting some horrid incident at Bemid, had said, "It was all due to misunderstanding. An order in a strange tongue is hard to obey." When that was said Madselin's interest was firmly centred on herself and her imagination was similarly limited. Now she understood. All over England, those who knew no French would be regarded and treated like animals. And how could men like Britt Four Ox and Wat, boys like Alfred and Child, learn a language which had seemed so difficult to her in the early days at Winchester?

Giffard had picked up his stool and carrying it came to her right hand.

"It is," he said, in English, "a time for me to try. I will talk and you will tell me what is wrong. Please. Thank you. This I like. This I do not like. Left, right. Meat, water, bread. I know many words . . ." He ran off a dozen or so, and then, reverting to French, said, "You do not mind, Rolf?"

"Somebody must learn. I have no knack. After two years in Spain I could ask for food and name tools, no more."

"You went about it wrongly. In any language bed is the best schoolroom and a pretty woman the best teacher."

Rolf grunted and gave his attention to cutting the meat which the dishbearer offered, going down on one knee and resting the dish on the other as though on a table. He served Madselin first, then himself. To Giffard he said, "Take what you need now. There will be little left when it gets down there." He nodded towards the other table.

Giffard helped himself liberally. Then Peter was served and the dish taken to the table on the floor of the hall where the men fell upon it ravenously.

"I like to eat," Giffard said, practising his English again. "Enjoy? It is a word? I enjoy food."

"I enjoy food, too."

"Too much?"

"Also. I also enjoy food."

When he had been trying to trick her by questions she had feared him and thought that his amiable look and voice were deceptive. Now happily guzzling, laughing over his own mispronunciations, he seemed a different creature, harmless, and, had circumstances been otherwise, amusing. She found herself wishing that he, not the silent, inscrutable man on her left, had been the new lord. She might then have been sure of her harp and perhaps even a change of clothing.

And then, abandoning the difficult English, Giffard shattered that illusion. He said, wiping his mouth, "Where is the convent?"

The mouthful of succulent meat went down like a stone.

"What convent?"

"The one to which you fled. Where the priest is waiting now. To deny its existence is foolish. You reek of the convent smell."

"How it adheres," she said, feeling clever. "The nuns at Bergholt stitched my linen, and wove the stuff of my cloak. And the priest who is waiting to bury my husband, and who was forestalled by you, waits at Bemid where Sir Volfstan permits him to go about his duties."

She looked at him, he looked at her and their eyes were like bared swords as liar faced liar. Then Alfred and Child brought the wooden bowls in which a pale mixture of wine and milk quivered. Wat's tears had fallen into the milk that had gone to make this frothy concoction. She waved her bowl away and Giffard said, "I will have both," and he said it in French, which Alfred did not understand and would have put down one only and would have been considered disobedient, surly, stupid . . . had she not been there.

The boys, she noticed, had not been branded; possibly even Normans did not wish to be waited upon by those with red wounds on their brows. She swivelled around in her chair and said to Rolf, "You are master here, now. I beg you, be tolerant with those who do not understand your speech and may seem stupid, disobedient." It was the first time she had ever given a serious thought to the well-being of anyone but herself, and— until his marriage—Stigand.

Rolf said curtly, "Those who do what they are told will come to no harm."

"But that is the trouble. So often they do not know what they are being told to do. At Bemid, not long since, Sir Volfstan killed a man for what seemed disobedience."

"I shall avoid killing, if I can. Dead men do no work."

Of all the hateful, churlish . . . She looked down hastily. Eitel had once said that when she was angry there were sparks in her eyes. She must not let him see that she was angry: she wanted her harp.

"Well," Giffard said, patting his stomach, "that gives me heart for the next job." He got to his feet. Peter rose too. A man from the lower table went to the fire, thrust in a stick and lit the candle in a horn lantern. All those who had gone out before, to search for enemies, trooped out again, led by Peter and followed by Giffard, who had picked up a large basket of woven straw. Snow blew in at the open door.

Madselin said, "I must go, too. Thank you for my supper. May I take my harp?" She looked into the hard, unyielding face and said, "Please. It is of small value."

"When you have answered *my* questions."

She waited.

"Where are you going?"

"Towards Colchester."

"You have friends there?"

"No."

"Elsewhere?"

He judged her to be well born and there was a section of the English aristocracy that had hastened to make terms with the Conqueror, who delighted to show them favour, take them about with him and make display of their friendship. Their acceptance of him substantiated his claim that England was his by right of inheritance, not by conquest. When they had served their turn he would discard them, but meanwhile if the girl had a lickspittle relative or friend she would be safe enough.

"No. My uncle died in the battle. His wife disappeared."

"How will you live?"

"I do not know. But that uncertainty I share with many." Fool, she thought; what does that matter; ask for your harp. "I play the harp well, and Hild sings. We might manage."

"On the roads?"

"Where else?"

He still stared at her.

"The roads are full of such as these." He nodded towards the lower table. "Mercenaries. Disgruntled by failure to find wealth or place. If I had not been here . . . I have seen women die, raped roughly by twenty men."

She felt sick again; the good tender pork regurgitated and she pressed her hands—suddenly gone cold—to her mouth, willing herself not to be sick or betray distress under these watchful eyes which were neither friendly nor hostile. Oddly coloured, the copper which matched his cropped hair, flecked with green like a hawthorn leaf in autumn. The effort to force back the retch brought water to her eyes and she was afraid that he would think she was crying. She brushed her lower eyelids with her fingers and forced—to give tears the lie—a bitter, self-derisive smile.

"We lost a battle," she said in a hard cold voice. "And if you will allow me to take my harp I shall have more than most."

He stood up, not without difficulty, removing his leg from the stool. Normans were stocky, but he was tall. He took a candle and limped towards the door of the sleeping chamber. She turned in her chair and caught a glimpse of the room, always so neatly kept. Now the contents of her chest and of Eitel's were heaped on the floor, all muddled with men's gear and muddied boots. Then the light moved inwards and she saw no more until the man Rolf came back with her harp in his hand. He put it down on the table so roughly that the jolt vibrated the strings into a faint, formless sound.

"Now," he said, "think of serious things." He spoke as though she were a fractious child or a dog, patience and attention to be purchased by the presentation of the toy or the titbit momentarily craved. Her naturally quick temper was provoked.

"And what could be more serious than this?" She put out her hand and from the harp plucked one string after another. "With rape," she said, "the most likely reward."

"That," he said, "need not be. You can stay here. If you wish." He made a deliberate effort to fight a lifelong sparingness with words. (The brutal old man who had fathered and trained him had checked his childish chatter—"Spare your breath for the bellows!") "You could be useful," he said. "You know the place. And the people. The house was well kept." Indeed for a place so poor in any other kind of wealth and so disorderly in its arrangements, Bradwald was in its domestic arrangements surprisingly well stocked and well organized. "If you married me," he said.

Something in her which always stood apart, capable even in moments of anger and other emotions of making its own individual comments and judgements, thought—This, for the third time! Stigand breaking the fierce embrace, the long engulfing kiss, "I will speak to your mother, sweetheart." Old Eitel, diffident and courteous, "Madselin, I have talked with your mother." And now this Rolf, this Norman, hacking his words as though they were wood, "If you married me."

Marry one of the enemy? Marry a man whom she had first seen how long ago? An hour? Two? The man who had branded the Bradwald men, killed Eitel, and at least stood by while her mother was killed? Impossible. . . . But compare it with the only alternative, the life on the road, or retreat to Wyck. Time to think, that was what she needed. Just a few moments in which to strike the balance between the dangerous life, but free, and the safe life, tied forever to this hard inscrutable man, sure of a roof, of food, of her own bed.

"By our law, widows may not remarry within a year." Think on that; and give me time to think.

"With us, too. Where there is property. Or dues."

What he did *not* say seemed to sound as loudly as what he said and she heard it clearly. Who cares about any marriage you make? You own nothing except the clothes you wear and that harp. She, the only living child of Scartoke; Eitel's childless widow. And until two days ago, a woman of some importance, ranking high in her little world. Nothing now. A beggar. And unless she took this strange, this almost incredible offer, likely to be a beggar all her days.

He was speaking again, wrenching the words out. And seeming in a way to answer what she had not said.

"I have no rank. I was the King's armourer. Two lords coveted this land. He gave it to me. I shall be poor. A castle to build. Two knights to provide. But you would be safe with me."

Marriage, as she had already learned, had little to do with love or liking; it was a business arrangement; but even so most people tried to hide that stark fact by pleasant words, or looks of admiration. And even in the most cold-blooded arrangement one party at least usually had some reason, some preference. She said, "Why should that matter to you? My safety?"

He wondered himself. His real reason was valid enough, but to put it into words was almost impossible. And his leg hurt him. His failure to find anything of value in the Rinland bothered him—with so much to do, so much to provide for. He had been pushed, by a few words from the King, out of his element; sitting here, lord of the Rinland, he was as much out of place as Madselin was in her rôle as mendicant. He said, awkwardly, "A man needs a wife. A woman needs a home. It is for you to say. Yes or no?"

"Hild came with me. May she stay, if I do?"

"You can have all that you had before."

"Then I will marry you," she said in a small voice.

"It must be done," he said, "tomorrow. Because of the others. We will go to Bemid where the priest is."

"He will not be there. He is at Wyck, waiting to bury Eitel." And then she knew that she had broken her given word. She said hurriedly, "It is a little house of nuns, in the forest. Ten of them, all old and so *poor!* But for Eitel and my mother they would have starved long ago. They sheltered me and Hild and I promised . . . What has happened to me I do not know. I came here to ask leave to bury Eitel . . . and then I was hungry, and ate . . . and there was the choice . . . to stay here or walk the roads. And what with that mule, and Hild and the brand on Wat's forehead . . . Too much for one day . . . Too much altogether." Her lower jaw began to shake and she clenched it with her hand, forcing it to be still. Above it her eyes met his level stare, with distress, but without tears.

"You should get to bed," he said. Leaning across the table he called, "Clear that room. Throw out *our* stuff."

A harsh male odour lingered in the room, tidy again; the alien stuff removed and her clothes and Eitel's replaced in the chests. There on a shelf were her own silver glass, Eitel's wedding gift, her own brush and comb and the little pots of stuff which Camilla had given her when she left Winchester; blue for the eyelids, red for the cheeks and lips; white for nose and chin and brow. And there was the wide bed with its mattress and pillows of finest goose down, its blankets of warm light wool and its great cover of wolf pelts. It was the symbol of comfort and of safety, and snuggling down in it she tried not to think that only three nights ago she had shared this bed with Eitel, and tomorrow would be sharing it with Rolf. To everything there was a price. Loving Stigand had held moments of great joy, paid for by other moments of misery and humiliation. Fretting was useless; she would not think about the past or the future; she would think only that she was warm and safe now. And she would sleep.

And then, on the very border of sleep, she became aware of Eitel, almost as though he were present in the room. The spirits of those who had died violently were said to linger sometimes, possessed with uncanny power—usually exercised in taking vengeance. Suppose Eitel had brought her here and influenced Rolf's mind because he wished her to be safe and warm and comfortable? A heartening thought.

The wind veered; the snow became rain. Eitel lay in his shallow makeshift grave. The old mule lay down and died. Madselin slept. In her own bed.

Rolf sat at the table. When the men returned it was rain, not snow, that showed through the open door. Giffard said, "All is well in the barn—except for the man I said would die. Now I will dress your leg." He looked towards the door of the sleeping chamber and said, "Who threw out my gear?"

"And mine? My diagrams and reckonings," Peter said, speaking as though his children had been thrown on the midden.

"I ordered the room to be cleared."

Well, it was his right. It was to Rolf the Armourer that the King had given the Rinland; it was Rolf who had chosen them, Giffard to be scribe, accountant, surgeon and physician, Peter the architect to build the castle which—with two knights, armed and mounted—was what the King demanded in return for the Rinland of which Rolf was now tenant-in-chief. On Monday night, and on Tuesday, they had all slept together in the room where one bed was wide, the other small; if now he chose to sleep alone . . .

"The stuff could have been handled carefully," Peter said; and he went to the pile, took out some rolled-up parchments tied with cord and smoothed them out.

"The fresh willow bark . . . for your leg. What did they do with that?" Giffard asked, digging into the pile. "Ah." He found it and pulled it out with satisfaction. "It took me an hour to strip off. And it serves. You have suffered little pain."

They stood there for a second, Peter clutching his parchments, Giffard the willow bark about which an old woman with no teeth had told him, calling it silicate.

"She is within there," Rolf said. "We are to be married in the morning." Get it over and done with!

Peter said, "Marry? One of them?"

Giffard laughed, the belly-laugh of a fat man. "Oh, very clever! Very clever indeed. If the scales tip—as they may, who can tell? Who knows what the Danes will do? An English widow, with property! And pretty, too. You are to be congratulated . . ." As he spoke his hands were busy, untying the cord, stripping off the old buskin of bark. "Doing well. I still hold with salt." He reached into one of the silver salt-holders on the table, took some on his palm, slapped it against the wound which, though deep, was drying, and put on the fresh, silver-grey cylinder of willow bark.

"Pitied," Peter said. "Duped. She came here for no other purpose. So meek seeming. *I have come to ask leave to take my husband's body and give it burial.*" He mimicked her voice, and did it well. "I saw, I listened. She lied; she is false to the core, as they all are. From the Aetheling down. If you do this you will have an enemy in your very bed. She came here to sell herself and her looks."

Peter had an inborn dislike of women and more than his share of the Norman contempt for those who were not Normans.

"She will be useful," Rolf said.

"Will marriage make her more so?" Peter demanded.

"It was necessary. I am having no woman trouble on my manor." It was true that in a number of places trouble had been sparked off by resentment at the way some women had been treated.

"She is young," Giffard said. "And very pretty . . ." He remembered the defect in sight from which Rolf suffered and which he took pains to conceal as though it were something to be ashamed of. Giffard had discovered it by accident and remembered the occasion as the only one in which he had ever seen Rolf show emotion. So it was pointless to say that her hair was almost the colour of an apricot, her mouth like a rose and the blue of her eyes much deeper than the average in her breed. "Slender," he said, rather deprecatingly since he admired full curves, "but she will fill out. Her hands and carriage show breeding. I think you have done pretty well for yourself." He added as afterthought, "Poor Alsi." There was nothing of reproach or pity in his voice, but some amusement.

Rolf had no wish to be reminded of Alsi, the well-built fisher girl in Avranches, who, whenever he was in that district, had made him free of her favours. She had sometimes dropped wistful little hints about marriage and he had always explained that moving about in Duke William's train as he did he could not contemplate marriage yet. If she had taken that as any kind of promise for the future, that was her misfortune.

"I have already learned something it might have taken weeks to discover," he said. "There is a house of nuns, deep in the forest. The old priest is there. The wealth may be too. To-morrow, while we are being married, you look around, Peter. If there is a well, search it. Keep an eye out for fresh plaster or loose woodwork."

"There now," Giffard said merrily. "And you'd have killed the wench as you did the old woman at the other place."

"That was her mother," Rolf said expressionlessly.

"They say that before marrying a girl you should look at her mother," Peter said nastily. "A harridan if ever I saw one."

"There were no men there," Giffard said thoughtfully. "She may be heir to that too; so if things should go wrong . . . Really, this calls for wine. . . ."

CHAPTER TWO

"I knew it," the Abbess said with bitterness. "She betrayed us! Look!"

The sound of hoofbeats and voices had drawn her to the window, where the old priest now joined her. Water dripped from the eaves and from every tree. Through the drops his long-sighted eyes saw the Lady Madselin, with four mounted men, ride into the open space between the garden and the wall of the little chapel which jutted out from the main building.

"God be thanked," he said. "They have not harmed her."

The thought of what might happen to her had haunted his sleepless night. He reproached himself; he had been weak and foolish.

He had refused to go to bed—it would be so horrible, he said, if the lady, having struggled back with her sad burden, found all the house asleep. The Abbess felt obliged to keep watch with him; but after the midnight service for which the nuns crept down to the cold chapel, she again suggested bed for all. "She will not come now." "We cannot know," he said. Grudgingly the Abbess had lighted another candle, and presently another, the time-keeping candles with the marks that told the hours.

"That one, with his leg in a splint, is the new lord," Father Alfleg said. "The fat man is the Latin monger. The one in blue hustled me out." He realized his own position and stepped back from the window, almost cowering, and then recovering. "I am within my rights here. Bradwald, Ing and Scartoke I was forbidden; Wyck was not mentioned."

"Because they did not know. Until she told them," the Abbess said. Then, because she was a woman, albeit one who had put the world away fifty years ago, she said, "She is dressed very fine. Under the cloak the dress she wore at Stigand's wedding; and her own." She had gone to both weddings, being Stigand's great-aunt and somewhat related to Eitel, through his first marriage.

"Go in there," she said, nodding towards the little room in which Madselin and Hild had slept, "and I will see what is afoot." Bustling to the door, ready to placate the new lord, if possible, she thought that she did not wish to be caught harbouring the old priest; and she thought that she and all her nine nuns were too old to provoke lust in any man, and their poverty was obvious. They might survive.

Informed by Madselin of what their errand was she was both disgusted and delighted. Widowed on Monday, married on Thursday to the man responsible for her widowhood—only of Madselin could such behaviour be expected, and the Abbess reminded herself that from the very first she had disliked the girl. But a wedding was a wedding and even a Norman was bound to have some respect for the place where his marriage vows were taken. When Madselin asked, "Is Father Alfleg still here?" the Abbess replied boldly, "Yes. How could he leave, in such weather? And on foot?"

So Father Alfleg emerged and within a couple of minutes angered them all.

"But how can I perform a marriage ceremony, the man unknown to me? He may have a wife living and be about to commit bigamy. It is unlikely, but not impossible, that there is some degree of consanguinity."

These were practical considerations. But there was more. Marriage was a sacrament to be approached only by those in a state of grace.

In the single room which served the poor house at Wyck as parlour and refectory, English, Norman-French and Latin flew about as Madselin explained and Giffard explained and Rolf fretted over time wasted. Assured by Giffard that Rolf was a bachelor, Father Alfleg said to Giffard, "For that I must take your word. But he is not confessed or assoiled. However . . . I will do it. Without blessing . . . But first I must have a word with the lady. Alone. My lady, come with me," and he led the way, not into the little guest chamber but into the kitchen.

"Now," he said, "if this is by force, go through that door and get upon a horse. Go to Bemid; to Frieda who keeps my house. She will tell you what to do. I will untether and scatter the other horses. On foot—and him so lame—it will take a day. . . ."

She had despised him too. Old, fumbling, muddled. But sharp now.

"It is by my own will."

"That is a harsh man. Child, do you know what you do?"

"I know. I thank you for your care for me. But I gave my word."

"You know what you are doing?"

"I know."

He tried to see her face, less clear to him now than when she was at a distance.

"Well," he said dubiously, "he will guard you from others. He is a man who will look after what is his own." Worse things were happening every day and the fact that the man had offered her marriage was something. Compared with his night's fears. . . .

He led her back and, selecting Giffard as the most civilized of the band, said, "You will act as father to her and when I . . ." He gave up the attempt to explain in his execrable Latin, but Giffard said cheerfully that he had seen a wedding or two. Then the old man said to Madselin, "Tell that one to leave his sword. I cannot allow arms at God's altar."

"They are here for another purpose," she said. "They are in search of treasure." They had talked openly of it as they rode and taken no notice when she said that Wyck was the poorest house in Christendom.

Some nun, long ago, clever with her fingers, had painted the walls of the chapel with biblical scenes, done in crude colours. Dampness and time had ruined her work, but enough was left to be something for Madselin to stare at while the words which she had hoped to hear said over her and Stigand, and had heard said over her and Eitel, joined her to Rolf so long as they both should live. Overnight she had learned the trick of survival—forget the past, which was gone; ignore the future, which was unpredictable; live for the day, for the moment that now was.

The Abbess had issued her hasty orders and when they emerged from the chapel the table in the parlour was prepared, spread with a white cloth in the centre of which sat a little crock holding a spray or two of ivy, shining damp. There were some cups, no two alike, and a jug of what, given time to mature, would have been an intoxicant, made from the honey of the convent's bees. And the nun who cooked came in from the kitchen, bearing, with modest pride, a dish of pancakes which could be made at short notice.

"Nothing," Peter said, disgustedly, answering Rolf's inquiring glance.

The Abbess, producing a smile of about the same warmth and quality as the pallid sunshine which shone across the table, lifted the jug.

"We have no time," Rolf said to Madselin.

Giffard said, "They have done their poor best." Rolf had much to learn. A lord, however dreaded, should have gracious moments.

"Say that we have no time. Thank her," Rolf said.

At once affronted because her hospitality had been refused, and relieved because there were pancakes enough for dinner and supper today and tomorrow, the Abbess saw them ride away. The seven nuns who were still mobile, though more or less senile, scattered in response to her order to make all tidy— an order which included pouring the jug of honey wine back into the barrel. Cheated of the little feast, they were as much disappointed as Rolf and Peter who had hoped to find silver candlesticks and bowls, a golden, bejewelled crucifix. At least.

"Well," the Abbess said, "and what do you make of *that?*"

"I do not know," Father Alfleg said. "She was greatly changed. Looking from the window . . . I saw. Yesterday she was sad and troubled, but alive. Today it was different. I thought she might be under duress. That is why I took her to the kitchen and offered her a chance to escape."

"Of all the foolish actions! How could you? Had she run away his wrath would have fallen on us all."

"We are old," he said with seeming irrelevance. "She is young. And like her own wraith. Certainly she *said* that her marriage was her wish, and how could I deny? And you may have noticed that I went beyond what was demanded. I gave them the full blessing, God forgive me, as though they had come prepared. These are strange times, strange things happen, and people do strange things." He knew, he had done a strange thing himself; he had completely forgotten to ask about his old mule, his beloved Martin. He had intended to ask about the animal, to give back the ring, but in the talk and the confusion he had clean forgotten.

"A young twig can be bent," he said dismally, "an old bough breaks."

"And the old walk slowly," she reminded him, anxious to have him gone by dinner time. "It is a long walk to Bemid."

CHAPTER THREE

Rolf helped Madselin onto a full sack of barley and said, "You know what to say?"

She nodded. From her small eminence she looked down upon the men of Bradwald with their wounds and their brands, huddled in the centre of the barn; at Peter and the Norman mercenaries, standing around, at Rolf's close-cropped, copper-coloured head on one side of her, Giffard's grizzled one on the other.

She would begin with the comforting things which she had not been schooled to say.

"Men of Bradwald. When you have heard me you can go to your homes and your families. No house that was lived in has been damaged and except for Old Bertha every woman and child is safe."

Some dull eyes brightened.

"Except for some that I shall name later, every man will go about his work as before; but there will be changes. . . ."

She enumerated them as swiftly and clearly as possible, announcing the death of a free society. Everything, *everything*, now belonged to the new lord. The land, the stock, the tools. The men themselves. No man must set foot off the manor of Bradwald, unless by order or by permission. No man might marry, or allow his children to marry, without permission. The new lord gave his word that, to those who were docile and industrious, no harm would come. Of what was grown or reared they would be given a portion for sustenance; the more that was produced, the more there would be to eat. Anyone who was idle or disobedient would be punished severely.

These were all men to whom fresh air and freedom were as essential as food, and they had been in the barn since Monday. Bread and water had been brought to them regularly, but in no plenty; none of them knew what had happened to his family, or what the future held for himself. Few were in a fit state to estimate immediately the full force of the calamity that had overtaken them. Their homes were safe, their women and children waiting. The general feeling was of relief. She realized that and thought—Poor fools. On her own account, she added, "If there is any order or any rule that you do not understand, ask permission to talk to me. I speak their tongue. And I shall be here because I was married to the new lord this morning."

Most of them assumed that she had had no choice. Some looked at her and thought—Poor lady.

She said to Rolf, "Now, if you will pick the men I will name them."

He picked, unerringly, the sturdiest, if not necessarily the hardest workers.

"The one with the gash on his cheek."

"Britt Four Ox," she said. There were several Britts and each had his distinguishing name, derived from some physical feature or from some possession. Britt Four Ox was—had been —a man of some substance. He was also, since the plague, the only able-bodied man in his family. Who would man that plough? His old father, so stiff that he could only just hobble about, tending his geese and his bees?

"The tall one with the bandaged arm."

"Aldret." No plough would miss his hands; he owned no strips in the great fields, but was much in demand at shearing time, at haysel and harvest; he kept himself and his mother by such casual labour and by making and mending shoes and harnesses.

"That one, hurt on the ear."

Another Britt. Britt the thatcher, a man with a wife and four children; one who at times when most men, harvest in, took things easy, would go around the Rinland or over to Bemid and Cressacre to mend thatches or lay new ones. Could Emma, his wife, till their land?

As Rolf chose and she named the men, Madselin realized how much knowledge she had acquired, in an uncaring way, about the men of the place to which she had come unwillingly and about which she had felt so little. Eitel's talk, of course, had been mainly about Bradwald, and it had bored her, but even her inattentive ear had absorbed more than it had seemed to.

After the tenth name Rolf stopped and said, discontent in his voice, "It is far short of what is needed, but it must serve. Point out Peter to them, tell them they will take his orders. They are to be by the stockade gate, tomorrow at first light."

"What tools should they bring?"

A good question, he thought: she had her wits about her.

"Spades," he said.

She relayed the order and then, before dismissing them, added more words of her own.

"You fought bravely," she said. "But we were defeated. We must make ourselves useful and pleasing to those who are now our masters. So we shall survive. Go now, and God go with you."

Rolf helped her down and Giffard beamed at her.

"Well spoken," he said. "I understand more English than I know—or know more than I understand. Either way, it was well spoken."

She said to Rolf, "May I now go to where I think Hild may be?"

"You may go where you wish, provided it is safe."

She sped to Wat's house, noting as she went that at the lower end of the commonland—the piece that lay between the hall and the houses, the forge and the mill that composed the town—pegs had been driven into the ground in a great circle and that cords joined peg to peg.

Wat's house was small; he and Edfu had no children and there had never been need to build on. In the single room, with the bed in an alcove, Wat and Edfu sat by the fire, and Hild lay on a makeshift bed on the other side. She seemed to be asleep.

"I hoped she would be safe with you," Madselin said. "I could not come before. I had much to do."

Wat said, "Is it true, my lady . . . what Alfred said . . . when I milked this morning and fed the cows?"

"I am married to the new lord."

The old man groaned and looked stricken. Then from somewhere he seemed to gather force and energy.

"It was by force. The vows have no hold, my lady. Even now . . . Better be homeless and hungry with the wild ones. I will set you on your way. . . ." As he spoke he looked for and found his hood. Edfu snatched it from him, dropped her hand to his shoulder and shook him roughly.

"Shut your mouth! I am weary of such talk." She looked at Madselin. "The hurt overturned his mind, poor man. He thinks we could run into the forest and be free. The wild ones he speaks of—there are no such people, except in his old head." She shook him again. "Talk like that will get us into trouble. Now be quiet or go to your cows. The lady must look to Hild."

"I will go to the cows," Wat said, and it seemed as though he spoke direct to Madselin.

"She has lain like that since Wat dragged her in," Edfu said. "Should a sleep last so long? Sunset to sunset?"

"We walked from Wyck. And she was so frightened that she swooned," Madselin said. But it was time the girl woke now. "Hild! Hild! Wake up!"

"I have shaken her," Edfu said.

"Shake her again."

Edfu went down on her knees and took Hild by the shoulders. The girl was as limp as a rag and did not wake, and now

that her head was clear of the bedding and in the full light of
the fire, Madselin could see that her face was twisted, the
mouth lifted at one corner, like a dog's before the first warning
snarl, the lower lid of the eye on that side drooping.

"Lay her back, Edfu. She took a fit. She may die." Poor Hild,
who had come so reluctantly. But as Madselin had stood on
the barley sack and looked at the men who would henceforth
be slaves in all but name, she had thought again that perhaps
the dead were the fortunate ones.

Edfu made noises of distress. It was unlucky to have one
who was not your blood kin die under your roof. Two others
would die there. That was one of the oldest superstitions—it
had prevented the killing of the stranger as he ate or slept.
This origin had been forgotten, but the belief had been
strengthened by the fact that it was generally strangers who
brought in sicknesses. Britt Four Ox's wife had allowed the sick
pedlar to shelter—and die—in their barn, and her father and
sister had been the first to die in Bradwald.

Madselin walked back towards the hall through a scene of
muted activity as men looked to see how their stock had fared
in their absence and women hastily prepared food. Here and
there men and women stood and talked, in muted voices
which hushed altogether as she approached. In the barn some
of the men had looked upon her as a fellow victim and pitied
her a little; the womenfolk had seen it differently—She is one
of *them* now! That remark had changed their attitude and it
was to be a long time before men forgot that it was through
her mouth that they learned of the new rules whose full im-
port and harshness they were to discover, day by day, in the
next few months.

Wat stood waiting to waylay her under the awning by the
byre. He had the yoke on his shoulders and two freshly
scrubbed buckets hanging from it; he was prepared to begin
milking if any Norman came by, and he was keeping a wary

eye upon Peter, who was again busy with the pegs and the cords and the measuring rule.

"My lady!"

She halted.

"It *is* true," he said in a hasty, low voice. "Men and some women, from places taken earlier, living in the swallow-holes and eating what they can catch. I wanted to go but Edfu would not. I can tell you how to find them." Looking furtively this way and that, he began to tell her and she interrupted him.

"You mean well, Wat, but I have no desire to sleep in a cave and eat half-raw venison."

"They are free," he said.

"Not for long. They will be hunted out."

He had meant well and was disappointed. He said peevishly, "Edfu also wished to *sleep in her own bed!*"

The reproach held no sting for her. In her early days at Winchester she had been anxious not to appear ignorant and rustic; she had been avid for Stigand's approval, and her mother's anger was something to be avoided if possible: otherwise what people thought or said about her had never mattered to her much, armoured as she was in self-love. And now she had other things to think of than the rebuke implied in the old cowherd's words.

In a grossly unfavourable market she had bargained for security and comfort, perhaps even for life, and as the short winter day faded and died, the hour of settlement drew near. Soon she must go to bed with a churl.

"The motte itself," Peter said, "will take only a few days. They dig, and throw the earth inward and make at one and the same time the moat and the mound. But it must be stamped down. Even a wooden fortress cannot be reared upon an insecure foundation." He said the word *wooden* with bitter contempt; his dreams were concerned with hewn stone castles such as he had seen in Italy. But this was a barbarous country and the Conqueror himself was content, it seemed, with a wooden tower in London, erected under the direction of Gandulph, called contemptuously, Gandulph the Weeper. But *he* was a bishop. Peter, with all his skill, had found no patron except Rolf the Armourer. That thought consumed him like a canker. "Even with the one-armed, one-eyed fellows assigned me," he said, "the motte can be ready in five days—if everybody stamps and rams. The question of timber remains. It will not be ready."

The men from Ing and Scartoke, who had put up no resistance, had not been branded or incarcerated. They had simply been sent into the forest to cut down trees not less than ten feet high with trunks of from twelve to eighteen inches in diameter. That order had been given, by gesture, by Giffard's small knowledge of English, some time on Monday or Tuesday, and already, on this Thursday afternoon, some timber had been hauled in.

"I cannot think," Giffard said, "that such haste is necessary. The King is a reasonable man. To take a place, settle it and begin building a castle, all within a week, is not reasonable and I am sure he would not expect it done."

"Did you ever stand face to face with him?" Rolf asked. "I did. He chose me to do the impossible. Because I had done it. On his coat of mail." The King was attached to his leather jerkin, closely sewn over with flat metal rings, and refused to replace it as he increased in girth; enlarging it, keeping it in repair had been a test of skill and ability to contrive, qualities which must now be applied to a vaster and very different task.

"I still think you misunderstood," Giffard said.

"You misunderstood me," Rolf said and proceeded with his supper in silence, brooding. Giffard, who had known him for a long time, knew better than to press the point. Peter brooded, too; in a lifetime of disappointments this Rinland venture had been the greatest. Nothing of value had been found; he must plan and overlook a makeshift, hurried job. Of the ten men who would start work on the motte tomorrow six were incapacitated by injuries; the timber, when it arrived, would be unseasoned.

Madselin was not interested in this talk of building and she was practised in ignoring what did not interest her; she had sat, scores of times, in this very place, but beside Eitel, and paid scant attention to his droning talk.

"It would save labour," Rolf said at last, "if all the sheep ran together under the care of one man. I saw good pasture, empty, at Scartoke."

The word arrested her. Ignorant fools not to have guessed why those meadows were empty in midwinter. Well, it was nothing to do with her. Let them drive the sheep there and watch them get foot-rot and all the other ills to which sheep were prone in such damp, low-lying places. As she thought that she cut a mouthful of smoked mutton ham and was about to lift it when another thought struck. Next year no fresh saddle of mutton at Whitsun, no haunches to smoke and hang up for winter use. Next June no shearing time, or a poor one. If she allowed *them*, through ignorance, to take this, or any other ruinous action, she would share that ruin.

"Sheep would not flourish there."

"Why not?"

"It is too damp; their feet rot away, and their insides. There were never sheep in quantity at Scartoke, just a few, here and there, kept in the garths beside the houses."

"Which is the best sheep land hereabouts?"

"Ing. It stands high." Having begun she might as well go on. "In summer those meadows have a use. The grass is green there. Cattle do well. And it was always reckoned that a week or two on those meadows would cure a cracked hoof in a horse." Whenever pasture was short elsewhere, the men from Ing and Bradwald would bring their cattle down to the water meadows at Scartoke to graze and in return gave her mother some share of whatever they had done well with that season. The meadows served another purpose too: twice a year a man and his wife came to collect the water snails which abounded there. Dried and pounded the snails were a cure for the cough. In return the Snail Man, as he was known, brought salt or a small, precious handful of spice, and once, in a little jar, something called hartshorn which he said was better far than burnt feathers for bringing anyone out of a swoon. The Lady Edith had rejected it with scorn; swooning was not encouraged at Scartoke, and on the few occasions when anyone seemed to be unconscious, a sharp slap on the hand had been effective.

These thoughts brought the past, sudden and clear, between her and the table at which she sat with the three men who represented the race who had overturned the old, comfortable, familiar world. And presently, with one of them, she must go to bed.

She had visualized it as a repetition of the necessary but distasteful procedure which she had already endured in this room, in this bed. Eitel, fine man as he had undoubtedly been in his prime, was, when he married her, shrivelled and hollowed out by age, and the gaps where he had lost teeth had been repulsive to her. She had married him under the combined compulsions of her mother's will and the need to save her pride in the face of Stigand's perfidity. Now she had another husband, utterly different, equally distasteful, whom she had married because he offered shelter. She had managed before; she could do it again.

She had come to bed early, leaving Rolf, Giffard and Peter talking. Peter had pulled the talk back to building and was drawing, with a stick of charcoal, on the white table-cloth which would, she reflected idly, need a good deal of washing and bleaching, with bleaching difficult in winter days, before it was fit to use again.

In the old days the door of the sleeping chamber had been kept open during the evening, so that some of the heat from the fire in the hall might penetrate. Today the door had remained closed and the room was chill. She missed Hild as she brushed her own hair and laid her clothes away. Rolf had promised her all that she had once had, and that meant a body-maid; but he had not noticed that now she had none; he had not asked if she had found Hild, alive or dead. She ran through her mind a list of possible replacements. In this new way of life, with even Britt Four Ox and Uffa the miller reduced to serfdom, a good sensible woman should not be hard to come by. See about it in the morning, she thought, getting into her bed-gown and, because now everything in the past had a special vividness, remembering that until she went to Winchester she, like everybody else in the Rinland, had in the old fashion slept bare, and the absence of bed-gowns from her baggage had been remarked. She had been quick-witted enough then to say that hers were all outgrown, not worth bringing, she would buy new. She had always been ready with excuses, quick to explain away anything that would shame her or call down reproof, sly in the evasion of duties she found tiresome; now she was in a situation where slipperiness would not serve.

Rolf came in, carrying a candle which, thriftily, he extinguished as soon as he saw that hers was still alight.

"Peter kept me," he said. There was nothing in his voice or about his movements, as he began to take off and lay away his clothes, to indicate that he was profoundly ill-at-ease and at the same time excited. He was thirty years old and not inexperienced; there had been others before and besides Alsi, but all more or less like her, solid, easygoing, earthy young women. This would, he sensed, be different, better or worse, who could say? Last night, when she had faced Peter and been frightened, and fought fear off, he had thought—That is the *kind* of woman . . . And within an hour he had offered to marry her and she had agreed to marry him. He had explained his incomprehensible behaviour to himself by thinking that she would be useful—and that had already been proved true—but he had been sorry for her too, and being sorry for people was not his habit; nor was acting on impulse, or being in a position to give way to a whim.

Madselin, from behind the shaggy wolf pelt, watched him undress. From the base of his neck downwards, and from midway between elbow and shoulder, his skin was white as milk, in strange contrast with the places in which it was weathered. He was very muscular, very shapely. She noted these things without a flicker of desire. She had once known how body and mind could strain together towards one end—in her case never achieved—and she was not likely to be content with less. Rolf might have physical attractions, but he was still the enemy, as unacceptable to her mind as old Eitel had been to her body. She noted, with cold approval, that he was tidy, folding and laying away his shabby worn clothing with more care than they merited.

Then he was in the bed.

In no time at all something outside them both had taken charge, lifting and shaking them, making mock of differences of nationalities and all past experiences, even of sex, since now, for a timeless moment, both were one. In the white heat of passion everything else melted away.

It was new to them both. Her dreams of Stigand had been limited by her youth and her inexperience; the ripple of excitement that had run through her when he kissed her had given little hint of what the full tide might be, this shattering thing which meant not merely a loss of self, or self-consciousness, but almost the loss of consciousness itself: like fainting, like dying. Rolf had looked upon Alsi and the others much as he had looked upon food—necessary, pleasant, taken for granted when available, important only when unobtainable. This was utterly, utterly different.

Then it was over. Madselin fell back into Madselin, slightly ashamed. A Norman! How could this be? Rolf fell back into Rolf, more than slightly cautious. An Englishwoman who would, given the slightest hint of her power, begin to twist him around her little finger. And he had more to think of. Peter's venom; Giffard's amusement.

Without a word, or even a conniving glance, they locked the

thing away; a secret to be kept behind the door of the sleeping chamber. Outside it cool and civil behaviour—you are useful to me, I am useful to you. Admit nothing by day; wait for the night; and in the morning close the door between the two worlds firmly.

"A girl?" Rolf said, using his knack of making one word serve for twenty. He looked at Hild and looked away, feeling some of the repulsion which more fanciful men admitted to where spiders, frogs, rats, cats were concerned. A mouth drawn up, an eye drawn down, a leg that dragged and an arm that sagged. One's wife's waiting woman lived close, could not be avoided. "Find yourself a girl," he said. "She could tend pigs."

Madselin could have said, and would have said to a less arbitrary man—but I owe her a place; she came with me, much against her will, and thus suffered the fit that maimed her. But to him she said, "You promised me all that I once had. And Hild is part of it."

She would have been glad to send Hild to tend pigs, for the girl had changed, gathering from her fit not only the look and infirmity of age but an insolence, a rudeness. One could only conclude that her wits were disturbed. Nothing else could account for the change in Hild.

"As you wish, but keep her out of my sight," Rolf said.

He had other things to think of. Peter had said that the motte would be ready in five days. Three weeks had gone by with rain or snow, sometimes both every day. The ten men chosen to dig had started and gone on until they were no longer lifting and throwing inwards spadefuls of soil but of mud, so loose that it fell off the spades as they rose. It seemed sensible, at that point, to let the men return to their ploughs until the weather cleared. Peter said, "I see now, with such a climate and such soil, why the English build nothing but wooden kennels."

Giffard said, "What of Westminster? You must wait for summer."

There was the question of supplies. The King, making the gift of this lost and forgotten corner to his faithful armourer, had said it would merely be a matter of walking in, but he should take enough men with him to make a show. So Rolf had hired his mercenaries. They had not been needed at Scartoke or Ing, but they had earned their pay at Bradwald, and he had paid them, with the savings of a lifetime, since the treasure everyone expected to find and to share had not been there. He kept two, both past youth and ready to settle, both wounded in the Bradwald fight. Arnulph was at Scartoke, seeing that the work was done; Roger was doing the same service at Ing. Twenty men in a week had made inroads into the Bradwald stores which could not be replenished before summer.

The matter of the two knights bothered him, too. The King had been generous; the usual lowest unit for a tenant-in-chief was five. But even two must be found—and who would wish to take knight service with a master not only of humble origin but into the bargain very poor? Once found they must be kept, and paid. They would make demands. They would have airs and graces.

Sometimes he felt that the only good the strange gift had brought him centred about the sleeping chamber, and even about that he must be careful. Men who succumbed too completely in bed lost authority out of it.

Early in March the weather changed; the east wind blew and at midday the sun had power. The ten picked men resumed digging, throwing the soil inwards and then spreading it. There was a new rule. Everyone, in the last hour of daylight, must cross the little bridge and stamp or ram the earth down. Some used spades, some a new tool, a heavy square of wood with a handle in its centre; and all used their feet. By the end of the month as the days grew longer the mound grew higher and Peter was selecting from the tree trunks that had been dragged in, even on the worst days, those of comparable length and thickness which would be driven in to act as foundation piles.

"I will go and stamp," Hild said.

"Hild, there is no need. You are lame. You have other things to do."

"Mending his shirt I leave to you," Hild said. "You are his wife. I will go out and stamp with the *English*."

That was the kind of thing she said nowadays: the words never such as could be challenged or rebuked, the meaning, the manner deeply malicious.

On this afternoon Madselin said, "Hild, you must be more careful. Giffard is mastering our language fast. Yesterday, when you called him a fat pig . . . I think he understood."

"So? And today I said I would go and stamp with the English. Is that wrong? I *shall* stamp. They *are* English."

"It is the way you speak, Hild." She looked at the girl, and out of her own feeling of depression and hopelessness, added, "If you fall foul of them, any one of them, I doubt if I could protect you."

Sometimes Hild's twisted face seemed to snarl, sometimes to smile mirthlessly, sometimes to sneer. It sneered now.

The evening sky was pale apple-green, and although the evening was cool it held a promise of primroses. The mound was in clear view as Madselin stood by the narrow window and watched the ramming and the stamping being done by people already exhausted by a long day's work. It was the season of seed-sowing and with the ten strong men back at the digging their labour was missed in the fields. Britt the thatcher's wife and her eldest—a child of about six—were scattering the seed in his furrows, while the three little ones, too young to be helpful, or to be left alone in the house, huddled in the shelter of the balk. This extra labour was an imposition and would have been done lethargically but for the fact that

Peter now carried a whippy stick which he used on anyone
who displayed insufficient energy. He looked upon them as animals and treated them as such.

The figures stood out like a frieze against the sky; largely
anonymous; those who used the rammers or the spades
were distinguishable by their movements: Hild's stamping—a
mere gesture of loyalty—was an uneven lurch; Edfu had a red
cloak which stood out against the general buff of the homespun, as did the blue hood of Britt Four Ox's wife. Madselin
could hear the thud of the rammers, the slap of the spades, no
sound of voices; and this at Bradwald where every communal
labour had always been done with chatter and laughter and an
air of festivity! She had tried to school herself to avoid all comparisons between past and present, but such thoughts would
occur from time to time, and when they did they made the
bed's secret all the more shameful.

Peter had never hit Hild; probably he understood that she
was a volunteer—the fact that she was lame would not alone
have gained her any consideration. This evening, however, he
hit Edfu, who, like Wat, was old and who, since Aldret had resumed digging, had been helping his mother with shoemaking.
Madselin saw the blow fall. Then she saw Hild move, snatch
the stick, break it across her knee and throw the two pieces
into the water of the ditch. She made for the door, gathering
up her skirts and ran towards the mound, crying, "Peter, no!"
crying "Wait. I will deal . . ." She had a strong feeling that
this was the kind of incident that Peter would welcome, an excuse for some cruelty. He would punish Hild in some terrible
fashion; probably punish them all. Those on the mound must
have felt the same fear; all work had stopped.

Then Madselin saw that there was no immediate need for
intervention. Peter and Hild faced one another; Hild seemed
to say something. Peter took two steps backward, almost as
though she had pushed him; and then swung about and
shouted one of the few English words he had acquired.
"Work!" Work began again and Hild went on with her lop-

sided stamping. It was a most inexplicable thing; Peter was the last person in the world to take such an affront calmly, or to control himself for the moment by the thought of what he would do later.

She turned back to the house, feeling, as she always did under any emotional stress, horribly sick. And not only sick, curiously heavy, and far more breathless than the short run warranted. She admitted to herself that she had not felt really well for several days.

"Hild, terrible things have started over smaller things than what you did today. He might have set about you and then a man with a spade might have lost his head. . . . It was a most dangerous thing to do."

"Nothing happened."

"We have not heard the last of it yet. He will complain to the new lord." To others she always spoke of him so. "You will be punished and maybe others, merely because they were there and saw him insulted."

"I think not. I cowed him."

"It seemed so. But Hild, how could you cow him? What was it that you said?"

"I *said*—Touch me and you'll be sorry!"

It sounded futile, pitiable; a cornered rat rising on its hind legs and showing its teeth. But as Hild spoke the eye over which she still had control narrowed while the other sagged; combined with the sneer . . . an expression of such malevolence that Madselin felt a chill at the back of her neck, between her shoulders.

"He did not understand what I *said*. He knew what I *meant*."

"And I know what this means. You will be sent to tend pigs."

Considering how timid Hild was about some things, and tending pigs included driving them into the edge of the forest

in autumn when the acorns were down, she took this with surprising calm.

"Maybe. Unless you ask for me. Unless *he* is unlike other
men. Most men, over the first child, at least, do not wish to
upset the woman."

"Hild!"

"Count the days," Hild said. "I wash your linen." Abruptly
her manner changed to a fawning obsequiousness, as alien
from her old manner as her recent insolence, but equally offensive. "Most ladies in your condition like to be tended by those
whom they know. But if I am sent to tend pigs, ask for Githa—
when the time comes. . . ."

"Hild! You know, I know . . . A cold in the head, losing my
temper . . . And when I first went to Winchester where there
was so much to learn . . . three months on end. And with all
this . . . I thought today I was not feeling myself . . . And
then the fear and the running . . ." She recovered herself. "I
cannot give that reason for keeping and shielding you, Hild.
Any other plea that can be made, I shall make." She could say
that since the fit Hild was as twisted in mind as in face; she
could say that when Hild took her fit Edfu had tended her. It
would none of it mean anything or carry weight. The Normans
were not human. Rolf, alone with her, behind the door of the
sleeping chamber, *seemed* human, but once on the other side
he was like the rest of them, cold, hard, thinking only of their
own well-being, or arranging things to their advantage.

The matter of Hild's defiance was never mentioned. Had
Peter actually been cowed for a moment and then, ashamed,
fearing that Rolf would say—Why did you not throw her after
the stick? Or that Giffard would say—Do you believe in the
Evil Eye? Nothing was said about the incident; eating in his
absent-minded manner Peter simply said that in two or three
days' time the mound would be high enough and the work of
driving in the foundation wood could begin.

Rolf said, "That is something. I hoped to have more to report at Easter, but the weather was against me."

"To report," Giffard asked, swallowing one of the mouthfuls which had made Hild call him a pig. "To whom?"

"The King. That was a condition. Easter, Lammas, Michaelmas and Christmas; to look to his mail. It means nothing. I trained Theobald and he is able. . . . But on me, as on the rest, he must keep his finger. I had hoped to say 'twice my height' when he asked how the walls went. Thigh high, Peter, by Easter?"

"Not less. I will measure up on the day before you go and tell you to an inch," Peter said.

Giffard said, "And he will be amazed. If you explain how few men; and no money." To that remark Rolf made no reply; it showed ignorance of William's character, manner, glance, none of which invited explanations that sounded like complaints.

"I need another twenty men. At least," Peter said. He began to explain that whereas ten had been sufficient to dig since it was useless to have more soil thrown in than could be properly rammed at the day's end, once the real building began he could use forty, fifty, sixty.

"Some might be spared from Scartoke and Ing, now that the seed is sown," Rolf said. "We will arrange it tomorrow." Whenever he said "we" in that way Madselin knew that he would issue blunt orders and she would put them into English. Useful, necessary and helpful work which had contributed in the last few weeks to the smooth running of the new methods in the three towns. But it was becoming more and more distasteful to her, because, as people experienced what alien rule meant, they became more sullen, resentful and suspicious, and looked at her, saying, wordlessly—You are one of *them*. The self-approval and self-interest that had buffered her against criticism from outside had begun to flake away. It had cracked on that first night, in bed with the enemy, and the process had continued.

She sat there, toying with her food, and thought of what this new order would mean to some men at Scartoke and at Ing.

Either a long walk in the dark of the morning, another in the dark of the evening, or leaving home and lodging in Bradwald. Neither way would be welcome. She knew how the chosen men would regard her—the bringer of more bad news. She shrank from the prospect and thought—Hild was right, perhaps; I have never felt this way before, all weak and vulnerable, even a little grateful that the supper-table talk had not turned upon Hild's behaviour. If Peter meant to complain he would have done so before supper, surely; and though I no longer like her, or find any comfort in her company, I should have felt bound to defend her and in this state I could not put up a good fight; I am not myself.

Hild, as though to make up for the weakness of one hand, used the other with force. Bringing the brush down heavily so that Madselin winced, she said, "Well? And am I to go to the pigs?"

"You were not mentioned. The talk was all of other things. It may happen yet. Hild, do not bang with that brush. My head has trouble enough. Inside."

"With what is to be said tomorrow? Child told me. None of this would have happened had you not been so handy with their tongue."

"And where should we have been?"

"At Wyck."

"And cold and hungry, you ungrateful girl! I doubt whether the place would have stayed undiscovered long. That Giffard has explored every path, hunting for what is not to be found. In any case, what is done is done . . . And if you must either use the brush as a rammer or too softly to serve at all, leave it."

Hild put the brush down and stood, as was her way now, resting her weight on her sound leg, holding her weak arm in her sound hand.

"I think you do not wish to ride to Scartoke and Ing tomorrow."

"Would *you*? The men there will hate what I have to say and hate me for saying it. I am tired of hatred."

"Let Giffard go; he understands English so well!"

"There is some difference between understanding a few words and being able to explain."

"A few words are enough," Hild said. With startling accuracy she mimicked Peter. "Work! Stop! Good! Bad! Fool!"

CHAPTER FOUR

Hild said to Giffard, "Now I have much to tell you." He was not repulsed by her appearance and often talked to her, because, apart from Madselin, she was the one English person with leisure enough for conversation. He was set on perfecting his English as soon as possible and since he had a keen ear and never forgot anything, he was making rapid progress.

"Speak slowly," he said.

Speaking slowly she told him that the Lady Madselin was with child. She aided speech with gestures, outlining an imaginary distended body, holding up her fingers to indicate the months and then cradling and rocking a child in her arms.

"The lord will be pleased," Giffard said. He guessed that Rolf did not know; such a piece of information even that uncommunicative man would hardly have kept to himself. Also there was something about Hild's manner that indicated that this was a piece of special knowledge. She had held up seven fingers—so the lady was only just aware of her state and had perhaps taken this roundabout way of informing her husband. Women were odd about such matters even in normal circumstances and this was, Giffard knew, a very curious marriage indeed. No sign of fondness or familiarity between them, merely a cool civility.

"You want me to tell him?" he asked.

Hild nodded.

"Not to please him. To spare her. Listen . . ." Speaking a little more quickly than allowed for instant translation, she told of Madselin's sister, Ethel, a stout, strong girl, who had ridden when she was pregnant and jolted the baby so that it came feet first and died when it was born. Ethel too. This tragedy was difficult to mime, but she did her best.

"Say it again," Giffard said. "Slowly, please."

Hild said it all again, and then, aping someone riding a horse, added, "Ing and Scartoke tomorrow . . . No! No horse riding for seven months." She held up her fingers again. "She goes on a horse and he will lose his son. Tell him that."

"His son?" Giffard said, his mind, as curious as it was critical, instantly diverted. Had these English people, in many ways so primitive, some secret means of divining the sex of a child seven months before it was born? "How can you say that?"

She could not give him the honest answer. She could not mention the age-old belief that children with *two* fathers were always boys.

"I feel it here," she said, and put a hand to her chest. "She will not speak. She says it is too early. But she must not go to Ing or Scartoke. Bad for her, here," she put her hand to her girdle, "and here," she touched her own head. "No horse . . . you understand me? Nothing to upset." She made a whirling motion about her own forehead.

"I will see to it," Giffard said.

Hild was satisfied. She had appreciated, in her own way, the kindness of Eitel, her old master, and it seemed to her that there was reason to think that the child might be his. She had, most reluctantly, come with Madselin to Bradwald to bury his body, but if within Madselin something of Eitel lived on, its life must not be endangered. It must live and grow and be born and be born a boy to inherit what was his own.

"Why did you not tell me, first of all?" Rolf said in the dark.

"I was not sure. I am even now not sure. Hild, since her fit, has been strange . . . and this afternoon—you heard what happened? I feared for her. I ran. And I felt sick. She takes too much upon herself. She had no right to speak of it."

Rolf found himself in the peculiar position of standing up for Hild, upon whom he could not bear to look.

"It was for your good. Your sister . . ." He repeated the story which Hild had told Giffard and which Giffard had told him. There was not a word of truth in it. Ethel had never been fond of riding and would seize any excuse . . . "So Giffard must make shift to do the talking tomorrow," Rolf ended. Madselin then saw the point of Hild's fabrication; it was to spare her that distasteful task. She was grateful, but mixed with the gratitude was wonderment. The new Hild, though surly and often uncivil, apparently still retained some feeling of loyalty, and had developed a quick-witted cunning not formerly much in evidence.

"She predicts a boy," Rolf said.

The intimacy of this talk, the hopefulness in his voice, was part and parcel of the double life they led; one on the other side of that door, and one on this. Underlining the falsity of both, it irked her and she said shortly, "It is far too early to know whether there will be a child at all." She rolled over and with her back to him pretended to be asleep, and presently was.

She dreamed that she was in some vast, frightening place; forest? Some building bigger than any ever reared? It was too dark to see. Out of the darkness a voice called, "Madselin!" and the word went echoing on; and then was repeated, the echoes following. It was Stigand. He sounded frightened too. He was appealing to her to find, to help him. She tried, but in the darkness she could not judge the direction; but she sensed that if she stood still and called, he would be able to find her. But it was dangerous to announce her presence. Nevertheless, she forced herself to it, calling his name, shaking with fear.

Then she was awake, Rolf was holding her and shaking her, not very gently.

"Wake up! You are safe. Madselin!" For a moment the real voice saying her name mingled with the voice of the dead man.

"Everything is all right," Rolf said. "You're safe. . . ."

"I was dreaming. A horrible dream," she said shakily. "I was lost. In the dark. Terrified."

"And shouting," he said, "to wake the house."

She was still shaking and was ashamed. Born and reared in the belief that courage was the ultimate virtue and that fear, if felt, must be concealed, she felt degraded.

And then she thought—How strange that I should dream of Stigand now! She never had before; never once during all those times of childish infatuation, despair, the later hope, the final hatred. Never once when he had figured in her last waking thought had he had any part in her dream life. So why now, when he was dead, the flesh rotting or rotted?

She said, "I am sorry I woke you."

"I know what bad dreams can be. I have suffered them myself."

His had always been of heights; from the tops of high towers, or high trees, or the last rung of scaling ladders he fell, clutching at air with hands gone numb and limp. Lately he had not been so troubled in his sleep, but he was able to sympathize. After a moment he said, "You shouted for Stigand. Who is he?"

"A dead man," she said. "He was lord at Bemid and died on Senlac Field. Once, when I was a child, he saved me. I was treed by a wolf and he happened to come along and the wolf ran away."

She said those things from the topmost layer of her mind. At a lower level she was thinking that she knew what Purgatory was, that blinding darkness, and fear, and the sense of responsibility and wish to help which was impotent and could only call out for help itself. All lost in the dark and calling to one another. She thought of Purgatory, of her own bad dream— now rapidly vanishing—and did not think to ask Rolf what form had been taken by his bad dreams which had made him so understanding of hers. He did not notice the omission. He had never known sympathy and any tendency towards self-pity had been purged from him years ago.

Life went on. The days lengthened. With infinite toil the foundation timbers were driven into the mound and some cross timbers hammered home. The castle would be rather more than thigh high, with luck, breast high, when Rolf went at Easter to his King. But before that the matter of the knights must be settled.

Giffard was despatched to London to find two knights willing to take service with an ex-armourer in an isolated place. "They will be either very young or very old," Rolf said flatly, "but I want no cripples or men wrong in the head."

"So narrow a choice makes my task easy," Giffard said sardonically. But in less than a fortnight he was back, very pleased with himself. The first full tide of the invasion was ebbing. The English Enterprise, as it was called, had attracted more people than it could provide for. The conquered country appeared to be settling down peaceably and there was a slight surplus of younger sons, cousins, men known to be of awkward disposition, even men who were too poor to replace the horse killed, the sword broken, at Senlac. Of these Giffard had hired two; one slightly past his prime, Sir Godfrey, who should by all rights have been by this time in possession of an English manor—but he had once, years ago, fallen out with Bishop Odo, King William's half-brother. The other was a young man, Sir Eustace, who had fallen out with his father.

"I was fortunate," Giffard said. "Both, in their way, are superior to most of those to be hired. Both were financially embarrassed . . . in debt to the Jews. For the assumption by you, of these debts, and a year's keep, both are willing to take knight service with you for a year."

"You did well, Giffard. And when will they arrive?"

"After Easter. A week. Ten days. There is an open tourney at Easter, at Winchester, which both, being free, wished to attend. And," Giffard said, delicately, "in the circumstances . . .

I felt it unwise to insist upon time . . . But they are engaged, I think they are both honourable. I think you may tell the King that you have fulfilled your obligations. The castle shoulder high, the two knights engaged."

"One does not *tell* him," Rolf said. "He may ask and, thanks to you and Peter, if he does I can give answers which I hope will satisfy."

"The King keeps Easter at Winchester," Giffard said. "You could look your men over." He looked at Rolf with a covert curiosity. He had not objected to going to London and fixing the business, haggling with the Jews he had positively enjoyed, but he did wonder why Rolf had not left the whole matter until Easter and at Winchester made his own choice.

Rolf said, "I shall have no time to hang about tourney grounds. I shall look to the King's mail, have a word with Theobald and start back. All in one day, with luck."

The whole business of the knights embarrassed him in a deep and secret way that he would have died sooner than acknowledge. In a society rooted and rigidly ordered upon a man's fighting capacity there was a wide, impassable gulf between a knight, however old and decrepit, or however young and inexperienced, and an armourer, even the best in the world—and Rolf knew he was the best; William would not have been satisfied with less. The King, from impulse, or perhaps from sagacity, had, with a few words, translated his armourer into a landowner, one who *employed* knights, housed and fed them, saw that they were well mounted and armed. Rolf's cold good sense and his pride saw the awkwardness inherent in the situation. It could not be avoided, so he had faced it. But he knew that both knights, reduced by disappointed hopes and penury to being in a position where they were willing to take service with a man who was not himself a knight, would feel their pride damaged and endeavour to make up for it in various small devious ways. He knew knights; all avarice and ambition.

Madselin, informed of Giffard's success in his errand, was first concerned with where Sir Godfrey and Sir Eustace would sleep.

"This place was not geared for the housing of knights," she said. There were the two rooms behind the little dais. One had always been a store-room but it was cleared now and Giffard occupied it. He had invited Peter to share it with him, but Peter said he preferred the little nook to which he had taken himself and his belongings on that first night. "Giffard must move," she said.

"No," Rolf said, concealing the reasonless anger that sprang up at this suggestion. "Giffard was first here. They can sleep as Peter does, between the wall and the posts. There is room for twenty."

Remembering Winchester and feeling responsibility as the mistress of this hall, she said, "They will not like it."

"Then they will dislike it."

"There is room now at Ing and at Scartoke," she said, intending to be helpful.

"That would not do," he said, not bothering to explain why. Give any knight an inch and he'd take a yard, as by right. Sir Godfrey of Ing; Sir Eustace of Scartoke. The manors were his, and the knights were his. They must live where he could keep an eye on them.

He spoke in a manner that never failed to infuriate her. Curt, dismissive. It not only denied and ridiculed their secret relationship, it made a sharp and ugly contrast with Eitel's behaviour to her. Eitel would consult her about so simple a thing as setting a broody hen over a clutch of eggs. So, angered again, she said, with intent to hurt, "To my mind an alcove like Peter's is good enough for them. They have failed in their duty to you. They should have been here, now; ready to ride behind you when you go to the King."

That aspect had never struck him, but it was true. He repudiated the idea, firmly, without showing the distaste it evoked.

"When I go to my King, I go as armourer," he said.

It was that kind of flat statement, his refusal to argue, or to wince at a verbal wound, which made a shared life by day impossible. He would ask her point-blank questions and sometimes she answered them with an imitation of his own brevity; "Yes," "No," "Never in my time." It was not in order to please him that she busied herself with arrangements for the housing of the knights; it was from a perverse form of pride. She did not wish the Norman knights to despise English Bradwald. But it was Giffard whom she asked to inquire of Peter whether it would be possible to wall in, at least partially, two of the alcoves along the west wall, and it was Giffard who gave her the answer. Quite impossible. There was neither labour nor material to spare for such nonessential work. She then remembered that at Ing there had been hangings across one wall, stiff, heavy things which some seafaring ancestor of Eric's had brought home and hung, with other trophies, on his wall. She sent Hild and Edfu and a pack pony to bring them back to Bradwald, which they did with some difficulty, Hild loudly complaining of being forced to do men's work, Edfu surly. Next day she set Alfred and Child to hang up the stuff, not against the wall but between the posts so that Sir Godfrey and Sir Eustace should enjoy some slight measure of privacy as they slept; but the boys were clumsy and stupid, also the hangings were too heavy for them to handle easily. She lost patience, climbed the ladder herself and was hammering away with the strength of anger when Rolf came in and said, "Get down from there!" Nobody except her mother had ever used such a tone of voice to her. She said, "Two more nails and I've done. Hold it up, Child, up! How can I manage, with you . . ."

Rolf took her by the knees—the highest he could reach—and pulled her backwards and downwards.

"Are you mad? Do you want a dead child?" He set her down on the floor as though she had been a child, climbed the ladder himself and, with maddening ease, finished the job.

She was still angry with him at supper time and kept her ears open, hoping that one of the three—preferably Rolf, though that was unlikely—would say something which would offer an opportunity to say the word that would make them all look fools. Something like the proposal to put sheep on the Scartoke water meadows.

They talked, Peter doing the most of it, about the castle. On that subject she knew nothing and had no wish to know. So, as so often she had done at this table, she sat and half-listened, letting some of her attention drift away. She thought about the child; she was definitely pregnant now and Hild had taken into her cracked head the idea that the child might be Eitel's. "You were the old lord's on Sunday night, the new lord's on Thursday," Hild said, sneering and venomous, "but we shall know. If it is the Norman's get it will be born with a tail!"

She heard Peter say, "And at the end what have we? A mere wooden fortress, vulnerable to fire."

"The King's own Tower of London is just that," Giffard said.

"You have never seen a proper castle," Peter said.

Rolf said, "I have. In Spain. And if there were stone here, or near, you should have had it." He used the almost placating voice which he sometimes used to Peter.

"Then be thankful that it is a chalk soil with a few flints in it," Giffard said. "Stone must be quarried and needs masons to work it."

The conversation might have ended there, but Madselin said, "There is stone, near here, and already quarried."

They all stared at her and she pretended indifference, giving attention to her meat.

"Far be it from me to contradict a lady," Giffard said amiably, "but this is not stone-bearing country. Even the shrine of the saint they regard so highly, at St. Edmundsbury, patronized by Canute as it was, is a mere wooden structure."

"For that I take your word, never having seen it," she said. She could be uncommunicative, too.

"Where is it, this stone?" Peter asked. She had hated him, even feared him a little from the first, and since he had taken to striking those who worked on the mound she had never vol-

untarily addressed a word to him. So now she looked at Rolf
and said, "Do *you* wish to know?"

"Yes."

"Then I will tell you. It is in the forest. Eitel found it. A
great town of stone, ruined, grass grown thick on its pave-
ments, the walls tumbling or grown through by trees. He spoke
of an oak, old he reckoned by its girth, that had carried a slab
of stone," she moved her hands, "so big, upward as it grew. A
solid slab of stone, carried up between trunk and branch to
twice the height of a man."

She wondered that she remembered so much. Whenever
Eitel rode out without her he had come back with something
that he hoped would interest her. She had seldom paid him
much attention but she had absorbed more than she realized,
and the idea of an oak, springing from an acorn and growing
upward, handicapped by the weight of a slab of stone, had
touched her imagination.

Giffard said, rather breathlessly, "Roman." Peter said,
"Where is it?"

"That I cannot tell you. Eitel was hunting a wild boar and
when he did that he never took me with him." There, she had
teased them, as she had so often teased Eitel. She had given
them a hint of something, established her own superior knowledge and left them little better off.

Rolf said, "Who went with him? Men do not hunt wild boar
alone."

Oddly enough, even in her present mood, she acknowledged
the good sense of that statement, and responded to it.

"No," she admitted. "Eitel was very brave but even Eitel
. . . He took three men with him. They were . . ." She
thought back. "Two died in the plague. The other was Britt
the thatcher."

"Send one of the boys for him," Rolf said.

She sent Alfred, telling him to be sure to tell Britt that all
that was needed of him was an answer to a simple question.
Despite this reassurance when the man came and stood un-

covered before his new lord his eyes were wary. He was one of those upon whom the brand mark had healed into a shapeless pucker; on others the letter held its shape in the scar.

She said in her kindliest voice, "Britt, it is a matter of remembering. Can you recall a day when you and the Lord Eitel hunted a boar and found a place where there were slabs of stone?"

"I remember it well, my lady."

"Where is it?"

His face took on the puzzled, slightly anxious expression which so many English wore these days—the look which the Normans called stupid.

"That was a cunning brute, my lady. He doubled back on his tracks and in the end got away."

Peter, in a fever of impatience, deduced from Britt's look and voice that the answer was unsatisfactory.

"Tell him," he said, "that there are ways of aiding memory."

She was about to tell Peter to be quiet in her old imperious way and then checked herself. She could do better than that. In a manner so sweet as to be poisonous she turned to Rolf and said, "Does my lord wish me to continue questioning the man? I cannot do so, nor can he think, if there are interruptions."

Rolf said, "Give them time, Peter."

Britt said: "I cannot say how the place is to be found. But, given time, I could find it."

She translated this statement and before the eyes of the three men at the table a vision reared itself: a castle of stone, the first in England. Giffard thought of a place, of stones, of inscriptions, relics of the Roman occupation. In England, as in all northern parts, the wild men who had come in when the Romans left had deliberately avoided the settled places, choosing their own and allowing the weeds and the wild to take over.

"How long?" Rolf asked. She put the question to Britt.

"A day, perhaps two. I know where we went in, and where we came out. There were beeches, with no undergrowth and then thicket, yews to our left and then to our right and open again, with hawthorn trees." He was remembering one of those happy days, so happy now in retrospect, when he had been a free man, able to take a day off to go hunting the boar that had ravaged the tillage.

And Rolf remembered that it was on the day after tomorrow that he must set out for Winchester.

"Tell him," he said, "that if he is back here by this time tomorrow, with directions, and some proof in his hand, he shall have a reward." He regretted that as soon as he had said it because he had nothing to give as a reward. Even food would be short until harvest; and the two knights to keep; the debt to the Jews to be paid off somehow. But a stone castle, the first in England . . .

Madselin relayed the promise and watched the process with which she was now familiar; a kind of shuttered look in the blue English eyes.

"I cannot promise," Britt said. "I will do my best. Good night, my lady."

"Of course," Peter said peevishly, "he could have directed us, and Giffard here—who does no work—could have gone. Or I myself . . . The man is one of the builders and aims to take a day, or even two, off from work."

"Giffard keeps tallies, he speaks for me, he found the knights, he tends the sick," Rolf said. He had the unlettered man's deep, if grudging, respect for learning; he had the skilled man's respect for another skill; he had chosen them both to share this new life onto which the King's whim had launched him; and he needed them both. There must be no dissension. . . .

Britt the thatcher was back next day at supper time. Sweat streaked his filthy face and he was scratched and exhausted. He carried an axe in one hand and in the other a piece of stone about twelve inches square with moss on one surface, soil on the other. At the sight of it Rolf's eyes gleamed but his face remained impassive, his manner imperturbable; Peter and Giffard bent over the stone and scratched at it with their knives while Britt told Madselin that in actual distance the ruined place was not far away and that there was much stone there. He had blazed the trail of the shortest route by using his axe.

"You have done well, Britt," Madselin said. She waited for the reward to be mentioned; but Rolf only said, "Ask him how *much* stone?"

The English shutter fell as behind it Britt made the kind of calculation never demanded of him before.

"Enough to build a hall like this?" she asked helpfully.

The shutter lifted. "Three or four such. Under the grass and small bushes the very road is of stone, my lady."

"You shall be rewarded, Britt. I will see to it."

For a second he looked at her with another expression familiar to her. It said, "Yes, you are one of *them* now!" To counteract it she asked, "What would you like?" A foolish question, a mistaken attempt to show goodwill. He would get—if anything at all—what Rolf chose to give and she was well aware that Rolf had very little to give away. He might perhaps be persuaded—on the other side of that door—to return to Britt one of his own confiscated sheep!

"As to that I should wish to ask Emma, my wife."

This Madselin considered a very right and proper, a truly English answer.

Peter and Giffard were arranging to go to the place of stone first thing in the morning. Rolf would leave for Winchester at the same time. "And you must ask the King for *money*," Peter said in his arrogant way. "We shall need masons, and masons must be hired."

Giffard said, "There should be no need to ask. When the King knows what you propose he will offer."

Neither of them knew anything about the King; or much about Rolf.

In the privacy of the bedchamber Madselin brought up the matter of Britt's reward.

"He can have what he asks—short of money. I have none."

On this side of the door she always felt more kindly towards him.

"None? You mean none at all? You cannot go to Winchester without a penny."

"I shall carry food and fodder."

"Where will you sleep?"

"On the ground." On this side of the door he always felt kindly towards her so he volunteered a statement. "It will not be the first time by many."

She went to her chest and after a second's hesitation between amber beads and silver belt, lifted out the latter. She seldom wore it nowadays and the time was coming when, even linked at its widest, it would be too small to wear at all.

"This is yours by right," she said, her voice gone hard again. "Had I not come . . . you would have sold it long ago. Take it and sell it as you go through Colchester."

His unhandiness with words did him ill-service.

"It is worth nothing," he said, stating a plain fact. "There was demand for such things once. Now too many are on offer." So many English people, expelled from their homes, had managed to take out a few trinkets and then, through need, been compelled to sell them. And the moment had gone when every Norman, down to archers, smiths and cooks, had been anxious to send or take home some English thing to their wives, sisters, mothers.

Rebuffed, her managing instinct as well as her generous impulse frustrated and her treasure said to be worthless, she dropped the belt back into the chest. Too late Rolf said, "It was a gentle thought, none the less."

Gentleness was not a thing of which either of them had much experience. She had not encountered it until she was married to Eitel—and then she had despised it. Rolf had never met it at all from anyone outside himself, and when he recognized it in himself, mistrusted it.

Next day, with Rolf on his way to Winchester and Giffard and Peter gone to inspect the stones, she was alone in the hall when Britt the thatcher, forgoing his midday meal, came to see her. It pleased her to think that she was empowered to give him whatever he asked for since he was extremely unlikely to ask for money, which had never been of much account in the Rinland. So she asked, genially, "And what have you and Emma decided upon, Britt?" Even if he wanted back his own cow, he could have it.

"My lady, we want our freedom."

That took her by surprise. But she thought quickly—Why not? Rolf said anything but money; and Britt, perhaps more than any other Bradwald man, was equipped for life in the outer world; he could go to Colchester and ply his trade. Immediately after that she thought—But he is strong and a good worker; Peter will grudge the loss! But the idea of a battle with Peter, who shouted and cursed and struck people as though they were animals, did not deter her; it sent a thrill of excitement through her.

"The Lord Rolf said, when I asked him, that you could have anything you asked except money, Britt. So what you ask, you have." The absurdity of it struck her. In return for a service you gave a man back to himself.

"And permission to work a bit of assart land," Britt said.

They spoke the same language; she knew what assart or intake land was. Every now and again a man, finding his strips in the field insufficient to support an over-large family, or not large enough to engage his full energies, would clear a bit of forest and make a little cultivated patch. She had seen it done at Scartoke, and at Bemid. But even with oxen it was backbreaking work.

"Where?" she asked.

"Where the path goes to Wyck, my lady. Beyond the com-monland. The trees are small there."

"The stumps of older trees are there too. They would have to be rooted out. And the briars and brambles are thick. And without an ox . . . Britt, it would take you a year to clear an acre; two before you grew a grain. You and Emma and the four little ones would starve. . . ."

"We spoke of that," Britt said solemnly. "Emma looked on the children and said better starve than to be slaves . . . And, my lady, in the times long past, it was all assart. The men who cleared it lived."

"There were many of them," she said, "and they must have had food . . . from somewhere." Oddly enough none of the old songs and stirring stories about the past had anything to do with so essential a thing as how the first settlers lived while the land was cleared. "Britt, it is in my mind that you will be ex-changing one kind of slavery for another, worse. And with hunger."

"All will hunger," he said, "while the best and strongest build instead of ploughing and beasts are tended by those who do not own them. And if I am a free man, to come and go, I can thatch, as I used to do."

"Very well," she said. "If that is what you choose, you have it. You are free."

Something flashed in his pale blue eyes. Then the shutter came down. He said, "My lady," and hesitated, lifting his big work-worn hand high enough to indicate his forehead. "I wear his mark. To earn bread I shall need to go abroad. There might be trouble in Bemid or Colchester. May I have a parchment?"

"A parchment?"

"With the words, to say that I am a free man and no runa-way."

"Yes. Master Giffard shall write it," she said, thinking how fast ideas spread, and wondering that this man, so ignorant, should know what a parchment was. *She* knew, because she had been in Winchester. Camilla could read and write, had offered to teach her, but she had seen no point in that—learning French was burden enough—and since she hoped and intended to return, at the first moment possible, to the Rinland, where agreements were made by word of mouth and always honoured, and counting was done on notched tally sticks, she had no need to learn to make marks on parchment.

Britt said, "I thank you, my lady. Emma said . . . Emma sent a message. She has borne four and all lived. She said, walk. Walk every day. Walk to the last minute. So Emma said."

"Thank her for me. Tell her I will walk."

But in which direction? She hated the garth now; there Eitel lay in his hastily dug, unhallowed grave. On the other side of the hall was the mound, the very symbol of change, rearing up on what had been the commonland with sheep and cattle and geese, all happy and haphazard. A horrid world; she preferred to stay indoors.

Peter said, "The best of them all! And *you* gave him leave to go. You had no right. If Rolf had been here . . ."

"You," she said, "would not be speaking to me in that voice. My lord said anything except money. Britt did not ask for money. Therefore I gave him what he did ask."

"And robbed me of a man, with men so scarce . . . To be," Peter said in a curiously shrill, almost girlish voice, "in a position where one man counts . . ." He put his hand to his head and Madselin saw his bulging pale eyes were full of water, tears that he would not shed. "And on the day, too, when we have seen the stone and know what can be done—you rob me of a man!" She thought, coldly, that no self-respecting page, however young, would demean himself with such a display of emotion. Then his manner changed. "Wait," he said, "only wait. We will see what Rolf has to say about this."

"If he is—as I think—a man of his word, he will agree that I am right," she said. Inwardly she was not sure. A Norman might not regard a promise made to an Englishman as binding.

Perhaps she had been hasty and would presently be shamed.

Giffard had watched and listened but taken no part in the exchange. As soon as it was over he began to speak of what he called the discovery. They had, he said, touched only the fringe of it; it had been a settlement of some size. Roman, as he had guessed from the first. And now he would make another guess—that the sound paved road ran in a straight line from the river up to Bradwald and probably on to Bemid. Once cleared it would immensely facilitate the hauling out of the stone. There was some marble, too, and alabaster. These and the stone, he thought, must have come in from the river and that was why he deduced the direction of the road. He talked on, happily and informatively, to two listeners both too preoccupied to pay him much attention.

Rolf arrived home looking thinner and tired. He came alone, explaining in a manner which in another man would have been sour that the great horses of the knights could not be hurried. His own mediocre mount bore evidence of having been considerably hurried.

"What did you think of my choice?" Giffard asked rather eagerly.

"Not much. The old one is arrogant. The other a pretty boy."

"I did my best. There was not much choice."

"I know. And so do they."

Peter lost no time in laying his grievance before Rolf. "*She* set free the best man I had. He has not done a stroke of work since!"

Rolf was silent so long that they all thought he intended not to answer at all. Finally he said, "I gave my lady my word. Anything except money."

"Did *you* get any?" Giffard asked.

"No." He could not be bothered to tell them what William *had* given him—a privilege many a nobleman would envy him when the new forest laws were strictly enforced—the right to hunt and to invite six other men to hunt with him in the Rinland forest. Just as Rolf had assumed possession of all the stock on his three manors, so the King had assumed possession of all the red deer in England and his claim was enforced by laws of the utmost savagery. But the ex-armourer, with no leisure, and no inclination, had permission to hunt! As he wryly considered the irony of this, Rolf hoped that his knights would be fond of the chase and willing to eat venison every day. Then he could sell cattle and sheep that would otherwise have come to this table.

"Then in the name of God," Peter said, "how can we hope to build?" He, like Giffard, like Rolf himself, had had high hopes of this meeting between William and Rolf, surely the poorest tenant-in-chief in existence.

"As we have done," Rolf said, calmly. "With what we have. Until June. When we have the fleece money we will hire masons."

Giffard thought the whole project impossible, but he took it lightly, certain that eventually Rolf must see sense and ask the King for a gift of money. Peter took a different view: the ways and means did not concern him, except that with an inadequate force he must do the best he could by extracting the last effort from every man and every animal—and from himself. The great, strong edifice, beautiful in stone, was his dream, had been his dream, even as the wooden walls grew. A freak of chance—a silly woman's memory, a churl's sense of direction, akin to a dog's, had brought the dream within touching distance. He could not be bothered about pennies. Rolf must find them, somehow. What concerned him, at this moment, was the business of transporting the stone. Presently he spoke of it.

"This is a different business," he said. "A felled tree, hitched to a brace of oxen, travels undamaged. With stone it is not so. And to build wagons, with wheels, will delay us further."

Sitting there, not much interested, her arm propped and her chin in her hand, Madselin remembered that Rolf had not shamed her or let her down over the matter of giving Britt the thatcher his freedom. And grateful for that, she said idly, "Use hides." Once before, as when she had mentioned that there was stone in the Rinland, they dropped their private arguments and looked at her with interest and inquiry.

"Two oxhides laced together," she explained, "make a bag which would hold as much stone as any ox could pull. Leather is tough and if, as Giffard says, there is a paved road to be found and used . . ."

She went to bed that night with a feeling of triumph; she had repaid Rolf for his support of her; she had scored over Peter who was so clever, but who could only think of wagons, with wheels. And Giffard had said, "Clever; clever indeed."

Her ebullient, self-satisfied mood lasted for two days. Until the knights came riding in and Sir Godfrey, looking about him with astonishment and disdain, said, "Where is my page?"

But she was cunning. She said, "I thought you would like to choose. This is Child . . . Alfred . . . Osric."

Looking down his long nose—that nose which combined with the round, closely clipped head and the bright eyes made all Normans look like birds of prey—Sir Godfrey studied the boys and chose Osric, saying that he looked teachable. "He will need clothes," he added. "My colours are red and white."

"Mine are green and blue," Sir Eustace said. "And I will have this boy." He chose Child.

"They shall be garbed tomorrow," Madselin said recklessly, knowing that pride had made her set herself an almost impossible task. There was not an inch of new cloth in the house, and contriving new garments from old ones was a time-consuming business.

At the first possible moment she said to Hild, "Run and ask Edfu to come and help us sew."

"For *them?*"

"No! For Osric and Child. And for ourselves so that we are not humbled. They spoke as though a cloth merchant kept shop around the corner with six apprentices standing ready, needles threaded. Run!"

She went into the sleeping chamber where some of Eitel's clothes still lay in the chest. The only red garment was the long, English-style robe which Eitel had worn on special occasions; it was old, dating back to that unimaginable time when Eitel had been young and fond of display. Lifting it out she realized suddenly that there was something poignant about a dead man's clothes; they had shaped themselves to the body which they had outlasted. She was even conscious of Eitel's personal scent, dry, slightly astringent, like chaff. With a gentler touch than she had ever used towards him, she laid it on the bed. White was easy to come by—not in wool, but in linen. So there was Sir Godfrey provided for. Now, blue and green; nothing of Eitel's met that need. It must be her own cloak, blue, and the gunna she was wearing, green. And she sensed that the items sacrificed from her own store would never be replaced. Rolf had no money. When she thought of money she still, sophisticated as she was, having lived in Winchester, thought of bartering—Rolf had nothing to barter with, and when he had, when the sheep were sheared, he would not think of cloth or clothes. He managed very well with his working outfit—scuffed stained leather—and one other, buffish brown and very ill-woven. . . .

Hild came in, with Edfu, and within a minute Madselin felt a momentary sympathy with Peter and, beyond him, all those who must deal, direct and govern a people who, not daring to be defiant, were at heart intractable.

Hild said, looking at Eitel's red robe, "I thought that the old lord's clothes were being saved for *good* purpose. This is silk. No wear for Osric. I cannot chop it about for him. Lay it aside. Until we *know*. Then maybe I shall cut it to small size with good heart."

Edfu said, in a meeker way, that she saw less well lately. Once upon a time she had helped the Lady Githa with her stitching, but now it took her a long time to thread her needle and she could only make large coarse stitches.

"I will cut the red silk. I will thread the needles. Are you both so stupid that you cannot *see?* The King demands that the lord has knights; the knights demand pages, properly clothed. I said tomorrow, and tomorrow they shall be properly clothed or . . ." She broke off, thinking—I sound just like my mother! That was the tone of voice I always hated in her. But with her there was power behind it. When she raged Scartoke trembled and hastened to obey. I have no power; I can only cajole.

So she cajoled them, praising Edfu's clumsy stitching, inviting Hild to competition—"Let us see which of us can get to the end of the seam first." All the time her natural impatience and irascibility crouched, growling and snarling, tearing at her inwardly because she could not tear at them.

But the two outfits were ready next day and Osric and Child wore them proudly, though with some bewilderment. Then Sir Godfrey said that their hair must be cut. He asked Madselin for her scissors, cut one lock of Osric's pale hair, and bade Child finish the job and then submit himself to the same treatment. When the job was finished he said, idly, "Now they look almost human!" Madselin overheard and was filled with impotent fury.

She said to Rolf, as though casually, "What is your favourite colour?"

"I have none."

She was almost too much exasperated to speak but she managed it in a gritty voice.

"Everybody likes one colour better than another. I have a reason for asking."

"Colour means nothing to me. I know the words. But you show me a bit of stuff now and say, red, and the same bit tomorrow and say, blue, I should not know."

"Then what do you see?" she asked, thinking—Imagine not to know that the sky is blue, the grass green.

"Shapes," he said, almost cautiously. "Light and dark and what is between, lighter or darker as the case may be. I see very well."

"In a grey world!"

"Yes. If grey is the word for what I see."

"You did not notice the change in Osric and Child, the one all red and white, the other green and blue?"

"To me they looked trimmer. And their hair shorter."

And then the thought occurred—He did not see her as she was; could not see that her hair was of a rare colour, her eyes a darker than ordinary blue, her skin very white, her lips very red.

"Well, no matter," she said, mentally sacrificing the yellow and tawny of her best clothes. "Tomorrow Alfred will be trim, too. For it is all wrong," she said, with conviction, "that your knights, your hired men, should be waited on by boys prinked out like popinjays while you, the lord of Bradwald . . ."

"I have no title." He said that as curtly as though they were in public. The whole business of matters of address bothered him. He could accept "my lord" from the English peasants, occasionally even from Arnulph and Roger, who owed their keep to him. Giffard and Peter, both of whom he had known in the past, called him "Rolf." With the knights it was different. Six months ago or less to them he would have been "Hi, you!" or "Fellow!" In the day and a half that they had been at Bradwald Sir Godfrey had—perhaps maliciously, with his kind one never *knew*—underlined Rolf's uncertain status by addressing him now as "My lord of Bradwald," and now as "my lord Rolf." Each time Rolf's pride had flinched.

"You *are* their lord," Madselin said firmly. "They are your men, and already in your debt. And tomorrow you shall be waited upon by Alfred, with his hair cut and brave in yellow and tawny." In fact, she thought, she would promote another boy from the kitchen to wait upon Giffard and Peter. Alfred should be in yellow decked with tawny, the other boy in tawny decked with yellow.

"No," he said.

"Why not, pray?"

He made a genuine effort to communicate. "Because it would seem to be aping them. As though what we had before was not good enough. There is this to mark, too. It may be many years before you get any new clothes."

It surprised her to learn that he had noticed that, save for the red silk, the boys had been dressed at her expense. Curious man: she would never understand him. And she would never—as this trivial incident proved—get her own way with him.

Soon began the coming and going between Bradwald and Bemid that was henceforth to be a feature in their lives. The great horses—which the knights called destriers—needed regular exercise and their riders needed constant practice. Also, it was presently revealed, Sir Volfstan at Bemid was a distant cousin of Sir Godfrey's, and so was Lord Bowdegrave, for whom Sir Volfstan acted as agent.

To begin with the knights were content to go to Bemid where there were what Sir Godfrey called facilities, which included a large apartment called the Knights' Lodging where there was room for half a dozen to sleep and stow their gear. Bemid had always been part of the outer world and both the old man and Stigand had been given to hospitality. Bemid suffered no shortages of manpower or of food; Sir Volfstan lived very comfortably. Whenever Sir Godfrey drew a comparison between the two places, he did so with the outward courtesy of his breed but both Rolf and Madselin winced—he for himself, she for Bradwald, though she knew and always had known that Bemid was infinitely superior. It also disturbed her to be thus constantly reminded of Bemid and therefore of Stigand, who was dead; and who, long before he was dead in fact, had been dead to her.

Then, presently, Sir Godfrey said that a tilting ground was

desirable at Bradwald. He and Sir Eustace could not forever be going to Bemid and imposing upon Sir Volfstan's hospitality, relative though he was; besides, when the days shortened and the one road, bad at any time, worsened, practice must be possible at home. He chose what remained of the commonland as a site for the tiltyard—unsuitable, he said, as it was, so very uneven. Osric and Child, stripped of the finery that made them the object of envious mockery from the other kitchen boys, worked, not very effectively, at smoothing out the worst bumps and filling in the holes into which a charging horse might put a hoof.

This was the time when every effort of man and beast was directed to hauling stone out of the forest. Giffard and Peter had traced the lost road and it had been painfully cleared. It ran straight and flat for about a mile between the old Roman town and Bradwald. Rolf worked with the rest both in the clearing of the road and then with the prying out of the stone slabs and loading them onto the hide skids which Madselin had suggested, and in unloading them onto the space around the mound. Every day it irked him to see the knights' great horses, each weighing almost a ton, sleek from being corn-fed, glossy with grooming, thundering about the tiltyard or setting off for Bemid, to thunder and prance about there while their riders practised their aim by thrusting lances through suspended rings, "A hit! Well done, sir!" or their swordsmanship by lopping the heads off dummy figures swinging from posts.

The oxen and what horses there were at Bradwald grew thin and slow from overwork. And there were losses, too. In the old days, when each man had owned his beast, a sick or failing one was cared for and cosseted; now every animal belonged to the lord and why bother? The foundering horse, the stumbling ox was prodded on, and died. It was the same with the sheep, now all herded together at Ing. Roger, whose experience with sheep was confined to the eating of mutton, knew nothing and cared less. A man who owned his ewes would sit up all night in the lambing season, would rear an orphan lamb by milking an-

other ewe by hand and giving the motherless one the milk
from a soaked rag. He was wary of wolves at winter's end and
on the look-out for fly-blows in summer. Now nobody cared
and the flock steadily declined in number and in quality.

Tools were similarly treated. *My* scythe was cared for, well
honed, taken in from the rain or night dew, because it was
mine and I would use it tomorrow. A scythe, belonging to the
lord and likely to be taken by the first comer tomorrow, was of
no importance and merited no care. Rolf in assuming ownership of everything had done himself an ill-service, and Madselin, the one person at Bradwald who could have seen the situation clearly, drawn comparisons and issued a warning, kept
to the house, grew heavy, and gave her attention to putting on
a good front when, as it was sometimes necessary to do, she
must entertain Sir Volfstan and some of his friends. The remark of the Abbess, so much resented at the time, about extra
mouths to feed, had meaning for her now. Rolf would not,
dare not, allow a lamb or a calf to be slaughtered and but for
the fact that Sir Eustace enjoyed hunting and also had a su-
perbly trained falcon, Bradwald would have been meat hungry. How the ordinary people managed she did not dare to
think. This year the hungry season had extended itself into
spring, and summer.

In one respect Rolf was fortunate; there was no landowner
in England whose knights' armour cost less to keep in repair.
He still had his tools and his skill and his pride in his job; and
once, putting a perfect edge to the sword which a rare mis-
stroke of Sir Godfrey's had not merely blunted, but nicked, he
entertained for a moment or two the idea that he had been
happier in his old life where nothing was demanded of him but
to do his own work to the best of his ability. No worries, no
demands to be met, no talk. He and Theobald had been capable of working together for two, even three hours at a stretch
without exchanging more than a few words, all in connection
with what they were doing. Now there was always somebody

saying something that had to be answered, somehow. Both the knights and Madselin and Giffard had a knack he lacked; they could talk at table without missing a mouthful.

He put this mood away, his good sense telling him that it was mainly the result of financial stress. By a singular combination of circumstances he, who had begun to earn his bread when he was six, wielding the bellows in his father's smithy and standing on a stone in order to reach, and since then had never known an idle day or owed any man a penny, had been made, by a gift and a promise, into a man with debts and liabilities. But all would be well once the sheep were sheared and the fleeces sold.

For the shearing the sheep were brought back to Bradwald. Upon that Peter insisted, saying, "Better a day spent by one man, driving a flock along, than the waste of time by men going to and fro."

The sheep still bore their owners' marks. In the old days, though the sheep ran together as they did now, each had borne the cross, the square, the triangle, the arrow or the spots which were the alphabet of the illiterate. When this year's fleeces fell the marks of ownership would be lost forever. The lambs dropped this spring were unmarked. The shearing day brought home once more the knowledge of loss; the awareness that here the English had been treated worse than at Bemid, even. There, though there were harsh new rules and impositions, something of the old structure had been spared.

In the old days the shearing had been a merry time, terminating in a feast of roast lamb, contributed by those whose sheep had done well, and of freshly baked bread and ale. Even the children had played their part, searching for the sweet little wild strawberries which grew in the forest clearings.

On this day the work was done in sullen silence, done quickly because in the long pasture the hay was ready to be scythed and done grudgingly. Time was saved because there was no necessity to re-mark the sheep that struggled up from under the shears, looking very clean and naked; but this year there were far more little wounds upon which the flies would fasten, in which the maggots would breed. Why be careful? The sheep all belonged to the new lord and the man Roger, who had taken upon himself the old, honourable title of sheep-reeve—once an elective office—would never notice.

Peter had agreed to cease the stone-hauling, just for this one day; but he had insisted that three men should continue to work upon the timber of the castle's interior. Between stone and wood he had been forced to a compromise. He would wish his castle to be all of stone, every archway, every stair, every inside wall; but he realized that if Rolf managed to employ masons long enough to rear the outer walls, that was as much as could be hoped for; and timber was plentiful. So although work on the outer walls had ceased, and they now stood shoulder high, inside, the partitions that would divide the castle into its separate compartments had gone on rising and now stood stark and high, a kind of wooden network, incomprehensible to anyone except Peter, who knew that here would be the Knights' Lodgings, here the Armoury, here the Solar, the great hall, the kitchen, the store palaces and sleeping chambers. Attached to the walls there were platforms upon which men stood to work, and between the platforms ladders were lashed to give access.

Britt Four Ox was one of those who had gone on with the building on this shearing day. Over the sheep he was not much concerned; he had never kept any. His pride had been in his four beautiful beasts, creamy white in colour, strong, willing, responsive to a word. When his own ploughing was done, he would plough for others who owned inferior beasts, or none; and it was the same at harvest time. He had kept the animals in the same condition as Osric and Child, under the knights' critical eyes and occasionally heavy hands, now kept the destriers. No mud, no sweat marks were allowed to remain long on their gleaming hides. Their very horns had been polished and often decorated by garlands of wild flowers. Now one was dead, one was failing, and the other two were dull-coated, dirty and gaunt. He thought about them often as he worked.

He was thinking about them on this shearing day as he hammered away at what was to be the partition between the Solar —the private room, not a bedchamber—which Madselin was one day to occupy and the large room, the hall, which Peter had said must be up one flight of stairs. The space on the ground floor, he said, must be reserved for defensive purposes.

Britt Four Ox had worked hard all day; he always did. Work was a refuge from thought and in some obscure way it eased his misery to think that he was sharing the weariness, the sense of doing more than could be rightfully demanded that had killed one of his oxen and would presently kill the others. And he was working when Peter climbed the third ladder to inspect and measure, as was his habit, what work had been done that day.

Britt said afterwards, and held to it, that Master Peter had said, "Good. Will do." He had then, according to Britt, seemed to miss his footing on the ladder as he turned and was about to descend. He fell, crashed into the lower platform, bounced off and landed on the floor, the floor which was the top of the mound, stamped and rammed until it was as hard as rock. Britt waited a little. This one enemy, representative of them all, lay very still. Presently, investigating cautiously, he saw that there was no blood.

Giffard was reckoning the weight of the fleeces, doing his best to gauge what the wool was worth and for how long Rolf could hire masons with the proceeds. Of all the Normans Giffard was best; he smiled occasionally and had never been known to strike anyone. So Britt ran to Giffard.

Giffard had not liked Peter much, had often teased him and sometimes bickered with him, but at the sight of him lying dead and in a curiously broken posture he felt a pang of pity and of compunction and of sadness. He also felt the irony— Peter, who had dreamed of a stone castle, dead on the very day when the sheep were shorn and there would be money to hire masons. Upon these feelings suspicion followed swiftly;

Peter had been very unpopular; and the death of any Norman needed looking into. And then professional curiosity took over; a fatal fall, from such a height, and yet no visible wound. . . .

Madselin and Hild were in the hall, busy with the interminable mending and re-making. Hild had been in a bad mood all day, returning short answers and fidgeting about, going now to the window, now to the door. She also was thinking of other shearing days, merry in themselves, and holding promise of the other, even more exciting, day when the wool-buyers would come and perhaps the young man with them. This year, if he came, she would not dare to show herself with her twisted face and dragging leg. She always came back from window or door with a remark about whose sheep were now under the shears; she could recognize the marks; finally Madselin said, irritably, "What good does it do? The sheep are all his, now."

"He has so much," Hild said darkly, "that he does not know what *is* his. But we shall know, eh? *They* are all born with tails."

"Hild; if you mention that again—just once more—I shall, I shall . . ."

"Complain of me to the lord?" Hild sneered. "Have me sent to tend pigs?"

Before Madselin could frame a proper retort or threat, Child rushed in.

"Peter the Norman is dead. He fell from a ladder and is dead."

"With all his bones broken," Hild said, softly, with satisfaction.

"They have taken him to the barn," Child said. "Britt Four Ox, also. They blame him. He was there!"

"Not within reach," Hild said, shrilly. "Not within reach. That I swear."

"And who would take *your* word, with a Norman dead and an Englishman within sight?" Madselin asked, driving home her needle and getting to her feet. She hurried out to the barn, across the yard smelling strongly of sheep dung and fleeces.

Peter, in a strange posture—*all* his bones broken?—lay on a piece of sacking. Rolf, expressionless as usual, but with his nostrils and lips gone pale, stood there with Giffard, plainly distressed, and with Britt Four Ox, the colour of clay and sweating.

"Not a sight for you. In your condition," Rolf said.

She said, meekly, "I thought I could help perhaps." Giffard, who had welcomed her arrival with relief, said, "There is no wound, Rolf. And in a matter of such importance it is better to be exact."

Britt Four Ox looked at her, appealingly, but without much hope. She was one of *them* now; but at least he would understand better what was asked, and she would understand what he said.

"What happened, Britt? Tell me all. Take your time."

"My lady; I was at work on one side of the wooden wall. He came up on the other and looked at the work and said, 'Good. Will do.' I had done much work; up to my chin. We could see one another when he stood at the top of the ladder, but when he turned and began to go down . . . My lady, I could not even see. I heard him fall. Then I ran down on my side and found him."

She translated rapidly.

"So I understood," Giffard said.

"Peter was as sure-footed as a goat," Rolf said; and, as so often happened, he had pressed a great deal of meaning into one simple statement.

Madselin said, "We can test the truth. He must touch the corpse. If he is guilty fresh blood will spurt from the wounds."

"You believe such nonsense?" Rolf asked.

"Britt does," she said simply. "Britt, are you willing to take the test?"

"To touch him? Ten times, in the sight of God and man," Britt said eagerly. She might be one of *them*, married to one, in time to bear his child; but she remembered the old ways, the old rules. He stooped and put his unsteady hand on the body; on the head, on the chest, on each limb.

Giffard said, reasonably, "But there are no wounds to bleed."

"Britt believes that blood would have sprung from the mouth, the nose, the ears. And he touched boldly. He is guiltless."

But they were not satisfied. Normans were few, the English many. And there had been so many cases . . . Nowadays any Norman dead in mysterious circumstances was savagely avenged, death and mutilation falling upon whole communities. Sometimes the English, in their cunning, would strip a victim, re-dress him in English clothes; so now the first process when a man was found dead was "the establishment of Englishry." It did not apply here. But the principle did. A Norman, accustomed to ladders, sure-footed as a goat, had fallen from a ladder. An Englishman had been nearby. Something more than resort to some ancient, superstitious rite was necessary.

She felt their doubt. Think quickly! She looked at Britt who had faced and seemed to pass the vital test and looked puzzled because it had not been instantly accepted as proof of innocence.

She said, "There is another way. Where did Peter stand? Where did this man? Could that be seen?"

Giffard said, "I *know* where this man stood. From time to time I lifted my head from those fleeces to take a breath of air. I saw him. I know where he stood."

She said, "Britt, go back to the place where you worked."

It was the first time that she had ever crossed the bridge that spanned the water which separated the motte from what had been the commonland and she went unwillingly, hating the embryo castle not only because it was alien, the symbol of Norman domination, but because it had contributed to the impoverishment of Bradwald; even at this stage a monster, gulp-

ing down men's energy and time that could have been better
employed, and threatening to gulp more. This year the fleece
money would go to the masons and the autumn meat would be
laid down only with the indispensable salt; no cloves, no cin-
namon, no ginger. . . .

And by now her back was aching. Except when her mother
had beaten her she had been a stranger to pain save for a
childish toothache. Nowadays her back hurt a little whenever
she stood upright and hurt more the longer she stood. So she
propped herself against one of the low wooden struts and said
to Rolf, "You had better mount the ladder, as Peter did. Remembering that you are somewhat taller."

It was plainly impossible that Britt Four Ox had had any
hand in the death of Peter the Norman. As Britt had said, the
wooden wall on which he had been working reached his chin.
Sensing that this experiment was intended to help him, Britt
stood on his toes, strained to reach over. But it was evident to
Rolf and to Giffard that Peter, two inches shorter than Rolf,
at the top of the ladder, had been well out of Britt's reach.

"A dizzy spell," Giffard said. "It was a warm day and he was
angry by the stoppage of work; and perhaps a little excited by
the thought of the masons coming next week."

"I should have been sorry," Rolf said, "to have hanged an
able-bodied man. A good worker."

Neither of them had seen what she had seen; the distance
between Britt's straining hand and Rolf's copper-coloured
head was just about a hammer's length. And Britt had been
using a hammer. . . .

She said nothing, and went, almost jauntily, to supper.
While she was eating it the English took the ladder from
which Peter had fallen and burned it.

"A good new ladder," Rolf said.

"But it is the custom," she said. "A sort of wergild. A death
for a death. Anything that kills a man must be destroyed, lest
it should do the same again."

Sir Godfrey said, "If I fell from my horse and he trod on me and I died, would he be killed?"

"Oh no, Sir Godfrey. This is an English rule. Your horse is Norman. No Englishman would be asked to ride him, so the precaution would not be necessary."

They all, except Rolf, laughed. Rolf said, "They will, in their own time, replace that ladder. And find their own wood."

That settled, Rolf and Giffard went on to talk about the immediate future. Another architect to be hired? No, Rolf said. Peter's plans were there, meticulous and complete. The masons could work to them and Giffard could see that they did so. Peter, his work done, his death shown to have been accident, not design, lay in the barn seemingly forgotten until Sir Godfrey said, "And who will give Peter burial?"

Madselin, pleased with herself because she had saved Britt Four Ox, and bored by the talk of the castle, the plans, the masons and the possible price of fleeces, had turned in on herself, thinking mainly about Hild and her odd behaviour. But with Sir Godfrey's question she came back to the table talk.

The Rinland had now been six months without a priest. A few pious people, mainly women, trudged to Wyck, or even to Bemid, to hear Mass or have a child christened and that was all. Peter was the first person to die since January. He was Norman, and he was known to Sir Godfrey, who was orthodox in his religion as in other things and who had more than once said that an area of this size should have a priest of its own.

"Giffard knows the words," Rolf said shortly.

"My lord of Bradwald," Sir Godfrey said in his stiffest manner, "knowing the words is not enough. If I died here," he looked around in a way which said—God forbid! "I should not wish to be buried by Giffard, able man as he is. We need a priest here."

"One day. Not English. They make trouble."

"Parish priests of Norman birth are not plentiful," Sir Godfrey said. That was true; it was the higher clerics who had come at, or soon after, the Conquest. "But I might be able to

find one. Richard, Bishop of Bywater, is my cousin, once removed. I will ride down one day and ask him to use his
influence."

Rolf, resenting the feeling that he was being organized,
wanted to say—How strange, with all your grand connections,
that you were on sale in London, in debt to the Jews! But he
restrained himself, merely saying in a noncommittal manner,
"Yours is a large family."

"My father was one of four. All married and had children.
One married a widow with children of her own. Is that exceptional?"

Sir Eustace, who held the elder knight in high esteem, copy-
ing his behaviour, trying to model his demeanour on his, said
quickly, "Not at all. My grandmother had twelve children,
seven boys and five girls. Their future was a matter of some
concern. But the second son went to Italy and was soon so well
established that he found estates for his brothers and husbands
for three sisters."

That set off some talk of the kind that both Rolf and Madselin found irksome, an eager clambering about in family trees
and an endeavour to find some interlinking branches. Rolf disliked it because it gave him, with no kin and no connections, a
feeling of being at one and the same time shut out and surrounded. Madselin disliked it for its tacit assumption that only
Normans had pedigree. On this evening Sir Godfrey and Sir
Eustace had finally traced a kinship of a kind, through one
Hugh d'Este, an uncle by marriage to Sir Eustace and a
brother-in-law to one of Sir Godfrey's cousins. Neither of them
had ever seen him, or ever would; but as Sir Eustace said,
blushing modestly—"Then we are akin."

Madselin said, "How interesting. Family relationships are
interesting. My mother could trace her descent, on her
mother's side, direct from Sweyn Forkbeard. By his first wife."

It was true. It had once been rather more than a family joke.
One day her first stepfather—the one who had not lasted long—
had jumped up and slapped the Lady Edith, her mother, cry-

ing, "Do not come the Dane over me!" She remembered it—the only time that she had ever seen anybody really defy her formidable mother.

And still, it seemed, Sweyn Forkbeard was a name that meant something. He had held the whole of northwestern Europe in fee.

Sir Godfrey thought—That accounts! A poor English widow, who married the armourer to put food in her mouth and roof over her head, but has dignity and grace which I recognized from the first.

Sir Eustace thought—That accounts for the colour, the rich honey-yellow hair and those blue, blue eyes.

Giffard thought—I wonder; there is a streak of mischief in her; she may have said it to put them in their place and make the one relative they have in common look small. Sweyn Forkbeard has been dead for more than fifty years. And he cast away his first wife.

Rolf thought—My child will have royal blood in his veins.

So there was a little silence. Into it Sir Godfrey said, "There remains the matter of Peter's burial. Would the Bemid priest come here? Or must Peter be carried to Bemid?"

"So," Father Alfleg said, "now I am called in. Like a cow doctor. To bury a Norman."

"No. To bury Eitel and those who fell with him. Father, I arranged that the Norman's grave should be dug under the apple trees, near to Eitel. When you commit him, will you commit them too?"

"You," he said, narrowing his eyes and trying to look at her sternly, "have never presented yourself—either at Wyck or Bemid."

"I know. How could I? I cannot walk. I am forbidden to ride. I was with child, within a month."

"He treats you well?"

"Very well."

"That is good." He was glad that she was one of the few fortunate ones. "When the child is born you must bring it for baptism. The lady should set an example in such things."

"We may by that time have a priest of our own."

"Ah, the *pro*per priest he spoke of. Poor fellow. He will have a hard furrow. The Church has suffered sore damage. Even in Bemid . . . Even in my own house. The good old woman who spoils my meat said only the other day that with Sir Volfstan and his like she would not share even ordinary bread, so how could she share the sacrament with them?"

CHAPTER FIVE

The wool-buyers arrived as usual. This year there was no excitement or happy haggling over the exchange of fleeces for salt, spices, needles, yeast, knives, whetstones, trinkets. Giffard stood amidst the wool, already weighed and bundled, ready to sell it for the highest possible price. He had in his hand a list of the barest necessities, and apart from this meagre exchange he wanted money. The masons, already bespoken by Peter, were due to begin work any day.

They arrived on Sunday, thirteen of them, one master mason and twelve men, a strange, close-knit community with customs and rules, even a language, of their own. They were of all nationalities yet they bore an almost family resemblance to one another, their bodies short and thick-set, their faces dour, their gait purposeful. The master spoke for them all. They did not wish to eat or sleep in the hall; they would make their own lodge and keep to it. They expected meat three times a day—and not the same flesh more than once in any one day. They expected to be supplied with all the ale they could drink and bread of first or second grade. It would speed their work if unskilled labourers carried the blocks of stone to the place where work was in progress, but they were not to loiter or pry. Behind his words and his manner hung the unspoken announcement that there was more work in the world than there were masons to do it and that unless his conditions were met absolutely the masons, being free men, would move on. Rolf grudged the three meat meals, but within a week saw that it was well earned. The masons worked with prodigious energy and concentration. There was no talk, each man seemed to know exactly what was required of him; every step, every movement had purpose. They were out at first light and worked for two hours, then breakfasted where they stood. Awkwardly, from the point of domestic arrangements, they dined an hour later than was ordinary, again eating on the site. They then worked on until dusk, when they retired to their lodge for supper. Over it, and sometimes for a little while after, they appeared to make merry in their own way, compensating for the day's silence with laughter and singing. Giffard, with his all-embracing curiosity, was interested in their songs, in their way of life, and in the mixture which they made, fresh every morning, for the fixing of the stone blocks together; but all his advances were rebuffed; so was Rolf when he ventured a natural inquiry as to when, roughly, the work would be done. "Am I God, to foretell the weather?" the master mason asked. "In hard frost we cannot work. Nor indeed can we work on such stuff as was served for supper last night. Cows that die of old age should lie where they fall."

But the walls rose, visibly, day after day, and the year moved on. In the fields the hay, and then the corn, was cut and carted, stored or marketed. Rolf and Giffard had worked out that just under half the year's produce could be sold. It meant short commons for every man and beast—even perhaps for the great horses—but money was needed to keep the work going. Giffard, who liked his food, made a protest, "If the King knew what straits you are in . . ." he said.

"I do not go to him as a beggar. I go to pay my rent as he himself arranged it. Overlooking his mail four times a year. I will not mention money."

"Then you will lack it," Giffard said.

The days shortened, the woods blazed, the wild geese came honking in from the north. Madselin grew heavier and bulkier.

One day the miller came to see her, shyly doffing his cap and reminding her of what she had said in the barn.

"Though it is not a question but a favour I have to ask, my lady."

"None are in my gift, nowadays."

"But if you would ask the lord. It is this way. My boy is at the monks' school in St. Edmundsbury. He was not strong enough for my job. In the old days, when I took a tithe of every sack I ground, I always, at about this time of the year, sent a sack of the best flour to a shoemaker in the town who made shoes for the boy as he grew. This year, with the mill and all the corn belonging to the lord, there is no tithe and I have no flour to send. But he will need shoes just the same."

"I see that. But I cannot see what can be done about it."

Her own child—she always thought of it as a boy—kicked vigorously; and she thought how, in the old days, she and Hild would be sewing on fine new linen, fine soft woollen, suitable for wear by the first-born, heir to Bradwald. Instead they were making over old stuff and that scarce enough, now. "The times are hard, miller."

"Yes. Yet I and my mill have worked as hard and as well . . . And now, like the rest, I have so much flour, doled out by Master Giffard . . . But that is what I wanted to ask, my lady. Would the lord permit me to draw the flour to which I am entitled for the next three months and send it to the shoemaker?"

"If he did, what would you live on?"

"The sharps," he said, simply. Then he realized that she did not know what he meant. "The waste, my lady. The husks, the scrapings from the millstones, the grains that fall through, however careful you are. It is called sharps and fed to pigs in winter. But I could live on it—and gladly—if the boy could have shoes. My lady, I am no longer young and what I eat is of no great concern to me. If he had shoes."

"It seems a reasonable request," she said. "I will put it to my lord. I think I never saw your boy. How old is he?"

"Fourteen . . . yes it is four years since I saw that he would never shape to haul and heave and took a sneezing fit every time he helped with the grinding or went into a hayfield. A

strange affliction. I hope, my lady, that any child you bear will
be sturdy and healthy. Much depends on him, if him it is. And
if not a boy this time," the miller said, tangling himself more
with every word, "the next. English blood should make for
tenderness towards the English."

She thought—What has Hild been saying? Then she remembered that there was no need for Hild to have given utterance
to any of her dark sly thoughts. Any child she bore would have
an English mother.

She said, "Thank you, miller. I will mention your matter to
my lord at a likely moment and the best way I can."

It was some time now since they had shared that strange joy
in bed, but still, when the door closed on the outer world an
intimacy of a kind was established. She felt able to speak
freely and Rolf, though he spoke little, seldom argued in this
room and would often—especially when she criticized Sir Godfrey's arrogant behaviour—give affirmative grunts. Tonight he
listened as she described the miller's predicament and his
suggested solution.

"How old?" he asked.

"Fourteen." At that age Rolf had been doing a full man's
work, proud to do it, straining himself, anxious to show that he
was his father's equal, and would one day be his better. "He
must come home. Make himself useful."

To show ill-temper or make a sharp answer was useless with
Rolf. She said, in a reasonable voice, "The boy is not strong."

"It comes with usage," he said. He had gained his strength
in that way and had no pity for the weak.

"The miller will be disappointed."

He did not answer that, but after a little brooding, said,
"He should know. If he could live on waste. Mixed with the
good flour, it would eke out. This priest will be another
mouth." Sir Godfrey's negotiations had been successful; a
proper Norman priest was on his way to Bradwald.

The rebuff neither surprised nor hurt her. There was none of the "Just to please you, sweetheart," about Rolf. Indeed, why should there be? And she had sense enough to see that his decision was sensible. Bradwald was short of men and the master mason had said that very soon, when the building had reached a stage where ordinary men would not get in the way of, or mix with his, the interior woodwork could be resumed. The miller's boy could help plough and sow.

None the less she went to sleep with the thought that she would have failure to report to the miller and he would think she had failed him. And she dreamed that her child was born horrible to look at, with a face not unlike Hild's and with a tail, a fox's brush. In her dream she repudiated it entirely—horrible, horrible, take it away; never let me lay eyes . . .

"It's all right," Rolf said, shaking and holding her. "You're safe in your bed." Holding her thus he could feel the child's movements. "It will soon be over now," he said.

The new priest arrived a fortnight before Rolf was due to make his Michaelmas visit to the King, and one glance showed him to be as different from old Father Alfleg as two men, ostensibly of the same rank in the same profession, could be. He rode a good horse and was followed by a manservant on one less good, leading a heavily laden pack pony. Sir Godfrey had explained to his cousin, the Bishop, the financial straits of the man with whom he had been obliged to take service, and the Bishop, bearing this in mind, had chosen to appoint a man with the necessary missionary fervour and with independent means. The new priest was the second son of a prosperous merchant in Rouen who was so pleased to have an ordained priest in the family that he had given him as much in the way of money and goods as he had given his first-born when he married.

Sir Godfrey led the way by addressing the priest as Sir Stephen, or Sir Priest, as though he were a knight, and indeed from his manner, his physique, his speech, he could well have been. Even his most private thoughts had a military tinge; he had been sent to an outpost where old ground must be held, new ground gained. In Sir Godfrey and Sir Eustace—slavishly imitative—he saw allies; in Rolf, who for eight months had had supreme power in the Rinland and had done nothing about its spiritual needs, he saw a near-enemy who must be bludgeoned into submission; and in Madselin he saw a possible hostage.

Prepared as he had been from what Sir Godfrey had said about the poverty and the primitive conditions at Bradwald, he was slightly dismayed by what he found and over the first meal said that he would like a house of his own as soon as it could be built.

"There is no labour," Rolf said.

An alcove had been cleared for him, adjoining Sir Godfrey's, but it had neither screen nor curtain and was open to the hall. Altogether unsuitable.

"Then I must hire from other places. Fortunately, I have the means."

"None nearer than Colchester," Rolf said. He had that old, hateful feeling of being surrounded, of being pressed upon. Sir Stephen—*Sir* Stephen!—was in every way, even in looks, one of the family to which Sir Godfrey, Sir Eustace, Sir Volfstan and beyond them thousands of others belonged; he had the courteous manner, the assurance, the ability to eat and talk at the same time.

"Britt the thatcher's house is empty. A good house, too," Madselin said.

It was a good house, built long ago around a living tree. Britt and Emma had abandoned it, unable to spare the time it took to walk between it and their intake land. They had built themselves a low dwelling of willow branches and clods.

"I will look at it. With your permission, my lord. I shall also look about to find the most suitable place for a church." He gave a smile, surprisingly pleasant. "Naturally I shall not be able to pay for the erection of a church, unaided."

"There is a church already. At Ing," Madselin said.

Sir Stephen spent the next two or three days riding about his parish while his man, Simon, made Britt's house habitable. The other Britt's two surviving oxen made a slow journey, dragging a cart first to Ing and then to Scartoke to collect what furniture Roger and Arnulph had never used. Madselin snatched the opportunity of bringing to Bradwald a heavy oak cradle, shaped like a swan. Eitel, after his first wife died, had given his family one away.

The church at Ing, very old and decayed, had collapsed entirely, as though sensing that its service was done.

"And in any case," Sir Stephen said, "it was too small and not central enough. The new church must be at Bradwald. A castle always draws population. Men from Scartoke and Ing come here to work, I understand. They can come to worship." He then talked on, almost as though to himself, pondering ways and means. His own father, he said, would certainly subscribe towards the church; his Bishop would do what he could—though he himself was faced with a building programme in Bywater. And perhaps the King, if the situation were explained to him . . .

"Not by me," Rolf said.

Giffard said, "With our lord, Sir Priest, it is a matter of principle. Even for that great leech out there," he nodded in the direction of the growing castle, "he will not ask a penny."

"As Giffard says," Rolf said.

The new priest then said something that wrung from Madselin an unwilling respect.

"And that brings me," he said in his smooth, courteous, but relentless way, "to another matter . . ." He had never met with, or heard of, he said, any place, either in Normandy or England, where things were run as they were here, where nobody owned anything, not even a fowl or the egg it laid. It was a unique situation and it made his task almost impossible. Where peasants, out of the little they owned, paid dues to their lord, dues were understood and what was due to God was recognized, an extension of what was due to man. But here, where there were no dues, no ownership, however meagre, there was, and could never be, any sense of responsibility. And was it wise? Could he be forgiven for suggesting that it was not? It was regrettable, but true, that a man looked after his own. A man should have something, however small, that was his to use, to dispose of, to care for.

Madselin listened and thought of Britt Four Ox's white oxen; two dead, two caked with filth, thin and failing; of the ill-sheared sheep; of the many lambs snatched by wolves.

Sir Godfrey said, "It is true that the owner is the best groom. Not that he must fill the manger or ply the brush. But, as a matter of principle . . . A man looks after his own."

"Common ownership," Sir Stephen went on, "was tried by the early Christian Church; and soon abandoned. An unworkable system, men being what they are. . . ."

Rolf let him talk, making no attempt to explain his reasons or defend his actions. Giffard loyally tried.

"Sir Priest, if you have never seen such an arrangement it is because you have never seen a place such as this; few men; no wealth. And a castle to build. The hardships are shared, too. I have seen food as good on a fisherman's table. My lady cut up her clothes that the pages might be clad. My lord has one other tunic, much mended."

Into the silence with which this speech was received, Rolf spoke.

"No need to go begging," he said, going straight to the point as usual. "When we move into the castle you can have this for your church."

Sir Stephen said, without gratitude, "It is large enough. It will serve for a time. But I hold that in every community the church, which is the house of God, should be the largest and the most beautiful edifice."

It was on that evening that Madselin realized that the stone tower was to be a dwelling place, and the old hall abandoned. She had thought of it as a place of defence, for housing knights and weapons and stores, a place to run to if disaster ever struck. The idea of living in that cold unfriendly place, built by those cold unfriendly men, appalled her. A stone cage.

"It will be so cold," she said to Rolf in the sleeping chamber where he now slept in the small bed, formerly reserved for honoured guests and unused for eight months.

"Peter swore not," Rolf said, tidily folding his clothes. "What he called the Solar, he planned to face the sun."

She had heard talk of a Solar, had not known what it meant and had not cared to ask. Norman talk and of no interest to her.

"Stone is a cold thing," she said. "And those walls are thick. No amount of sun . . ."

"And no draught," he said, "every time the door opens."

He had had enough of talk for one day.

CHAPTER SIX

"There is just one thing," Giffard said. "If it should happen while you are away, and if it should be a case of mother or child, which is your wish?"

Rolf looked blank, but Giffard understood him a little and guessed at what the blankness concealed.

"It is woman's work," he said. "Even the long-gowned physicians avoid it. And she is young and healthy. You may well be back. But I should *know*. It sometimes happens that the head is too large to pass naturally. One can make way for it— and the mother dies—or one can crush the head, then the child dies. And that is contrary to the ruling of the Church. I say again it is unlikely to happen but I should know."

"Yes," Rolf said. He looked down at his hands with their long, thin, clever fingers that had done so many tricky jobs. Out of a whirlwind of thinking he snatched two simple statements. "I hope to be back." And, "A man can always get another child."

"So I see it," Giffard said. He thought—You hide yourself, even from yourself, my friend. He said, "Hild would die for her. And Edfu claims to have delivered forty, all thriving."

On the second evening of Rolf's absence the knights went to Bemid—the last time until spring that they would make a day's outing, Sir Godfrey said. Winter was coming. One sign of the changing season was the slaughtering of cattle which could not, like sheep and swine, fend for themselves off scant pasture. Most of the meat was preserved, but of every animal some choice portion was eaten fresh. In the kitchen the supper roasts were already slowly turning on the spits, and Sir Godfrey suggested that it would be courteous to invite the priest to share the meal. Madselin agreed readily; the habit of asking one's neighbours to eat a fresh roast was deeply ingrained, and Sir Stephen, by criticizing a system that took everything from the English, had somewhat endeared himself to Madselin.

She looked forward to the meal; for one thing she was hungry and hoped that the hunger would last until she had eaten; she was suffering the variable appetite of the gravid woman, ravenous, easily satiated; unable to eat at set times and then waking in the dark craving a crust. For another thing she hoped for some lively conversation to distract her mind. She was now longing to see and hold and possess her baby, to be her own shape and lightfooted again, but she dreaded the ordeal of birth, fearing not only the pain but that she might not bear it well and thus be shamed. The knights would come back with news of Bemid, the new priest's conversation was fresh, Giffard could talk on almost every subject and Rolf's absence would lighten the atmosphere. There were often times when his silence became infectious.

However, they were hardly seated and served before she realized that something had gone wrong. Sir Godfrey talked, but in a strained, artificially animated manner, every now and then looking at Sir Eustace, who seemed to avoid his eye and if asked a question gave answers as short as Rolf's. His face lacked some of its bright young colour and he was making slow work of his meal. Finally Sir Godfrey said, with a note of irritation in his voice, "And who *benefits* if you let your meat grow cold?"

"I have no appetite."

"Drink some wine then and stop behaving like a green girl."

Sir Eustace looked directly at him then, his mouth hardening into an expression of scornful disgust, his eyes so full of deep hurt that he might have been about to cry.

"Did you take a fall, Sir Eustace?" Giffard asked kindly.

"I have witnessed behaviour unworthy of a knight," Sir Eustace said.

It seemed that they had quarrelled; probably about some transgression of the knightly code understood by nobody else at the table.

"It is a coil about nothing," Sir Godfrey said.

"It is not about nothing. It is a matter of *principle!* If such a thing can happen to one man, it can happen to all. Even *you,* Sir Godfrey. There are rules governing the treatment of prisoners. They should be ransomed, killed out of hand, or set free. Not kept in a hole and fed carrion and made mock of."

"I think," Sir Godfrey said, "that it would be as well if you left the table, Sir Eustace."

"I have taken my last order from you, sir! If my lady desires me to withdraw, I will do so."

"I should prefer that you eat your meat," she said, giving him a look and a smile, almost maternal. He was older than she was, but had always seemed young to her; his boyish good looks, his enthusiasms, his deference to the elder knight made him seem youthful, and when they first met she was pregnant, twice married, mistress of a household, her youth long past.

"If it pleases you," he said, and cut a piece of the good beef, conveyed it to his mouth, chewed and swallowed.

"That way lies indigestion," Giffard warned him. His curiosity had quickened: a quarrel between the knights, how diverting—and what about? "Whose prisoner?"

"Sir Volfstan's," Sir Eustace said, laying his knife down again. He threw Sir Godfrey a dark look. "That is what sticks in my throat. You are related; you were the senior knight present. Had you added your protests to mine . . ."

"We will not," Sir Godfrey said, "go through all that again; at table, and in the presence of a lady."

"As a priest," Sir Stephen said, in a very firm clear voice, "I am interested in the condition of prisoners. Does the priest at Bemid have access to the man? Has he not protested?"

"The priest at Bemid is English, kept on sufferance. He is

half blind and about a hundred years old," Sir Eustace said bitterly. "He knows that if he said a word he would be down in the hole with the rats and the toads. And fed on dung!"

Madselin said sharply, "Oh!" The words—and what they called up, hurt her mind's inner eye, and then, she realized, her body also. Not a pain exactly, but a discomfort that might sharpen into pain. She shifted her position slightly. Giffard threw her a glance and said with less than his usual amiability, "Such talk spoils the meat, Sir Eustace. Even mine!"

With genuine anger, Sir Godfrey said, "For that breach of courtesy you will answer to me tomorrow. In the tiltyard."

"Willingly. If it is in earnest. I shall never joust for pleasure either with you or with Sir Volfstan again."

"Challenges are also out of place at table," Sir Stephen said. There was authority in his voice. "As for the man, Bemid is not my parish, but I shall take it upon myself to point out to the priest in charge that it is his duty to urge Christian compassion. And certainly, whatever the man's fault, he should not be denied the consolation of religion."

Sir Eustace made a noise that could have been a snort of scorn, the beginning of a mirthless laugh, a smothered sob.

"You mean well," he said, "but it is worthless. Ill-usage has driven the poor wretch past the point where he hardly recognizes his own name."

"In all my days," Sir Godfrey said, "I never heard such exaggeration. The man seemed to me to be an idiot, kept under control for safety's sake. He probably has no name."

"Then why should Sir Volfstan mock him with it and call him Stigand of Bemid?"

The threatening pain struck, a stake impaling her. She clutched at her body and gave a faint, mewling cry.

Giffard said, "Call the women."

Edfu took the child by the heels and in the traditional fashion slapped its buttocks until it cried out. Then she said, "Alive, thanks be to God. And a fine boy."

Hild held out a blanket.

"Give him to me. You see to her."

She wrapped the child and cleansed his face with a moist linen rag and carried him to the window. It was as she had thought. People laughed at the old ways, the old sayings, but there was truth in them. She kept well away from the bed until she could say to Edfu, "Now she will need wine to strengthen her. Mulled, not boiled. See to it yourself."

"She will sleep now," Edfu said. It had been a long labour. "Do as I say."

When Edfu had gone Hild carried the baby to the bed and said, not unkindly, but with a certain force, "Look upon your son."

There was Eitel's old face, puckered and anxious below the domed hairless skull.

"And no tail," Hild said. "So now we know. But it is between us. The likeness will not last long. And I have a little cap for his head. . . ."

CHAPTER SEVEN

"Your star," Giffard said to Rolf, returned from the King, "was certainly set in a lucky quarter. A healthy baby, the lady recovering. And now this."

He looked, almost with awe, on the gold pieces, newly minted. "Did you *ask* him?"

"No. No need. He noticed my mended sleeve and asked was I so hard put. I told him how things were."

Giffard could imagine the stark stripped sentences falling like stones.

"You did well," he said.

"Tomorrow you can go to Colchester or beyond if needs be, and hire more masons. To finish by Christmas or soon after."

How, with the masons holding themselves so aloof from ordinary men, did the master mason know within an hour?

"It has come to my notice," he said, "that other masons are to be brought in. My lodge has no quarrel with that. But the other lodges must be ones we can work with."

"They will be ones that we can get at short notice," Rolf said.

"Oh, no," the master mason said sternly. "Not if we are to continue. Any to be hired now, at a day's notice, would not be those *we* could work with."

"Why not?"

"Because those to be hired at a moment's notice are not worth hiring at all," the master mason said with a direct simplicity that struck Rolf as dismal truth. First he had lacked money; and now, when he had it, good workmen were all engaged.

"The building is one to be proud of," the man said. "I shall put our mark on the last stone with satisfaction. That thought has held us here, despite the unsatisfactory conditions." He allowed that reminder of inferior meat and sour ale to sink in and then took a more cheerful line. "There are ways and means," he said, almost benevolently. "If you leave it to me . . . Though the bread, lately, has been poor." It had declined in quality since what the miller had called "sharps" had gone to the dough trough instead of into the swill bucket.

"It will be better," Rolf said.

"Where did he find them?" Rolf said to Giffard when the two new gangs moved in, hastily built their lodges and set to work with the same intensity of purpose and precision of motion as the first one.

"They have their own methods," Giffard said, "and their signals, I have no doubt. I should guess that both lots were engaged elsewhere and seized on some excuse to leave. One bad dinner is enough; as we know."

Rolf grunted. Then he said, abruptly, "What ails her?"

"Nothing that I know of. Two nights and a day and a half in labour. It will take a little time. Feeding a child makes demands, too. I never saw a cow in milk that was fat."

Giffard was half a physician and his words should carry weight. Rolf took from them a superficial comfort but his dumb sense of something being wrong remained. A woman, safely delivered of a healthy son, should be cheerful and contented, surely. Madselin was neither. She ate very little and slept badly and often wore a stricken look. Once he had watched her actually feeding the child and looking down upon him with the soft, doting look exactly suitable to the circumstances—like a picture, he had thought. And then she lifted her head and stared straight ahead of her, looking at a blank wall as though she saw on it, or beyond it, something that caused her distress. Once he asked, "Is anything wrong?" It seemed to him that she deliberately banished the stricken look and put on one of brightness. "Wrong? Oh no." She hastily drew his attention to the baby, "He is gaining flesh," she said. Rolf, whose joy and pride in the child was boundless but quite inexpressible, said the boy reminded him of his own grandfather, especially about the mouth. She realized that she should have been pleased by that remark; but nothing pleased her now.

She had emerged from the deep sleep of exhaustion after the long labour and entertained for a moment the blurred hope that the scene at the table and Stigand's name had been part of a particularly horrible and vivid dream. That hope did not survive the full return of consciousness. It was true. Stigand, by some means or another, had fallen into Sir Volfstan's hands; was alive; was being ill-treated in a way that had drawn disgusted protest from Sir Eustace. So, lying in bed, safely delivered, the mother of a son, at a moment when she should have been supremely happy, she had been obliged to pick over, remembering every word, every glance, every intonation, all that had taken place in the time it took discomfort to change to pain. Apart from the shock and the horror the thing that stuck in her mind most firmly was that Sir Eustace had protested, apparently without result. Sir Eustace was a knight, a Norman, and up until that day, a friend of Sir Volfstan's. She was a woman, English and, even when obliged to extend hospitality to Sir Volfstan, had done it coolly with the necessary civility and no more. So any protest she might make would be doomed from the start. What could she do? Nothing. Yet something must be done. What? Something must be done because it was impossible to live indefinitely with the thought of Stigand in such plight; the dung and the carrion coming between her and the dainties with which everybody sought to tempt her appetite; her own cosy bed every night transformed into a cold dark hole with loathsome inhabitants.

And she had sensed, rather than gathered directly, some

kind of mystery about the whole affair. Sir Eustace, she
thought, had offended not only in mentioning unpleasant
things at table, but in referring to the matter at all. She remembered how Sir Godfrey had tried to make him withdraw
from table. Her feeling that there was something secret and
unusual was confirmed when, five days after her confinement,
Sir Stephen came to see her.

He brought offerings; a little silver medallion of Mary and
the Child to be hung on the cradle; dried plums and apricots
and raisins from his father's warehouse. He admired the baby—
she and Rolf had agreed that he was to be called William—and
spoke enthusiastically about his christening. Sir Godfrey, he
was certain, would ask his cousin the Bishop to perform the
ceremony. What Bradwald needed was some splendid and im-
pressive display, something to look at and at the same time to
bring home to the people a realization of the power of the
Church.

She listened to him impatiently, waiting for the moment
when she could slip in her question. She put it casually and in
a manner that had made old Father Alfleg say that she had a
way with her.

"You were concerned, Sir Stephen, about the plight of some
poor prisoner . . ." The tone of voice, the look in her eyes
approved his concern.

"Oh yes. I went to Bemid next morning. And I was relieved
to find that of all Sir Eustace said, the only facts were that the
old priest there is purblind and extremely old. Sir Volfstan was
playing a trick on his company. The man was a mummer,
feigning madness as others swallow swords or seem to eat fire.
He had deceived them all and gone on his way."

If one could only believe it; rest easy again; eat, sleep, take
joy in one's child; think of Stigand as dead; renew the bed-joy
with Rolf.

"So you were satisfied," she said, not as a question, as a con-
gratulation on duty well done.

"The priest at Bemid," Sir Stephen said, "for all his age and

infirmity, is active and conscientious. He eats in the hall three
or four times a week and he had never heard of a prisoner.
Also, I noted this . . . Sir Eustace spoke of a hole—meaning, I
suppose, a dungeon. And at Bemid there are none. There is not
even a cellar for the keeping of wine . . ."

Comfort yourself; comfort yourself. But why had the man,
prisoner or mummer, been called Stigand of Bemid? In
mockery?

"I shall get up today," she said.

"My lady, no, I beg you. Fourteen days and this is but the
seventh."

"Move about," Hild said, "and you will lose your milk."

Her anxiety and uncertainty and misery loosed itself in a
burst of ill-temper.

"Much you know about it, having had so many children
yourselves! Emma the thatcher's wife was up and at work on
the fourth day. I took her a custard and she was in the field."

"I warned her," Edfu said. "And she has never since been
the right shape. Or borne another."

"My girdle," Madselin said, "can be tightened." Up and
dressed, resuming ordinary life, she must, sooner or later, find
herself alone with Sir Eustace, who had seen the man and
sympathized with him and could tell her something by which
she could identify him.

When the opportunity came the boy wasted a little time in
making an apology and in apologizing for not having apolo-
gized before.

"Sir Godfrey ordered me to and I would not give him the
satisfaction of seeming to obey. But, my lady, I do apologize
from my heart for speaking of such unpleasant matters within
your hearing. And at such a time. I allowed my feelings to
overcome my judgement. If you can, my lady, forgive me."

"You gave me no offence. None at all." She smiled and
added lightly, "And after all that, the man, I understand, was

a paid mummer." She watched his face intently, saw it darken
and then assume a deliberate blankness.

"So it is said."

"But you do not believe it?"

"My lady, once my first anger wore off it did not need Sir
Godfrey to point out to me that ladies with gentle hearts are
hurt to hear of such things." Let her think that his misery was
pretence. And so forget the man and forgive *him*.

She said, "Sir Eustace, if I ever had a gentle heart I parted
from it years ago. You may be honest with me." He looked into
her eyes and saw that what she said was true.

"No. I do not believe it. I saw the man. He was no
mummer." In her breast the heart which life had hardened
banged.

"How could you tell?"

"By the man's condition; mummers walk from place to
place. This man . . . my lady, are you sure you wish to hear
this? . . . he could not have walked a mile."

"How tall?"

"About the Lord Rolf's height. Perhaps more."

"Yellow-haired?"

"I could not tell. He was so dirty," the boy said miserably.

Stigand, whose hair and beard had always been so well
cared for and glossy.

"And you heard his name?"

"Stigand. Calling him of Bemid was one of the things Sir
Volfstan found amusing. . . ."

"It was truth. Bemid was his. My mother knew him well."

"Then I am doubly sorry. But," his face lightened a little, "I
have done what I could. There is some mystery here. Sir Volfstan was drunk or he would not have shown the man at all.
When I protested he regretted the display. My father and I are
at odds but he bears an honourable name which I have not
disgraced—our quarrel is about a private matter—and as my father's son I have inquired of Lord Bowdegrave whether he

knows what is being done by his agent. For all his pretensions
Sir Volfstan is but an agent."

"You have seen Lord Bowdegrave?"

"No. I sent a letter. Giffard wrote in my name and I signed
it with my name and estate."

"You are a true knight, Sir Eustace," she said with feeling.
The boy blushed.

"How did you send the letter?"

"I carried it to Colchester and there hired a man to carry it.
My Lord Bowdegrave has a manor in Kent which he favours
above his others. It will take time."

Yes, it would take time. But in so dismal and hopeless an
outlook the slightest ray of cheer was welcome and must be
clung to. And surely, in the meantime, it should not be beyond
the wits of a normally resourceful woman to alleviate Stigand's
state by some means, however trivial.

She tried to resume her casual conversational tone.

"Sir Stephen was inclined to doubt your story because he
could see no dungeons at Bemid."

"I said a hole. And it is a hole, in the floor of Bemid hall."

She thought—Ah! The well that went dry. The well actually
inside the hall had seemed an enviable convenience, and
Madselin, about seven years old at the time, could remember
with what spiteful pleasure her mother had received news of
its sudden failure. "So!" she had said, "now those at Bemid
can carry water in all weathers like everybody else."

She said to Rolf, "At about this time of the year, before
the bad weather, I always used to take something to the ladies
at Wyck for their Christmas table. I should like to do so this
year."

Things were easier at Bradwald now, but there was no room
for lavishness and Rolf's impulse to charity was very small.

"Can you ride? So soon?"

"It would restore me. Of all things I have most missed riding abroad. I shall come back so hungry that I shall take food from your trencher."

"In that case . . ." he said. And indeed the mere prospect of the ride seemed to have enlivened her. Riding for pleasure Rolf had never understood; for him it was a means of getting from place to place.

"What may I take?"

"Of that you are the best judge. There are the three lodges to feed until Christmas. At least." Again she looked pleased.

"Giffard will go with you," he said.

Near the path to Wyck was Britt the thatcher's intake land and clod hovel. It was astonishing what a determined man and woman, working for themselves, could do in a few months. A plot was already cleared and in the centre of it a sow was tethered. Four young pigs ran around her. They would not stray; they rooted in the soil as she did, nosing, trampling, dunging the patch on which corn would grow next year; and on the edge of this cleared ground Emma and her eldest were burning out a tree stump, too large to be uprooted until the fire had eaten down and reduced it to a hollow brittle shell.

"I must just speak to Emma," Madselin said.

It was a heartening exchange. Britt was away, thatching at Cressacre. The sow, Emma said, had been payment for such a job, earlier in the year. "God blessed us; she was in-pig, but that they did not know." And neither Britt nor Emma would ever, ever forgot what the lady had done for them. Every time they prayed they mentioned her name to God; and the fine boy proved that He had heard.

Now to make certain that Giffard was occupied while she talked to the Abbess. He liked old things. He spent much of his spare time poking about in the place where the stone for the castle had come from. To ears unappreciative because of ignorance or self-absorption, he had sometimes spoken of what he had half discovered, half guessed at: a great temple to Mithras and around it the baths for the ritual cleansing before the temple could be entered, the buildings to house the priests, the worshippers, the traders. He liked old things. So she told him, as though it were fact, the legend of the hermit who had cut the zigzag path, leaving the oaks. And she said, "Giffard, you must see the convent well, built around the spring. The lady Cecily should show it to you. She has the longest memory and her aunt, and *hers*, were at Wyck. She can tell of cures which came of drinking the waters, once upon a time."

"Listen now," Madselin said to the Abbess, "we have little time. Father Alfleg still visits you?"

"Wyck was not forbidden."

"I know. That is why I am here. Mother, this may shock you. Stigand of Bemid is alive, starved and ill-treated, at Bemid. But Father Alfleg, if he were determined, could demand access to him."

"Vain talk and ridiculous. What put that into . . . Stigand died, with his king, in the battle. . . ."

"It seems not. Listen . . ." Swiftly she told what she knew and showed what she had brought. This and this for the ladies, almost but not quite their usual Christmas dole; and then the manchet bread so white and pure that though it might grow stale and hard it would never sour or moulder as coarser breads did; the pounded beef paste, food in its most concentrated form, salted and spiced and sealed in its little clay pot by an inch-thick layer of solid mutton fat; and another similar pot of honey and the best butter blended together.

"Nothing bulky," she said. "If Father Alfleg insists that even prisoners should have the sacrament administered, he can take his basket . . . and these. And this . . ." She lifted her cloak and unwound from her body the fine light blanket of pure wool. "He is spare," she said, "it will not show. And in the cold nights . . ." It all seemed so small, so furtive. "It is," she said, "merely a matter of keeping him alive in less discomfort . . . *They* are not all bad, one of the knights wrote a letter . . ."

Outside a dog yelped sharply twice and then sent up a whimpering howl soon mingled with a woman's weeping.

"What is now to do?" the Abbess said, rising and going to the door.

"But you understand," Madselin said. "Father Alfleg must *insist*. They will put him off . . . but if he insists he will have the support of the Bradwald priest who holds that all prisoners . . ."

By this time the Abbess had the door open. Outside Giffard wiped his knife, first on a tuft of grass, then on his sleeve, and Dame Cecily knelt, clutching and trying to comfort a hound which was trying to break away from her hold and to lick its bleeding paws.

"What did he ever do to be so treated?" Dame Cecily sobbed.

"It is the law," Giffard said, glancing at Madselin. "I thought it better done by a skilled hand. Dogs in or near the forest must be disabled to prevent them hunting."

"He never hunted so much as a rabbit," said the Abbess who had held this against the hound for seven years.

"And now so old," Dame Cecily said.

"Then he will not miss running," Madselin said harshly. She resented the interruption; she felt that she had not had time to convince the Abbess, who was, after all, Stigand's great-aunt. The willingness with which the old woman had broken off the talk by going to the door proved that she had not understood the seriousness of the business.

"Come," she said, "my son will be wanting me."

For a little while they rode in silence, Giffard thinking that her displeasure arose from the dog's mutilation. But presently the thought that she had done something, done what she could, allied with the riding in the crisp air, cheered her. When they came to the oak tree where she had been saved from the wolf, she began to tell Giffard about that adventure. And since Giffard had written Sir Eustace's letter it seemed safe to say, "The man was Stigand of Bemid. I was always grateful to him. I do hope Sir Eustace's letter has the effect he intended."

"That young hot-head will come to grief," Giffard said, for him very gravely. "I made him promise not to mention the man, nor the letter, to anyone at all. And he has already told you."

"Only because we were speaking of the man. I confessed to some concern for one who was once a neighbour and Sir Eustace said he had done what he could."

"It is a very dangerous business for ordinary people to meddle in," Giffard said.

"I know."

"If you believe the man is named Stigand you do not *know*, my lady, forgive the contradiction."

"What is there to know?"

"Guess would be a better word. I have interested myself in this—but very cautiously; and I do not believe the man is Stigand of Bemid. I believe he is Brithric of Gloucester. As a young man he was loved by Queen Matilda. He scorned her, so she has a grudge; and the King has a grudge too, putting down the Queen's unwillingness to marry him to her love for the Englishman. Brithric is said to be kept in conditions exactly such as Sir Eustace described—but whereabouts is uncertain. What the King wishes to keep secret it is not safe to know, far less talk about. It was the utmost folly in Sir Volfstan to let the man be seen."

"Sir Eustace says he was drunk at the time."

"Wine in, wit out. With him I am not concerned. For Rolf I am. Sir Eustace is Rolf's man and Rolf is the King's. If the case is as I think, it would do Rolf no service for the King to think that his knight was busying himself with how Brithric of Gloucester was fed and housed."

She knew, in a fashion, that it was wrong to feel so relieved, so elated that it was Brithric, not Stigand, who lay hungering in the old well. A man was a man, suffering was suffering, but the fact was that Brithric, only a name to her, never known, never loved, was difficult to visualize in his horrible state, whereas Stigand had been all too real; she knew even the shape of his fingernails and the shape in which his hair grew from his forehead. She felt suddenly light and free. And able to give her mind to other aspects of the matter.

She said, "Yet, feeling this, you did Rolf the disservice of writing Sir Eustace's letter."

Giffard hesitated for a second or two. "I wrote two," he said. "The one he signed—rather touching—Eustace, Knight son to Richard of Brecey—I held back for the sealing and super-scription. Then I wrote another, begging Lord Bowdegrave to give something towards the building of the abbey at St. Edmundsbury and signed with a scrawl that no scribe could decipher. *That* was the one which Sir Eustace took to Colchester. So no harm was done."

She said, "How clever! Giffard, how very clever!" But that part of her mind which always held off a little and always made its own, sometimes contradictory judgements, said—And how *dangerous*. Had it been Stigand there, and his only hope of relief a letter . . . and all dependent upon the integrity or the trickery of one man who could write.

She said, "To be able to write is a great thing, Giffard. I had the chance to learn once. Being young and foolish, I refused."

"You could still learn. If you wished. Few women have the capacity. I think you have. I would teach you—if you wished."

Father Alfleg cupped one hand around his bowl, took his spoon, supped and said, "Ah. There is good beef suet in this broth." The Abbess allowed him to take six or seven spoonfuls and then said, "Now. What is this I hear about a prisoner at Bemid?"

"You too! How do such tales take wing?"

"Madselin of Bradwald was here."

He took some more broth, not savouring it, and then put down the spoon and, staring at the blur which was the Abbess' pale squarish face, said defensively, "I know my duty and have done it. I know that even murderers should not be cut off from the confession of sins. It did not take the proper priest from Bemid to tell me that. I know my duty. . . ."

For him Wyck had lately been the exceptional place. Banned from the rest of the Rinland, he was allowed here; it was a place remote from the world, untouched, just as it had been. And although he now rode on the new, hard-mouthed, ignorant and seemingly unteachable mule, his visits had always been—despite the bad food—enjoyable; little re-entries to a vanished world. Now this.

"Is the prisoner the son of my nephew, Stigand of Bemid?"

"No. How could it be? Stigand died in the battle."

"He *fell*," she said, in her contrary way. "His body was never found."

"Nor were thousands of others. But for Edith Swan-neck King Harold himself would not have been recovered. Stigand died. And Mass was said for him, here and at Bemid." He spoke as though a Mass for a man's soul guaranteed his death. Because he seemed so sure the Abbess was bound to argue.

"Madselin of Bradwald said that Stigand was a prisoner at Bemid."

"So! They are using her now; poor lady. This is a tale concocted to discredit me. That new priest at Bradwald wants one of his own for neighbour. That is what it is. So it cuts both ways . . ." Into the old dimmed eyes there flashed a look of shrewdness. "This new man makes out that I am so old and senseless that I do not know my duty to those held in durance. Or he hopes that, by asking, I offend Sir Volfstan, who, although a harsh man, has borne with me and allowed my office. There is no prisoner at Bemid."

"How can you know?"

"Because, reprimanded by the Bradwald priest, I did not rush about, making accusations. I said, 'Come with me' and he came. Sir Volfstan said—*Find* a man in a dungeon! Find a dungeon, even! I admit that I see less well than I did—little things, under my nose. But I should not overlook a man . . . I suppose," the incongruous shrewdness flashed again in his eyes, "they thought that a message from the Lady Madselin would send me running back, making a nuisance of myself again. It will not." He felt about for his spoon and resumed eating with determination.

"I am glad," the Abbess said. "One does not like to hear of such things." She was glad for another reason. There was now no need to hand over the little delicacies that Madselin had brought. They would brighten the dull convent fare; and the blanket would be very welcome to old Dame Blanche, who was bedridden and always complaining of the cold.

"Old Frieda at the priest's house sent me," the little boy said. "To tell you, my lady, that Father Alfleg is about to die and anxious to see you."

He was an ill-clad, skinny little boy of eight or nine years old, breathless from running but panting without distress, like a puppy. To have come from Bemid and to arrive at Bradwald at first light he must have run through the dark. He had the bony, hungry-looking face that was the English face these days.

"You must go into the kitchen and tell them to give you something to eat. You have had a long run."

"Not so far. There is a short cut through the woods."

"And you could find it; in the dark?"

"I can find my way by the stars," he said, rather proudly. "And no wolf would touch me. I carry a charm." Again proudly he dived into his single homespun garment and pulled up a narrow string of wrinkled leather on which hung a wolf's paw, very old, worn hairless.

"Tell Alfred to have my horse ready." She must feed William. She must tell Hild that if the child woke and cried in the hungry way before she returned, to pacify him with a clean rag dipped in milk sweetened with honey and just warm.

When she emerged into the bright cold morning air her

horse was ready, and, waiting with it, Sir Stephen, walking his own horse up and down.

"I thought that if he is indeed dying," he said, "I could be of some service. No priest is nearer that I know of." She realized then that in her haste she had forgotten Rolf's order that she was not to ride alone.

"I shall be glad of your company, Sir Priest," she said.

He had hoped to snatch this opportunity of having a fruitful talk; beginning with the matter of the baby's baptism as soon as the hall was dedicated as a church and then moving on to the necessity for the lady in every community to set an example in piety and charity and devotion to the church; but they rode too swiftly for any real conversation. Both horses were fresh, exhilarated by the cool, bracing air, and she was, for a woman, a reckless rider. The homily must be reserved for the homeward ride.

Madselin was anxious to reach the old man's bedside. She had accepted—the more easily because she wished to do so—Giffard's assertion that the prisoner was not Stigand; as a consequence both her spirits and her appetite had so much improved since her visit to Wyck four days earlier that Rolf had been astonished at the restorative effect of a single ride. But as she was feeding the baby she had concluded that the old priest's anxiety to see her must be in some way connected with this affair. Giffard could not *know;* he had only guessed; and she perhaps had seized on a comforting theory too eagerly, simply because it was comforting.

They clattered briskly past the turnings to Wyck, Ing and Scartoke; over the low-lying place where in wet weather the water gathered, and then at a slightly slower pace up the gentle slope into Bemid.

"This is the priest's house," she said, reining in by a low clod cottage. Sir Stephen knew it; he had been there to talk to the old priest about duty to prisoners. And he had thought—How can ordinary people truly respect one who is housed like a serf? In a properly constituted community the church would

be the best edifice, then the hall of the lord of the manor, and
then the presbytery.

Madselin dismounted, swiftly and unaided. Sir Stephen took
the reins of both horses and tethered them to a post while she
rapped on the door. It was opened by an old woman who
looked as though she had been crying for a week. She was still
crying, wiping her eyes and her nose on her sleeve.

"He *is* dying," she said in a choked voice. "Only waiting to
see you, my lady." Then she saw the Bradwald priest and a
look of the utmost venom came over her disfigured face.

"Not *you!*" she said, rudely. "Nobody sent for *you!*"

"No," he said, agreeably. "I came on my own accord, hoping
to be of some service."

"Not here!" she exclaimed and slammed the door in his face.

The door opened directly into one of the two rooms that
with a little lean-to kitchen comprised the house. Here the old
priest took his meals and Frieda had her bed. Another door,
even lower than the entry, opened to the left. Frieda put her
hand on the latch and said, almost in a whisper, "My lady,
whatever it is, promise to do it. Promise anything so he dies in
peace. Poor, good old man. To end like this." There was a fresh
gush of tears.

The little room beyond the door was as bare as a cell, and as
cold. But it was clean. Father Alfleg lay on his back, propped
by two pillows. His body was hardly visible under the covers;
his face was the colour of beeswax, the closed eyes sunk in
purplish hollows, his nose and lips just tinged with blue. Without opening his eyes he said in a weak voice, "Dear woman, go
away. The weeping bothers me. God will take care of you."

"Father, it is Madselin."

He opened his eyes then and she was just far enough away
for him to see her clearly.

"Thank God," he said. "Come here. Sit on the bed." When
she obeyed he could no longer see her and moved his hand and
said, almost fretfully, "Where are you?"

"Here, Father." She took the hand, some bones in a loose

casing of skin, burning hot. The thin fingers tightened on hers, weakly. Even so much effort seemed to exhaust him and he lay quiet, except for the noise of his shallow, difficult breathing.

"I was wrong," he said. "There is a man at Bemid. And it is Stigand. As you said." Her heart took a sickening, downward plunge.

"Are you sure? I heard that it was, and then that it was not. How can you be sure?"

"I saw him. At a distance I see very well. He will die unless something is done . . . and soon. And only you can help him."

She wanted to cry—How? What can I do? But she remembered her promise to Frieda. She said, "I will do my best, I promise."

He seemed to sense the lack of confidence in that statement. His fingers tightened again.

"You must," he said. He drew some more shallow noisy breaths. "You owe Stigand something, you know."

I? she thought wildly. I owe Stigand? It is the other way about! All those long years of lonely loving; the handsome young men at Winchester, so ready to admire and meaning nothing to my fixed, single-hearted love; the beatings; the filth in the dovecote. And all to what end? Jilted for Gundred.

"I knew his heart and his mind. Both set on you. You were so young. And he waited, reining a young man's heat. But you chose Eitel."

Her heart cried out against that—Untrue! But of course that was the impression that she had intended to give. Emerging from the dovecote, bathed and cleansed, dancing, brave in yellow and tawny and amber beads at Stigand's wedding and then going defiantly to her own.

"You are well placed," the old man said in his innocence. "You have friends among them. And you work well in the dark . . . this is a dark thing, and secret. I blame myself. So blind. So easily fobbed off. And then so rash. Child, you must not be rash. You are English too. . . ." His hot fingers attempted one last pressure and then fell flaccid.

"I promise you," she said, "I will be careful. And I will do my utmost."

"I knew . . ." he said, and he closed his eyes and seemed to grow even smaller against the pillows. For a moment she forgot herself, and Stigand and everything else except that here, under her eyes, the old man whom she had known all her life was dying.

"Father Alfleg," she said, "the Norman priest rode with me. He is here. Would you wish . . . ?"

"No!" the word rang out with astonishing force. "The viaticum . . . from one of *them* . . . sooner go to my God . . . unassoiled . . ."

His next breath had a curious rattling sound. Then his eyes opened and focused, not on her, but on something above and behind her. The furrows and lines in his face seemed to smooth out. He appeared to be looking on something surprising, pleasing, almost amusing. The noisy breathing ceased.

She said softly, "Go with God," and sat there, still holding the rapidly cooling hand, thinking and thinking, wishing that she could cry. A warm wash of tears would have eased the ache in her throat and the feeling of constriction in her chest. No tears came, but presently a thought did, dropping into her mind, complete and hard, like a stone.

She loosened her hand and stood up and, remembering to duck her head at the doorway, went into the outer room where Frieda was. Through the narrow slit of window she could see Sir Stephen, sensible man, walking the horses up and down.

"He is dead, Frieda. He died happily." She opened the door and went out to the priest.

"He died before I could call you," she said. "Now I must console the old woman, who is distraught."

"I tried again to enter. She would not admit me."

"Nor will she now. To force her would be unkind. Sir Stephen, it is about dinner time, I think. Go to the hall; take Sir Volfstan's hospitality for yourself and the horses and then

come back for me." Before he could either protest or agree she
turned about and went in again by the low door.

"Frieda, is there a way out at the back? Good. I need a
knife. Now listen. I shall not be long, but if I should not be
back before the Norman comes, keep him out and pretend that
I am still here. Do you understand?"

The kitchen was not even furnished with a door; there was a
hole in the clod wall, serving both as entry and window and
access to the midden. She scrambled through and landed in
the noisome pile of refuse accumulated over the years. Then
she ran directly over the tussocky grass towards the river and
dropped, with more speed than caution, over the edge of what
had, years ago, been its bank on the Bemid side. The bank and
about half the width of what had been the old riverbed was
now waste land patched with grass and weeds and dotted here
and there by willow trees and clumps of brambles. There had
been, about ten years earlier, a season of very wet weather; the
river had flooded and its turbulent waters had scooped out the
bank on the farther side and when the flood receded the river
had changed course. It lay there now, slow and brown, hugging the southern bank.

She walked rapidly along the stretch of deserted bed, looking neither to right nor left. Then she pulled herself up the
bank and took a reckoning. She had guessed well; another few
paces would bring her level with the lower end of the hall. She
lowered herself again, took the few paces and then, slackening
pace, began to search the surface of the exposed bank with the
same intensity that she would have given to the hunting for a
needle dropped amongst the rushes on the floor.

The thought that came to her as she sat on the old man's
deathbed was simple and reasonable: the well in Bemid hall
had been fed from the river and had gone dry when the water
changed course. She was searching now for some sign on the
bank of the place where the water had made its entry—a chan-
nel, a tunnel, perhaps even a pipe. If she were right the entry
would be directly in line with the hall, and below what had

once been water level; so the area to be scrutinized was limited, a few feet to left or right, a few feet up or down.

She found nothing. The bank at this point presented the same face as elsewhere; tufts of grass, clumps of briars, some small willows, nettles. Yet surely water flowing in at one point for countless years must have left *some* mark. Combined with the feeling of deadly disappointment there was agitation because she had so little time. She broke into a sweat. She climbed the bank again and looked at the hall standing dark and low across the commonland. She reasoned again: the water would have been conveyed by the shortest route and just where she stood was in direct line with the hall's lower end. There *must* be something and it must be here, concealed by the growth of ten years. She stamped on and kicked at the nettles, tore at the briars, scratching her hands without feeling the pain. Nothing. She thought of the priest returning to the house, perhaps imposing his will upon Frieda and wondering what had sent the Lady Madselin running from a deathbed to a river bank. He must not be allowed to suspect anything. He was a Norman and although, as a priest, he had concerned himself, in a limited way, over the prisoner's state, he was not likely to bear any sympathy with plans for his escape. And back at Bradwald the baby would be hungry. She thought wildly—I have no time. Given time I could clear this space with my bare hands! As though to prove this to herself—but also to relieve her pent-up feelings—she seized one of the willow trees and tugged at it with manic strength. It did not, as she expected, come up, yielding to the pull of her scratched and urgent hands, but the earth around its roots shifted and a few clods broke off and rolled down the slope. The effort and its frustration exhausted her frenzy. The whole idea, the wonderful thought which she had looked upon as a gift, an inspiration dropped into her mind by the old priest's spirit as it passed, had after all been nothing but the product of her own mind, searching too eagerly for some way to help Stigand, and seizing too eagerly upon any proposition that offered any slight hope.

So all that was left to do was to use the knife that she had borrowed, and cut two strips of willow bark to make a cross to lay in Father Alfleg's hands. That was the excuse—should excuse be needed—for her running to the river bank. She cut one strip and had half cut another when she noticed that where the soil had moved and fallen away it had not fallen in a rough haphazard shape, but had left an arc, a small segment of a circle, with just a gleam of red against the dark soil. In a second she was on her knees, using the knife vigorously. She dug with it and she used it to slash at the young tree's roots. When she had damaged it enough she pulled at it again and this time it came away. She said, "Holy Mary, Mother of God!" in an awed voice when she saw what the uprooting had revealed. Almost the whole mouth of a pipe made of some hard red substance about an inch thick and in circumference somewhat larger than that of a man's body.

Through the dizzying mingling of thankfulness to God and to the Blessed Virgin, and superstitious thoughts about the old priest's soul informing her as it passed, and self-congratulation at having been right in her reckonings, caution still wove its way. She righted the half-uprooted tree and stamped the mangled roots in again and retrieved the two strips of bark that she had cut. Then she turned and ran back along the way she had come and re-entered the little house where Frieda, still weeping, had begun the laying out of the corpse. Two circles of lead, kept for the purpose and lent about, and called pennies because in well-to-do households actual coins were used, held Father Alfleg's eyelids down; a strip of linen held his jaw in place. There was nothing left of the expression which his face had assumed as he died. Peeling the outermost skin of the bark and making a thread flexible as wool, Madselin bound the two strips together and placed the cross thus made between the thin hands which Frieda had arranged across his breast.

"Frieda, I promised him so much. I promised that you

should have a home with me . . . You will be very welcome at Bradwald."

"He had more on his mind—at the end."

"I know. Stigand. You knew about him?"

"I knew from the first. I hid it from him; to save him distress. I blame myself. Had he known and been prepared the shock would not have been so great and he would not have acted so rashly. I blame myself."

"Frieda, there is so much to say, and no time. I have found a way, but it took me longer than I thought. Listen . . . yes, he is back already. Hold to not letting him in. He might pray for an hour and my child is hungering. But Frieda, as soon as all is done here, come to me. Come to Bradwald. There is so much to arrange . . . Come as soon as you can."

"Death comes to all," Sir Stephen said.

"I know."

"He was old; and very blind."

"I know."

"You were fond of him?" he asked curiously. Women easily transferred loyalty from one priest to another. On the other hand she had never shown any sign of either loyalty or affection towards the old man. She had actually sided with that demented old woman who had so firmly excluded him.

"I had known him all my life."

"I blame myself somewhat," he said. "Perhaps I should have insisted and not been put off by the old woman."

"There is no need," she said. "He passed so easily. The words, the oil would not have helped."

But there lay the danger, Sir Stephen saw. Where no need was felt . . . There was something wrong with a community where even a priest could die, easily, happily, with the Church excluded. He knew that this should have been the ideal moment for his saying all that he had to say to her. Death softened even obdurate hearts and brought home to the most frivolous minds that life was merely a brief prelude to eternity.

This should have been the moment, but a glance at her face, ivory pale and bleak, set in a preoccupied expression, made him think that he would not get far, today. So he postponed his talk again and contented himself with small, would-be comforting remarks as the horses, headed for their own mangers, sped along.

Madselin heard him and made brief answers now and then. But she had perfected the art of inattention and her mind was crowded. Plans for the future, and, intruding now and again, thoughts of the past. Looking backward was useless, but as the turn-off to Scartoke came near, was there, was passed, it was impossible not to look backwards and be puzzled. To wonder. To speculate. "I knew his heart and his mind. Both were set on you." Then why? From the moment of her return from Winchester she had made her feelings very plain. So had he . . . so had he . . . They had met often, in public at neighbourly gatherings, and in private. They had ridden together with lively talk and fond glances, and finally with kisses. At the point where the path to Scartoke turned off, they had parted on that never-to-be-forgotten day of their last loving encounter and she had clung to him with all the fierceness of a passionate, single-minded love. And he had said, "I will speak with your mother." And the next thing she heard of him was that he was to marry Gundred. It had not made sense then; it made less now, after what Father Alfleg had said.

CHAPTER EIGHT

William tugged at what had always been a source of satisfaction, let go, baffled, and tried again. Then, going red in the face, he roared to the world that he was hungry, and ill-done-by.

"So!" Hild said. "This is what comes of bouncing about on a horse!"

"It was not the riding. It was the shock of seeing the old man die."

"If you had thought of your milk and stayed at home you would not have had the shock."

"And he would not have died so peacefully. I promised to look after Frieda. She is coming here."

"To live? That dirty old woman! She is not to lay a hand on this child."

Madselin was about to say that such things were for her to decide, but she remembered that she would want to talk to Frieda alone; so she said, "No. It would be as well if they were together as little as possible."

"Now we must wean him and trouble will begin," Hild said darkly. But as she went off to warm milk and sweeten it with honey she realized that in the future there would be nothing that Madselin could do for the baby that she could not herself do. She came back in a more cheerful mood.

William, after a few squawks of protest, accepted the substitute and sucked vigorously on the rag which Hild dipped and offered. Madselin looked at him sadly; such a beautiful baby, such a good little creature, and except for four brief days after her ride to Wyck she had never been able to take full joy in him or give him her whole attention. Now she could not supply his simplest need.

Presently she said, "Hild, do you remember that day when my mother beat me and put me in the dovecote?"

"That was not a day to forget," Hild said, dipping the rag again.

"What happened?"

"What happened?" Hild repeated. "You know. You were the one it happened to."

Madselin saw that this must be approached cunningly.

"I angered my mother by not welcoming her choice for me. I remembered that as I rode past Scartoke today. I remember the beating, but the rest of the day . . . no, I cannot."

"Well, I can," Hild said positively. "There had been a clearance of doves and you rode with a bunch of them to take to the ladies at Wyck."

"Did I?" Madselin said, remembering how, setting out on that ride, she had hoped, as she always did, that she would meet Stigand.

"Yes. And we were to have doves for dinner. I had to help Bertha to dress them. We had almost done when Stigand of Bemid rode up—dressed very fine—and Bertha said we must dress more doves because he would be asked to dinner. But they were hardly spitted before he left, looking as a man would who had not been asked to dine."

"In what way?"

"Cast down," Hild said. "A bit put about. So was Bertha, having made ready, but I said you would eat for two after your ride. As you would on any other day."

He had kept his word. He had asked her mother, been told that Madselin was pledged to Eitel and gone away—perhaps on that very morning—to ask Eric of Ing for Gundred's hand.

She said, "You have a good memory, Hild."

"It is not so long ago," Hild said. "It is what has happened since that makes it seem long."

He will die unless something is done—and soon.

The plan which had fallen into her mind would take a little time to put into operation. Some immediate expedient must be tried and here, if he would, Sir Eustace could help her. It was not easy to catch him alone, but she managed it.

"Sir Eustace, I am going to ask you to do something for me. It is a *hard* thing. A very hard thing indeed."

"My lady, whatever it is, and however hard, look upon it as already done."

All young knights must have some object of devotion, some lady upon whom to lavish a romantic, unrequited affection. He had settled upon Madselin, though up to this moment she seemed not to understand the part she was supposed to play in this pretty make-believe game. That was because she had been pregnant, forced into a matronly manner that sat ill upon her. Now, slender and young again, speaking coaxingly and setting him some task of skill or daring, she fitted the role exactly. Whatever it was, he would do it, and then she would give him favour, a knot of ribbon, or a sleeve, or a flower . . . He knew all the rules.

"It is," she said, "to make your peace with Sir Godfrey and Sir Volfstan."

She evidently knew the rules, too; she had extracted a promise which he could not take back, before explaining what it concerned.

"This is your wish?"

"It is a way to help the man at Bemid."

"But the quarrel is on his account."

"I know. But absenting yourself from Bemid does him no service. Your presence there might do good. What he needs now, and needs immediately, is food."

"And how can I . . . ?"

"By stealing out in the night, lifting the cover of the well and dropping down what I will provide—and anything else you can lay hands on, saved from your dinner or supper."

It was so simple, so practical—and in such sharp contrast with his own behaviour, cutting himself off from the company of his peers, forgoing all knightly exercise, dictating an angry letter: he almost laughed. But he did not, because between such a simple, easy action and the position in which it would be possible lay the humiliating business of admitting to those two heartless older men that he had been too extreme in his views and begging their forgiveness.

"For your sake, my lady, I will do it," he said.

"Today; there is no time to lose."

Sir Godfrey made the whole thing wonderfully easy. He had missed the younger man's company, his adulation, his admiration. It was not pleasant to be ignored by one whom he had looked upon as a son, and with whom conditions of living forced him into close contact all the time.

"Say no more," he said heartily. "It is natural for youth to be soft-hearted. And I will tell you this for your comfort. The wretch could free himself with a few words."

"How so?"

"He knows something that Sir Volfstan wishes to know. I do not know what it is. Some secrecy is involved here. I do know that Sir Volfstan has reason for what he does, harsh as it seems."

Sir Eustace noticed that the pretence that the man was a mummer had been dropped.

"We will go to Bemid tomorrow," Sir Godfrey said. "Sir Volfstan will be delighted to see you. That I know."

More manchet bread, meat paste, honey, butter and, since this time the stuff need not be fitted into the priest's small basket, some cooked ham and some of Sir Stephen's dried fruit, all tied into a neat bundle inside another fine woollen blanket.

If this minor scheme could work while the other one went forward, all might yet be well, Madselin thought, moving restlessly about, watching William suck vigorously at his weaning

rag and Hild's face transfigured as she offered it. And where is
Frieda?

Frieda arrived, riding the old priest's new mule. She brought
her poor thin mattress and her blanket, made into a roll, and
everything else she possessed was contained in the basket
which Father Alfleg had always carried. It was a pouring wet
day and she was soaked to the skin, which gave Madselin good
reason for taking her into the bedroom to give her a change of
clothing, leaving Hild, with the cradle, by the fire in the hall.

"I should not," Frieda explained, carefully and ungratefully,
"have put myself under a Norman's roof had it not been his last
wish. Or one of them."

"One of them," Madselin agreed, diving into the depleted
clothes chest. "The other was more urgent."

"Stigand the Younger?"

"Yes, Frieda, as Father Alfleg died, and I sat there, holding
his hand, a thought came to me—as though from him. As
though from Heaven. But it is a thing I cannot manage by myself. I do not know the Bemid men and I am not free to come
and go."

"But, my lady, you and I and a thought from Heaven cannot
help a man in such a plight . . ." She began to cry again.
"Beodric said better a thousand times he had died on the field
and it was the sight of him rather than the blow that killed the
good old man, my master. The sage plaster would have drawn
out the bruise, it was his heart that broke so that he died."

"At peace, Frieda, in the end. Because I promised to save
him if I could."

"He was not himself, or he would have seen the useless-
ness . . ."

"Listen . . ." She explained swiftly about the pipe that ran,
she was reasonably certain, straight into the old well. "He
probably lies below where it opens, and does not know . . .
And in the dark . . . At the river end the pipe is full of earth
and weeds and roots. Farther in it should be clear. A night,

two nights, of digging. You speak of Beodric; is he to be trusted? Would he dig?"

"Beodric was crippled at Hastings. He was Stigand's servant who went with him to far places and learned strange tongues. It was Beodric . . ." Some terrible, racking sobs shook her. "Uffa would dig. Yes, Uffa. He is young and strong and his absence at night would not be noticed—there is that to think of—his wife is used to being left. Uffa is a cow-doctor. My lady, in the pipe it will be dark. We shall need candles. . . ."

Hild, who had resented Frieda's coming and her being reclad, perversely resented her going.

"Is it that the mule, like the great horses, needs to run to and fro every day?"

"She has gone back to clean and set the house straight," Madselin said.

"She could have done that before she left. She came to be reclad. In the blue gunna," Hild said viciously, "that I meant to cut about for *him* so soon as he could stand. With fringes all teased out. It would have matched his eyes."

William had his mother's eyes, changing from the indecisive grey-blue usual in babies into the definite blue of a cornflower. Oddly, the downy fluff sprouting on his skull had, in some lights, a copperish sheen. Eitel, as Madselin remembered as part of the virtually unnoticed background of her childhood, had always been pale-haired, the flaxen, almost primrose colour which merged imperceptibly with the silver of age.

"By the time he can stand," Madselin said, "maybe we can afford some new blue cloth."

Tonight, if Frieda managed well, the digging would begin. And tonight, unless something extraordinary happened, the knights would be back and she would hear from Sir Eustace whether or not he had succeeded in performing the task that she had set.

They came home with rather more than their usual clatter.

A third great horse, a black with scarlet trappings, was led by Sir Eustace.

"Nothing was ever more timely," Sir Godfrey said in a jubilant tone. "We did not know, when we set out for Bemid, that Lord de Lacey was at Cressacre and had arranged a meeting, with the horse as prize. And Sir Eustace won it. Congratulate him! Congratulate me also, who has had some hand in bringing him on!"

There were congratulations. Under the cover of them Rolf muttered, "Another useless mouth to fill," and Madselin's eyes sought Sir Eustace's. He very, very slightly shook his head.

Nothing I plan ever prospers!

Sir Eustace, too, was a little sorry for himself. Never before had he acquitted himself so well, never earned such applause or won a prize of anything approaching such value; but his triumph was tarnished by the thought that he had failed to perform the first task ever set him by his lady. By the curiously double standards of chivalry the failure counted as much as the triumph.

"Coming back through Bemid," he said, "I bought a little gift for William. Nothing of value. The market there is new and small as yet."

To institute a new market had been Sir Volfstan's idea. Lord Bowdegrave had applied for and received the licence and the dues were rightly his, but—unlike the ordinary manorial dues— the market dues, being variable, could not be calculated exactly beforehand, or checked with precision afterwards. Sir Volfstan was feathering his nest and looking forward to the day when Cousin Bowdegrave would have to find himself another agent while his old one enjoyed the sun in Sicily.

"Come and give it to him before he sleeps," Madselin said, leading the way into the inner room, where Hild sat, rocking the cradle.

"You can go to your supper now, Hild," she said.

"It is early yet," Hild said unhelpfully. "He is not yet asleep." But she limped away, though unwillingly.

"I had no opportunity. None at all, my lady," Sir Eustace said. "It was a large crowded meeting and those who could not be accommodated at Cressacre were lodged at Bemid. The Knights' Lodging was full and so was the hall. The bed of a knight from St. Edmundsbury was spread over the very stone . . . that was the first night. I was given a place nearer the fire, Sir Volfstan affecting to be so pleased to see me. The St. Edmund's man was considerably older than I, so in the morning I approached him and offered to change places, saying that as the younger knight I should take the less favourable place. And then," he said miserably, "I won the horse and as the day's victor was entitled to a place in the Knights' Lodging. I protested and at that they called me an over-modest fellow and slapped me about the shoulders. So I failed you. To have insisted and gone against custom would, I felt, have been unwise. I was aware of Sir Volfstan's eye upon me. There is something so secret and so mysterious . . . and deadly about it all. This, too I must tell you. Before we set out on Tuesday, Giffard took me aside and warned me very gravely to be careful what I did and said, because . . ."

"I know Giffard's theory," she said in such an abrupt way that he knew that she had taken his failure badly and would never entrust him with another errand. Or show him any favour.

"When he told me what he believed, I said, 'God in Heaven, if that is so, if this is indeed the King's business, *what of my letter?*' And then he told me what he had done."

She was about to say—I know that too. Then she realized what that would mean. So she stood there and listened again to an account of what Giffard had done. And when it was told, she said, "We have all acted as best we could, Sir Eustace. I thank you for trying—whether the man is Stigand of Bemid or Brithric of Gloucester, we did what we could . . . And what a pretty toy!"

He had laid it on the blanket at the foot of the cradle: a globe of bone or ivory, the size of a large apple, hollowed out and carved to the fineness of lace. Inside the globe, three little balls like hazel nuts. And from it a handle, shaped like a badger's tail, not smooth like the rest of it, but bearing the marks of the little teeth that had been cut upon it.

"It is," she said, "the prettiest thing I ever saw. I thank you, for myself, and on his behalf." She shook it gently and the three little balls jogged together and made a gentle sound.

I am here, safe, warm and well fed; and Stigand is where he is. And my joy in my child . . . this lovable kind-hearted boy's joy in his victory, all smeared and spoilt.

She said, "Will you stand sponsor for him, at his baptism, Sir Eustace?"

"Most gladly. I did not count upon such honour." She had forgiven him. "That black horse," he said, "is two years old, broken, but untrained. It shall be his. In eight years' time, so schooled that a thread of cotton will control it, safe for a child, fit for a man . . ."

Everything reduced now to one old woman, engaging a man who could dig; a night's digging, two, and Stigand would be away to what Frieda called a safe hiding place that she knew of, but seemed disinclined to say much about.

It was another shock to see, through the door by which Sir Eustace went out, much restored in his self-esteem, Frieda, looking humble and sad, warming her hands by the fire, near to the place where Hild was eating her early supper. As the door opened both women turned to it. Frieda said, "My lady . . ." and Hild, cramming food into her mouth, got up and said, "I have done. I will sit with him." She went into the bedroom and closed the door, leaving Frieda by the fire, where Madselin joined her. They were alone, yet not alone. In Giffard's little alcove he and Rolf were talking; behind their curtained spaces the two knights were moving about, calling to one another in their old way. Alfred brought new wood for the

fire. Osric and Child were putting trencher bread and napkins
and salt upon the table.

"If Beodric could dig," Frieda said in a low, bitter voice, "it
would be done by now. Uffa—he was away, tending a cow,
that is why I have been so long—Uffa needs some assurance
that should an accident befall him or anything else untoward
happen, his wife and children would not starve."

"Could he not have trusted me to see to that?"

"Nobody, these days, trusts anyone," Frieda said flatly.
"Beodric would have worked for love of his lord. Uffa asks
money, or money's worth."

"I have no money, Frieda. Must it be Uffa? Would no other
man at Bemid . . ."

"None that I know. I ran through my mind. Those who cannot keep a secret; those who must lie by their wives every
night; those who now use Sir Volfstan's market and so hold to
him; those who would dare nothing; those to whom Stigand
the Younger with his spendthrift ways did not endear himself
in his time; those who held Stigand the Elder in reverence, but
are now too old. I was left," she said simply, "with Uffa,
young, able, willing to do anything for pay. I offered him the
mule. My lady, he said it was not enough. A known bad animal
—that was why it was so cheap. Uffa asks a milk cow, a sow
and six geese. With them on the common, breeding and
profitable, he reckons his wife could make shift."

"I own, in this world, two things. A belt of silver and a
string of amber beads. Those, with the mule . . . It was good
of you to offer your mule. . . ."

"The Father's," Frieda said. "And even so; no, not enough.
And it would take time. A week, all but a day, to the next
market where such exchanges are made . . ." She waited as
though hoping that Madselin would suggest something else,
and then sighed. "Well, I will take the goods and do the best I
can."

The obvious need was for money, and the only people at
Bradwald who had money were Rolf, the masons and the

priest. It was useless to ask Rolf, no matter on however good
an excuse; he was already fretting over the fact that unless the
masons finished work at Christmas he would be obliged to borrow money again. Sir Stephen, she realized from various little
things he had said, was more likely to beg from her than give
to her. All his hopes were centred about getting possession of
the hall in time for Christmas and to draw the people to the
church he intended to distribute alms with a lavish hand. That
left the masons. And again the thought of Christmas, season of
charity, of alms and doles . . .

She was thoughtful all through supper and when the meal
was over left the hall as though to go to the kitchen.

It was a clear night, full of stars and very cold. She had no
cloak and shivered, hugging herself as she crossed the open
space between hall and castle which now rose, high and dark,
against the sky. The first-come masons had chosen to build
their lodge at the south side; the later comers were on the west
and east. She had never been near them, no woman had. While
on a job they lived monastically. Giffard said that they made
up for this by living riotously during times of leisure between
jobs, spending lavishly, patronizing brothels and drinking
freely.

The south lodge was nearest from this approach; she could
see the firelight through the chinks of the clod and wattle
walls; she could hear singing, a rather wild blending of voices
in some strange song. Her step slowed as she remembered how
even Rolf had been rebuffed, he, their employer, approaching
on a legitimate excuse. They were peculiar people. And beg-
gars were never welcome. She was inviting a snub, and worse.
It was not that she was afraid that they would offer insult or
assault—her inborn sense of superiority shielded her from such
a fear—but they might choose to make a great fuss about their
rights and privileges: she could imagine the master mason
stamping into the hall to say that his men could not possibly
continue work in a place where even their leisure time was disturbed. Then Rolf would be very angry, rightly so.

She stood hesitant. Then she thought—*This is for Stigand*, and moved forward.

The lodge, like Father Alfleg's kitchen, boasted no door; there was an arch-shaped opening in one side; the whole construction was singularly like a giant beehive. She walked well into the opening so that the light from the fire should fall upon her and composed her face into a pleasing expression. The men sat in a circle around the fire, the master directly opposite the doorway, and as they chanted they made gestures, all in unison, all rather stilted as in a singing game, except that everything seemed to be serious.

The master mason saw her almost at once and said a word which brought silence. He rose to his feet and came, outside the circle, towards her. Men turned their heads or twisted around to stare. There seemed to be a hundred of them.

She made a curtsy, as Camilla had taught her.

The master mason said—"My lady! What brings you here?"

"I am begging for the poor," she said in her sweetest voice. "Good master mason, the season of Christmas is coming and I thought that perhaps you and your men would like to give me some small charity for widows and orphans and the afflicted." Who was more afflicted than Stigand?

His face, tempered by weather, responsibility and authority, wore a naturally severe look which did not alter now; but he said very civilly, "I will ask them." He turned himself about and spoke in what Giffard called "masons' language," a mixture of several, for they were of varied nationalities. Eight men promptly raised their hands in a way that reminded her sharply of the way things had been done in the old days in Eitel's hall when any matter was debatable or such office as hay-reeve or sheep-reeve was being settled for a year.

"They will," the master said; and she noticed that even the four who had not raised their hands joined in the foraging into pouches or bedrolls and put their offerings into the master's cupped hands.

When he turned to her he said, "You have no bag? Had you

so little faith in us?" He took off his cap and shot the coins into it. "You will visit the other lodges, my lady?"

"Oh yes; I came to you first because you *were* first; and because I looked upon you as friends. I thank you all. And when Christmas comes I hope it will be happy for you."

It was necessary to visit the other lodges because she had no idea of the value of what she had collected here. In fact she had little idea of the value of money at all. Eitel had collected the old silver pennies for tax dues; Rolf had come home with some new-minted money, gold pieces which the masons would not accept because a gold piece could not be distributed, so Giffard had been obliged to ride into Colchester and dicker for what he called "small change."

"I will come with you," the master mason said. "They will be swayed by our decision; we are the senior lodge."

"And very kind," she said, smiling upon him, and upon them all, consciously exercising the charm for which there was so little use in these hard days. An outmoded currency, like the old pennies.

Frieda, though she had spent her life in much humbler circumstances, was far more knowledgeable. She scrabbled about in the masons' offerings—and Madselin thought idly that Hild was right, the old woman was dirty, every finger ended in a long curved nail with a rim of black. I should not care to eat the bread she kneaded!

"Enough and more. This for the milk cow; for the sow; for the geese. And to spare. For this Uffa would dig for a month. . . ." A curious look, almost sly, came into her face. "Beodric," she said, "would have dug for love of his lord. But he was not able. Uffa *bargained.* My lady, now that we have such plenty . . . Beodric could hold the candles . . . and be paid, perhaps?"

"It is for you to say, Frieda."

"Then Beodric shall hold the candles, Uffa shall dig and I

myself will take Stigand the Younger to the safe place that I know of."

"And come to tell me. At the first possible moment, Frieda. I promised Father Alfleg and I shall not rest until I know that promise fulfilled—thanks to you, and Uffa—and Beodric."

"Gone again?" Hild said. "Restless as a butterfly."

"She is old. She remembers things she should have done."

Nobody else noticed Frieda's comings and goings. Madselin had explained to Rolf that she had promised to give a home to the old priest's housekeeper and he had said, "*Another* ugly old woman about the place," but he said it with resignation, adding, "When we move we shall be less in a hugger-mugger. There will be not more space, but better used."

Two days; three.

Without help, he will die—and soon.

Life went on all around her, largely concerned now with the imminent move into the castle. The frosts which would have delayed work had not come this year and the master mason of the senior lodge had given his word that the work should be finished on the eve of Christmas Eve. The date did not please Rolf, because it meant that he would not be there to supervise; he would be waiting upon the King. ("And if you could go in real rags this time it might be to your advantage," Giffard said, only half in joke.) The date did not please the priest, because it gave him only one day in which to transform a secular dwelling into a church. The masons were not pleased either because unless they walked through the nights they would not keep Christmas in Colchester as they would have liked to do. But as the master mason said, that was how things had worked out, and he doubted whether any other three lodges in England, or anywhere else for that matter, could have done so sound a job in the time. Madselin dreaded the move, but could spare hardly any thought for so trivial a matter. How well and how

fast was Uffa working? Would Stigand be free, with the wild
men in the woods, for Christmas? Please God . . .

"So! Back in time for supper, as usual," Hild said nastily,
turning from the window.

Madselin looked out and read failure, worse, disaster in the
very way Frieda climbed down from the mule; the slow, painful movements, the dragging, lifeless walk were not those of
one who brought good tidings.

"She is not well," she said and made this an excuse to run
out to join the old woman who was stabling the mule. Frieda
turned stiffly, revealing her damaged face, the left cheek so
bruised and swollen that the eye on that side was almost invisible, a long gash sealed with dried blood across her forehead.

"You had a fall?" Madselin asked. The mule was known to
be a difficult animal.

"The pipe fell in upon us," Frieda said.

"Was he with you?"

"No." In the fading light, in the chilling wind, they stood
and stared at one another, hopelessly. Then Frieda said, "Beodric is dead."

Would that Stigand were. I could take my food, sleep in my
bed, live my life when I thought him dead—and should again,
in time.

Then something about the profound dreariness with which
Frieda had announced Beodric's death caught up with her rac-
ing mind and she remembered how the old woman's voice had
always changed when she spoke his name.

"You were fond of him?"

"He was my son. Nobody knew, but he was mine."

"Poor Frieda. Here, lean on me. We must get you into the
house. Are you hurt otherwise?"

"Not enough," Frieda said with the utmost bitterness.

"Uffa?"

"Scarcely bruised."

At the door Madselin said, "We will say that you fell from the mule."

Once again she was aware of the shocking lack of privacy. She wanted to hear everything: how far the work had progressed, whether it could be resumed. Frieda needed to go to bed forthwith, but to drag her roll out and spread it in the open space of the hall would mean that no talk would be possible for a long time. She thought quickly and then led her towards Giffard's little alcove, explaining to Hild as they crossed the floor. Giffard, halfway to being a physician, would surely understand; he could have the small bed from the sleeping room.

"Hild, can you make a sage plaster?"

"I hope so."

"Then please make one."

Frieda said, "Chopping the sage hold the knife north and south and then east and west so that the cross is signed." She dropped on to Giffard's bed and lay for a little while in silence.

"We were so near," she said at last. "At the end of every night's work Uffa measured inside the pipe and then paced the ground above. We were no more than ten paces away. There was less to clear as we went in, less dirt . . . but roots. They should have warned us that there were cracks above. Uffa was first; he had cut some roots away and pulled them clear. I was next, holding the candles. Beodric was behind me, gathering what Uffa had cleared—we cleared as we went. And then there was a noise above . . . and bits of pipe and earth fell in on us. Beodric took the full weight and died. I was bruised and cut."

Madselin visualized it as well as she could. Presently she said, "If Uffa was first, he was nearest the hall. . . ."

"Yes, where the pipe was not broken," Frieda agreed.

"Then how did he get out? Why was he not trapped?"

"He crawled out . . . Oh, I see. After the fall, there was a space above us. Uffa crawled over me and then pulled me clear. But Beodric was dead."

"Then the way is still open. The way is not blocked?"

"No." She thought of what lay there. "Only by Beodric. Uffa said best to leave him there. But we got past him."

"Then Uffa must go to work again," Madselin said positively.

"He says no, my lady. He says nothing would make him take such risk again."

"But he must. He was paid to work and to take risk."

"So I told him. I said, Beodric is dead and if we stop now he is dead for nothing. Uffa said he was also paid to hold his tongue and sooner than go back into that pipe he would go to Sir Volfstan and . . ."

Hild came up with the plaster and while Madselin was pressing it against the swollen face Giffard appeared, saying genially, "Who is usurping my place? *And* my function?"

She had no appetite for her supper, no ear for the talk. She sat with her chin in her hand thinking thoughts that were sometimes sensible, sometimes so desperate as to be ridiculous. There must be other men than Uffa to be hired; one must be found. If not at Bemid . . . perhaps Britt the thatcher; he was poor; he would surely welcome any job that offered reward. But what had she to offer? That was the line her sensible thought took. The desperate one was that she could clear ten paces of pipe herself; she knew that she had within her the determination, and the determination would give her strength; but how could she be away for the necessary time, by day or by night? Give out that she was going to stay with the ladies at Wyck—that that had always been her custom at Christmas time? Impossible, of course, ridiculous.

In the end her thoughts were so muddled that they no longer hung together either as sense or nonsense and in a way it was a relief to find in the morning that Frieda was quite incapable of getting out of bed. Nothing could be done until she was sufficiently restored to take Stigand if, and when, he should be freed, into the company of those who had learned to survive in adverse circumstances. "There are no bones broken," Giffard said, "but a fall of such severity, at her age . . ."

"Is it the thought of the move that troubles you?" Rolf asked. He was aware of her decline in spirits, and what other reason could there be? "You will be comfortable there." He wrung out the few extra, unnecessary words. "More comfortable than ever in your life."

Let him think what he liked; better that he should give himself a reason than press questions.

"It has been my home," she said, looking around the place to which she had come so unwillingly.

"It is a pity that I shall be away," he said. "But mark this. You are to lift and carry nothing. Let others do it. Walk across when all is prepared. And you will not be lonely. The knights were all set for Christmassing in Bemid, but I said they were to be back on Christmas Eve."

Surprise jerked her out of her depression. Neither knight had said a word in her hearing about going to Bemid either before or over Christmas. Or perhaps she had not been listening. That was a silly thought, too. Nobody could have said the word "Bemid" without arresting her attention.

"You never told me, Sir Eustace, that you would be at Bemid before Christmas." The reproach in her voice was genuine, but it was also exactly the match of the exaggerated reproach with which ladies, knowing the rules of the game, rebuked their chosen knights for the most trivial lapses.

"It was mentioned, I am sure. Yes—we said there would be quite an exodus on the morning of the eve of Christmas Eve; my lord, the masons, Sir Godfrey and I . . . I think, my lady, that at the time you were feeding the old woman her broth."

"Well, now that I know, I think you know what I am about to ask."

"To try again."

He would, naturally, do his best to perform whatever she required of him, but he wished she had chosen some other task, because his heart was no longer in this one. And the lack of enthusiasm showed in his voice, in the look on his face.

"Are you no longer sorry for the man?" she asked sharply.

"Not as I was. When I made peace with Sir Godfrey he said that the man could free himself with a few words. . . ."

"How so?"

"By telling Sir Volfstan something that he knows and that Sir Volfstan wishes to know."

"What could that be?"

"There lies the secret. I paid the words scant attention. I was so taken up with the doing something to please you. Then, raw from failing, I did think—if a man chooses to suffer, it makes his suffering more bearable for the rest of us. Do you not agree?"

"That is another put-about tale," she said. "Like the mummer. Would any man suffer so when a few words could end it?"

"I only know, my lady, what Sir Godfrey said."

"Look back," she said fiercely, "to the moment when you first saw him. Ask yourself, is this a likely tale or something invented to make you, and perhaps even Sir Godfrey, feel better?"

"It could be," he agreed, rather reluctantly, thinking how very blue her eyes were when she was angry. "In any case, my lady, whether his condition is due to misfortune or to his own conduct, if you ask me to feed him, I will try to do so. For *your* sake."

She mustered a smile. "The thought that an old neighbour had some small cheer for Christmas would make my own merrier, Sir Eustace."

"The thought that I had pleased you, my lady, would make mine the merriest I have known."

For the third time she prepared the offering of love.

"All that must be cleared," Sir Stephen said, waving his hand at the south wall. Madselin raised her head and looked, for the first time with really seeing eyes. In a place where so little storage space was available it was customary for things which, for this reason or that, must be preserved, but were not of immediate use, to be hung upon the wall and there, too familiar to be consciously noticed, was the record of generations of Eitel's family.

"Such stuff has no place in a church," the priest said.

She had always looked upon it as stuff. Eitel could tell a tale about almost every item and during the early days of their marriage had done so. She had listened with the minimum of attention. There was the harness of the almost legendary horse brought to the Rinland by Eitel's great-grandfather; there were weapons of his time too, round bossed shields and terrible battleaxes; there were tusks and horns and antlers, commemorating some special hunting days; a harp with no strings, tails of wolves and foxes, a corn dolly made from the first harvest ever reaped in Bradwald field. Most touching of all—though this was the first time she had ever seen them as so—were some miniature tools and weapons that had belonged to children. Even the spaces were eloquent; the weapons so hastily snatched down on that fateful Monday had never been replaced.

"William may take some pleasure in the toys," Madselin said. "Put them in the chest, on top of the clothes. The rest take to the barn." There would be no place for them in the castle, no pegs or nails in those stony walls.

The whole hall was soon cleared. Giffard carried away his tally sticks, his surgical and writing tools, his bits of parchment. The trestle tables and the bedrolls were removed, the chests from the inner room. Presently there was nothing left except the bed on which Frieda lay, and the cradle. Every footfall, every voice, now rang hollow and somehow doomed. Another ending.

In the central trench the fire died. Sir Stephen had ordered that it should not be mended again. As soon as the stones had cooled the declivity was to be filled in with some of the stuff which the masons had used for welding stones together. The making of it was one of their most closely guarded secrets; before they left they had mixed a tubful as Sir Stephen had requested, saying that as Christian men they would wish to contribute to the making of a church.

Of all that had once been in the hall, eventually only the table on the dais remained. It would serve, for a time, as an altar and the scarlet cloth was suitable to the season. "But, my lady, there will be other seasons, and changes will be needed. It is a pity that you do not take pleasure in embroidery. Many ladies find it absorbing and restful." Many ladies indeed spent their leisure hours in making beautiful altar cloths and vestments and he would have liked to see her thus employed, partly for her own sake. He attributed some of her low spirits and sad looks to lack of occupation; she had Hild to look after the child; she had a comparatively small household, no women friends; and entertainment was kept to the minimum.

"I never liked it," she said. "And the mending takes as long as I can bear to spend with my needle."

She went across to the alcove where Frieda lay.

"It is time for us to go, Frieda. Do you think you can walk?"

"I can try."

But even with Madselin's aid walking for Frieda was still a slow and painful business and before they had reached the door the women whom Sir Stephen had persuaded or bribed to come and help with the thorough cleansing of the hall had begun to arrive, some armed with brooms of twigs tied together or bunches of stiff feathers at the end of long poles.

Crossing the space between hall and castle, Madselin reflected that it would be a week, perhaps two, before Frieda would move easily enough to play her part in the next attempt to rescue Stigand.

The bridge that spanned the moat was still only a makeshift affair; Rolf planned to have one that could be drawn inwards and even the thought of it increased Madselin's feeling that a

castle was no place in which to live. In the old hall one
stepped from the door and turned in one direction to the garth
and the apple trees under which daisies grew in the grass, in
the other direction to the yard with the byre and the stables;
one was part of the life of the place. Inside the moat nothing
grew, the mound had been stamped so hard that not even a
weed had rooted there. Grey stone, grey mound, grey water.

The entrance was arched, fitted with heavy doors, now
open. Beyond to the left was Giffard's room and another; to
the right the Knights' Lodging. On the far side another arch
gave upon the kitchen quarters and also accommodated the
first three or four steps of a stairway, built in a spiral. The open
space was littered by things brought over from the hall and not
yet assigned their proper place.

It was, as she had known it would be, very cold. The stones
of which this place was built had lain for years on the forest
floor—Giffard said for six or seven hundred years. They had absorbed the dampness of all those springs and autumns, hardened in the frost of the winters and, because of the foliage
above them, hardly felt the summers' sun. All they had to give
back was the chill. She shuddered—and immediately thought
how much colder it must be at the bottom of a well.

Then, for a little, her mind was diverted by the problem of
getting an infirm old woman up a spiral staircase designed for
defence. Peter had so arranged the stairs that at each turn
one armed, determined man could hold a number at bay; no
stair was wide enough to hold more than one man at a time.
And neither Frieda nor Madselin had ever mounted stairs before. Except for a step up or down, English houses were built
low and on one level.

"I do not think . . . that I can manage," Frieda said.

"You must, Frieda. Perhaps if I were behind you and
pushed . . ."

In the outer wall, on the side where each stair was wide
enough to take a foot, there was a groove in the wall, just

enough to cling to. "Hold to that," Madselin had said, "and pull as I push."

Then Giffard came bustling from his little room—the first really private place he had ever owned—and said, "Allow me, my lady!" For all his bulk he was nimble; he got himself into position on the stairs, lifted Frieda as though she weighed no more than a cat and carried her away. He had already helped Hild, who had insisted on coming ahead with the baby, and so Madselin was alone when she entered a new and very beautiful world.

The main hall of the castle was hardly more than half the size of the old hall. A great fire blazed, not in the middle of the floor but on a hearth, set under an archway in a side wall. There was a dais, somewhat higher than the old one, with a new table and the old chairs set out upon it. Behind the table was a window, not a single opening, but five, set close together, each narrow in the wall, widening on the inner side so that light was caught and enhanced. Daylight and firelight combined to illuminate the warmth and colour of the wall hangings, the like of which she had never seen before.

There had been hangings at Winchester, and there were the two she had sent for from Scartoke to make a little privacy for the knights, but they were dim and faded and even in their best days had shown patterns, not pictures. On these walls trees grew and flowers bloomed, and there were birds with plumage incredibly bright. She looked at them with wonder and admiration.

Giffard came through the arch beside the hearth and said genially, "Well, how do you like them?"

She said, "They are very beautiful," in a tone that made him glad that Rolf was not present to see how his surprise was taken. For by that time her mind had run down the well-worn track and made the inevitable comparison—Here am I, warm and surrounded with beauty, while he . . .

"You have seen nothing yet," Giffard said. "Come through."

Beyond this arch was a smaller room, also with a hearth and a window and two hangings.

"The Solar," Giffard said, watching her face. "That window faces the sun."

"Oh, yes . . . I remember." For a moment she thought of Peter; he had planned all this and not lived to see it. And then immediately came the thought—There is no daylight, even, where Stigand lies.

There was the sleeping chamber and, in a niche beyond, a little cell with a built-in stone bench with a hole in it. A new-fashioned house of easement. A vast improvement on the board over a hole out of doors; necessary too, with all those stairs. Stigand existed in the conditions that she had herself once briefly known, in the dovecote!

Oh, stop it! Stop it! This way madness lies.

She was aware of Giffard's gaze.

"It is all so beautiful, so different from what I expected. I am stunned," she said.

"Sir Godfrey obtained them," Giffard said, when they were back in the Solar where Hild had already installed the cradle. "He has connections in the Vexin where such things are made. They are very costly." He eyed her again.

"That also was on my mind," she said. "How could Rolf . . ."

"He put himself into the Jews' debt again. What he owed before—to clear the knights—the King paid, you know. I hardly think that *he* will shoulder *this* load. Unless something fortunate happens Rolf will be in debt for years."

Not a spark of gratitude! Not a look of surprise!

She was thinking, whether it was another Bemid man or Britt the thatcher to be hired so soon as Frieda was able to walk again, some reward would be required, and all she owned in the world was the belt and the beads, virtually worthless.

"Will the Jews lend to anyone, Giffard?"

"Anyone who can offer security. The knights had their horses and their armour; Rolf has his tenure."

"Where," she asked abruptly, "did you place Frieda?"

What Rolf had said about no longer living in quite such a hugger-mugger was true. There was far less actual space here but it was put to better purpose. Around another corner there were two or three narrow niches: Frieda lay in one of them and Madselin, saying aloud that she hoped the walking and the carrying had not increased her pains, thought—Here we can have a talk at any time.

Late in the day, with the hall thoroughly cleansed and scoured, the women ran away, talking and laughing. They had worked on the hall-about-to-become-a-church with some resurgence of the communal spirit which had governed so many of their activities in the old days and which, but for Peter the Norman's presence, might even have touched the mound-stamping. Company and a common purpose were dear to most women. Sir Stephen reflected complacently that every woman who had worked here today would feel that in some measure the church was her own.

On the scarlet-clothed table now there was a crucifix, flanked on either side by candlesticks.

The women came scampering back, laden with great boughs of holly, bunches of mistletoe, trails of ivy.

"For Christmas," they said. "For tomorrow!"

He knew a rare moment of indecision. These were people who had never been far from pagan and in a year had slipped backwards, towards the past, towards the worship of trees and streams, rocks, even animals. But he must not be hasty. The leaves and the berries were at least evidence of goodwill. He was a man of some learning and knew his Scriptures. "She hath done what she could," the Lord Jesus Christ had said of the woman whose waste of the ointment had been criticized. And these women had done what they could. And after all, he thought, if a sprinkling of water and some words could convert a living hall into a house of God . . . He poured fresh water into a bowl, blessed it and sprinkled the greenstuff freely.

Then the women ran about hanging and laying their offerings. The holly berries of the boughs laid at the altar's foot matched the scarlet cloth well; the mistletoe berries were almost the waxen colour of the candles.

"Very pretty," he said when they had done, and he hoped that God would think so too and understand that when one was a lone soldier, in a difficult outpost, one could only do one's best and use what was to hand.

Once again the knights came home from Bemid and this time she knew from the bright, conniving glance with which Sir Eustace met her that he had been successful. He supplemented the look with a few careful words, "In our fine new quarters, it will be a more comfortable Christmas—for everyone," he said. Relief and pleasure dizzied her for a second; little though it was, it would be extra, and tonight when she lay down she could think of Stigand wrapped in the blanket, eating bread and meat. She began to speak about the new apartments and the beauty of the hangings with such enthusiasm and animation that Giffard was convinced that earlier in the day she had truly been overcome by surprise. Rolf was unlikely to ask, but if he did, Giffard could say, "She was dumbstruck."

After a few minutes Sir Godfrey said, "My boy has thrown my gear in as though he were making a haystack," and clattered away to overlook the rearrangement of his new abode.

"The hangings in my Solar are even finer, Sir Eustace," Madselin said. "Come and see. . . ."

As soon as they were alone, the boy said, "It all went sweetly, my lady. I loosened my belt and dropped it near the stone on my way to bed. A good deal of wine had been drunk; Sir Godfrey and the other two in the Lodging were soon asleep. I waited and then stole out. There was still light from the fire. The stone came up easily and I dropped the bundle down. Nobody woke and had they done so I was hunting my belt. . . ."

"You are brave, resourceful and kind. All that a knight should be," she said with such warmth in her voice as only Stigand had ever heard. "Would that I had some great jewel to give you, but you know how we are placed."

"My lady, your approbation is the most precious jewel in the world." That the pretty speech was all part of the game did not detract from its sincerity.

"I will make you a knot," she said—her practical mind asking, what of?

"I shall wear it with pride," Sir Eustace said. Then, in a different voice—not part of the game—he said, "My lady, perhaps you should not worry overmuch about the fellow, wretched as he is. It is true, as Sir Godfrey said, he could free himself. I renewed my apologies to Sir Volfstan and so brought the subject round. He said it was not to be spoken of, but the man knew something of importance. An answer to a simple question, he said."

"What question? What could Stigand know of such importance that he bears such punishment?"

"That I cannot tell. With Sir Volfstan it is a sore subject. I could not press."

"Wise as well," she said, smiling and reverting to the tone of the game.

"There is one drawback to this way of living," Sir Godfrey said pontifically. "The boys will have to be much livelier on the stairs if the food is not to be lukewarm."

"They have never encountered stairs before," Madselin said. It was true that the food was tepid but tonight she ate with appetite.

"Frieda, try to eat. I sent for a little pan and warmed this broth especially for you. You will never be strong again if you do not eat."

"I always had more hunger than I had meat," Frieda said, "except when I worked in Bemid hall. Just a year or two. The

old man always said I spoiled his meat, but the truth was it
was tough and stringy before I laid a finger on it. And now
. . . I think of Beodric and find it hard to swallow." Madselin
knew the feeling all too well.

"Beodric died trying to free his lord, Frieda. For his sake we
must try again. And for that we must be strong. And to be
strong one must eat." It was not an argument that she had applied to herself when the thought of Stigand eating rubbish
had come between her and her food, but she was not aware of
any inconsistency.

"I think I do not wish to be strong or to busy myself with
this again," Frieda said. "Two good men have died, Beodric,
my son—though nobody knew—and my master, my *second*
master and almost as dear to me."

"The ins and outs of that I never knew."

"I blame myself," Frieda said. "Beodric knew and told me
but I said nothing, thinking to spare Father Alfleg, who was always so fond of Stigand the Younger. The priest here, the Norman, came and roused him and together they looked and
found nothing. But he ate in the hall, often, to spare our meat
so that he could give to the hungry. He was blind close to,
but he saw very well at a distance. Sir Volfstan did not count
on that. So the night before he died . . . there was company
and Sir Volfstan lost caution and said, 'Would you like to see
a man eat a rabbit skin, fur and all?' So they brought him out,
and the Father rose up with a great cry and tried to go towards him. Somebody, not a servant—they had sent the servants away—held him and hit him in the chest. They threw him
out and he crawled home to die. Old Stigand, Father Alfleg,
Beodric, all dead. And I am willing to die too. And all for a
spendthrift who displeased my good old master. . . ."

Old woman's muddled talk. Out of it, most clearly of all,
emerged the eating of a rabbit skin, fur and all. She averted
her mind's eye from that, sorted the other statements into
some sort of order, and said, "Was Stigand the Elder ever your
master?"

"He was the one who bought me. I was young, a slave at Wallingford. He came on a visit and bought me. We came to a bridge over a river and he said—I hear him now—east of this water, he said, there are no slaves. So I was free. Free to come and go though I lived in the hall. For him I would have shed my blood . . ." With a shocking abruptness she gave a kind of cackle. "In a way, I did . . . The Lady Alice had lost patience with him and must not be upset again. So I was *lent to* Scartoke, and there I had my baby and Father Alfleg arranged for Beodric to be taken into a family where I could see him but not claim him. And he took me to his house so there should be no more temptation." She paused for lack of breath.

An old sad story, Madselin thought, and my mother knew . . . this was not old Stigand's only infidelity. My mother thought—Like father like son . . . But this was no time to think of that, all over and done with.

She said, "Frieda, we must look to the future. You know so much—so much more than I do. Can you think of any secret that Stigand knows, that Sir Volfstan would wish to know and wring out of him?"

"I only know what Beodric told me. This is a strange thing, my lady. Nobody knew he was mine, he did not know himself, but between us there was always a liking. Even as a little boy, when things went wrong with him, he would come to me. . . ."

"Yes, yes," Madselin said impatiently, but Frieda would not be hurried; she stayed with her memories for a moment. "So when this happened, he came to me."

"When what happened?"

"Beodric went with Stigand the Younger to far places and learned strange tongues. Then he went with him to the battle; he saw Stigand fall. He was wounded himself. And because he knew their talk he was useful sometimes in the hall. He listened. He knew when Stigand the Younger was brought there and he said—Better a thousand times he had died where he fell."

"So you told me. But you have not told me *why* Sir Volfstan treats him thus."

"It was said that Stigand brought back, from wherever it was he went, a great treasure of jewels. Emeralds and rubies, whatever they may be, as big as hazel nuts. And hid them at Bemid."

"What nonsense!" Madselin said sharply. "He brought back a fine sorrel horse and a new sword and many fine clothes. And that is all. I know because . . ."

"If there had been treasure," Frieda said as Madselin checked herself, "Beodric would have known. And however stubborn Stigand chose to be, Beodric would have pointed out where it was. He would not have seen his master suffer so for lack of a few words."

"That is true. That is very true."

"I wanted Beodric to feel that he had helped to set him free. And now he is dead."

"But Stigand is alive. Frieda, can you think of no other Bemid man who would help?"

"My lady, if there had been any other I should not have picked Uffa."

Britt the thatcher, then; but what to offer him?

"We must try again, Frieda. I will find somebody. And you must eat, and walk a little every day, so that when the time comes, you are ready to play your part."

"Yes, my lady," Frieda said, but she spoke wearily.

Next morning, for the first time in Bradwald, a church bell rang, scaring away the evil spirits and summoning the people to church. The bell had been provided by Sir Stephen's father. It had been cast in Bruges, and though not large was heavy, intended to hang and to be pulled by a rope. But there was no place to hang it and no time to make a place, so it hung inside a wooden cage that held it just clear of the ground and it was sounded by two men who pushed and pulled a beam as though they were working a saw.

Madselin stood and knelt, knelt and stood with the rest.

Hail Mary, blessed art thou . . . Help me, help me. You loved *Him!* If you had set your mind on saving him, and come close to doing it and failed . . . Blasphemy! And in church! Mary, Mother of God, pity me. Pity him and help me.

Our Father which art in Heaven . . . Father of all. Father of Stigand, knowing and seeing all. Can it be Thy will that he should rot and die in that hole? Help me to help him. . . .

Church is no place for me. I have no place anywhere. No thoughts, no feelings apart from Stigand. I am not even myself any longer. I do not own my mind, my body or my soul. I am locked in and tormented, cut off from life and from other people. I share his misery. And who will help me?

And then, as she stood between the knights after the priest had spoken the dismissing blessing, the thought came. Not direct and whole and sure as the thought that had come as she sat holding Father Alfleg's hand, but a tiny uncertain thought which would need careful examination and might, being handled, dwindle and die. So much of chance was involved, so much persuasion and cunning was needed that every now and then, as she thought, her heart would flutter. If this . . . if that . . . Far less simple than using old Frieda and bribing Uffa, the new plan depended upon her ability to manipulate men. But all men had one thing in common—greed. And somebody had once told her that she had a way with her. And even that was a tool that must be used with caution. Rolf must not suspect.

Giffard said, "And was he generous to you again?"

"He had other things on his mind. The Danes plan to attack in the spring."

"Bound to come," Giffard said. "They have not resigned themselves to the loss of England."

The knights sniffed war in the air and were elated. It was the thing for which—like their great horses—they were bred and trained and only in battle could they justify themselves.

Sir Godfrey saw another chance—there was much still un-
settled land in the north and he would distinguish himself so
markedly that even Odo's grudge against him could not, a second time, prevent him having his reward. Sir Eustace also
imagined himself winning such renown that his father would
be mortified and the Lady Madselin proud of her knight.

"You will not be called," Rolf said. "This area is threatened
too. We may be reinforced."

Madselin ignored the threat; had she thought about it she
would have thought that the Danes were far more akin to the
English than the Normans were. One's enemy's enemy was
one's friend. All she thought was that Rolf had come back
without money; any reinforcement would mean more mouths
to feed; he would be anxious to have the proper bridge in
place.

She had not made the mistake of changing her public attitude towards him; she had said, dutifully, that she was glad to
see him safely back and that the new hall, the Solar and the
bedroom were far warmer and more comfortable than she had
expected them to be. But when the bedroom door was closed
she paused in front of one of the hangings, all roses, red, white
and some striped with both colours, and said, "They are very
beautiful. But they must have cost a great deal."

He paused in the folding of his poor mended clothes.

"What has Giffard been saying?"

"Giffard? Why should he say anything? I can tell that they
were costly. Without aid from him. And there may be more
knights to keep. And the bridge to build. . . ."

"Let me fret about that," he said. He placed his shoes side
by side. "Managing is my business," he said.

Eitel in similar circumstances would surely have said—You
must not bother your pretty little head about such things. And
she would have given him a tart answer. The thought alighted
and sped away again, vagrant as a butterfly, that this, all of
this, was punishment for what she had made others suffer.

"I know," she said. "I spoke of it only because while you

were absent I have put this and this together and thought of a
way in which you might obtain some small wealth."

And that was not altogether a false or deceptive statement.
Thinking it over she had borne in mind that Stigand had gone
east, to Byzantium; and if emeralds and rubies the size of hazel
nuts were to be found anywhere it would be in Byzantium.
Frieda's argument that Beodric would have known was valid
up to a point, but it was not incontrovertible. How much did
Hild know of her mistress's secret ways and motives?

"Listen," she said.

When she had done he said, "Similar tales of hidden treasure are told of any place of any size in England. Silver dishes,
gold torques, jewels the size of pigeons' eggs. Few have been
found."

"Those who knew about them being dead, or run away. This
man is *here*. Sir Volfstan has tried to wring out the secret, and
failed. But I truly think that if I could talk to him I could learn
whatever there is to be learned."

"Even so, Bemid is not mine. How should we profit?"

"By asking a share. Two-fifths, I think, would not be too
much. I shall be doing him a great service."

"He would agree and then not share."

"I should ask for a parchment." Rolf gave his difficult, unac-
customed smile, and because she was set on a course of ca-
jolery Madselin smiled too.

Asking for a parchment had become, if not exactly a joke, a
household word. Britt the thatcher, more knowledgeable than
most because his work had sometimes taken him abroad, even
as far as Colchester, had asked for a parchment showing that
he was a free man and owned his assart land. Giffard had written it, throwing himself into the half-mocking spirit of the
thing, the best level script, the decorated capitals, the sonorous
legal phrases seeming to please him—"This testifies to an
agreement between Rolf, lord of Bradwald, and one Britt,
known as the thatcher. Whereas the said Britt has rendered
singular service to his lord . . ." Rolf, who could write his

name, wrote it and Giffard said, "You should add, *of Brad-wald*, since in the deed you are so named." With more difficulty Rolf wrote, "of Bredwuld." Sir Eustace then witnessed the signature and Giffard, scattering sand over the signatures, said, "It was made by a humble fellow for a humble fellow, but it is so made that it would stand up in any court, even the Pope's." For a moment his face lost its cheerfulness as he looked back over his life and thought of the talent he had frittered away to end up part-priest, part-physician, part-lawyer. Then he thought—But I have enjoyed myself; and smiled again. Afterwards it had become customary to say, over the simplest promise, the smallest wager, "I should want a parchment." So Rolf smiled, very briefly.

"I should not trust Sir Volfstan, even with a parchment."

"Nor would I. Giffard must hold it."

"And how would that help if he set his mind to cheat?"

"I think," she said slowly, and with venom, "that this is Sir Volfstan's private enterprise and one about which Lord Bowdegrave might not be pleased to hear."

Rolf could not see the sapphire colour of her eyes under the fall of amber hair but he thought that she looked extraordinarily like a cat about to pounce.

"There is truth in that," he said. "But I do not like it."

"Why not?" It was difficult to sound detached.

"It means dealing with him."

She looked back and realized that any hospitality that Rolf had extended to Sir Volfstan had been forced upon him, that any friendly or even flattering remark made by Sir Volfstan had been coldly received and his jokes ignored. And never once had Rolf accepted an invitation to Bemid. Until this moment she had not seen that Rolf's attitude towards all Normans save his own chosen few had made her position as an Englishwoman more tolerable than it might have been.

"I dislike him heartily," she said. "But I cannot see why that should prevent us making a bargain with him to our own advantage."

"Why should the man tell *you?*"

"Because I am English and was once his neighbour. I shall put in the parchment that, having told, he is to be set free. He will take my word for that." And if there is nothing to tell, he will still go free, she thought, testing her latest plan again and finding no flaw.

"It needs thinking," Rolf said. "Come to bed."

Contrary to his custom he lay wakeful. Jews were patient, but inexorable and certain of the King's support; there was the bridge to complete, the possibility of more knights to maintain. Nothing would come in until the next sheep-shearing, in June. Sir Volfstan plainly believed in the tale of treasure—why otherwise had he kept the man alive? And Rolf knew a little about Byzantium; a rich place. The Emperor there was always threatened by the Turks and could not trust his own mongrel subjects; he had many mercenaries—Danes, Normans, English and Germans—and paid them lavishly. It was just possible. . . .

In the morning he gave his verdict. "I do not like it but it is worth trying."

"You could invite him for a day's hunting," Madselin said. She felt, just for a moment, a fleeting pang of pity for him because he was being used and did not recognize the fact. But that feeling was gone, swamped by others: excitement; the certainty that this time she must succeed.

This feeling that the time was ripe at last was bolstered up by the arrival that morning of Sir Volfstan, accompanied by two servants. He explained his errand courteously. From Bemid a man named Beodric was missing. Not a valuable man, in fact a cripple, able only for sedentary work, but if one man could run away and not be recaptured and punished, others would be encouraged to follow his example. Sir Volfstan did not, he said, for one moment believe that the lord of Bradwald would harbour a runaway, but some of his people might. Could his men have permission to search?

"They will not find him," Rolf said. "Let them look. But

here, with food doled out as it is, nobody can feed a stranger."

"Do you find the system workable?" Sir Volfstan inquired; he knew from his own experience, and from the knights' talk, how inadequately Rolf's own table was spread. "At Bemid," he said smugly, "we had a surplus. That was the beginning of the market."

"My way was necessary. With building to do," Rolf said shortly. He was not blind to the drawbacks of his system and planned changes as soon as he could afford them. Despite himself, he thought of the hoard of jewels and then put the thought away. Too much chance was concerned. And yet, in a world where an armourer could become owner of three manors, marry a descendant of Sweyn Forkbeard, and build a stout castle, all within a year, almost anything was possible.

With no change in his cold, short-spoken manner he invited Sir Volfstan to set his men to work and then to come in, take an early dinner and discuss a bit of business. It was thus that he thought of it—Madselin had so well concealed any motive except desire for gain.

To hear the hidden hoard spoken of by the armourer's English wife took Sir Volfstan by surprise.

"What do you know of this matter? And how?" he asked, dropping the elaborate pretence at courtesy with which he usually addressed her.

"I *know* nothing," she said.

"You know what the treasure consists of," he reminded her. "How many other people share that knowledge?" He had never mentioned rubies and emeralds to anyone, and the man who had sold the man and his secret to him had gone back to Normandy.

"The man from whom I heard the rumour is dead," she said.

That was true, in its way: Beodric was dead.

The wretch whom nothing could persuade and this girl's former husband had been near neighbours, Sir Volfstan remembered: and three-fifths of something was better than the whole of nothing. The very way she was looking at him, intent and eager, hungry almost, helped to convince him that she *knew*.

"Your terms are steep," he said, after a little thought. "But I accept them . . . my lady."

"And will sign to that effect?"

"Sign," he said, "sign what?"

She produced the parchment which Giffard had written, hastily and unwillingly, at her dictation.

"It is a contract," she said, "setting down what I must do and what you must do in return. The terms I spoke of . . ."

He bent his thumb in the crook of his first finger and flipped the bit of parchment away.

"Scribbled rubbish," he said. "A man's word is his word. That," he said, with a scornful glance at the parchment, "might, for all I know, entitle you, once I had signed it, to graze a hundred geese on Bemid common. I can make my mark. But I would never put my mark to something of that sort, something which I do not understand."

Then Rolf, who had sat silent, leaving, as he always did when possible, the bandying of words to others, surprised Sir Volfstan by saying, "Very wise. Nor would I."

She was by this time so anxious, so fevered and tremulous, that she could only just manage to say in a calm, judicious voice, "If it is permissible for you to suspect me—and Rolf—of tricking you about geese, Sir Volfstan, you must not be offended if we suspect you about the conditions and the sharing which are set forth in this parchment."

"My word should be good enough," Sir Volfstan said stubbornly.

She saw what a vast difference there was in taking a risk when one had nothing to lose and taking a risk where so much was at stake, but she hesitated for only a fraction of a second.

"Then we will waste no more time on it," she said.

"You will not come to Bemid and question the fellow?"

"No." I have ruined all, she thought, trying to make too sure. She felt sick.

"What I will do," Sir Volfstan said, after a moment's

thought, during which he had looked at the ex-armourer and his English wife with distrust and profound dislike, "is to give you my word, as a knight, in the presence of a knight. That is binding on a man of honour and that is how such things are conducted."

"That I will accept," she said, thinking rapidly. Of the two she trusted Sir Eustace more; doubtless Sir Volfstan favoured Sir Godfrey; and although she could give an order in English, she must use a name. No, she need not. She could simply say to Child, "Find your master and bring him here."

The conditions were simple enough; she dictated them as she had done to Giffard. The man was to be immediately taken out of the place where he was now confined, washed, freshly clad and fed. "So that he is in a condition to be questioned," she explained. "I do not wish to talk to a man reeking of the dungeon."

"Agreed, sir?" Sir Eustace asked.

"I give you my word," Sir Volfstan said.

She was to be allowed a private talk with the prisoner and unlimited time. If the man gave the wanted information he was to be set free at once, and not pursued. Any profit resulting from the interview was to be divided; three-fifths to Sir Volfstan; two-fifths to Rolf.

"All this on your honour as a knight?"

"On my honour as a knight. I swear."

Rolf, though he had hardly spoken, had been observant. Sir Volfstan was, at heart, eager for Madselin's help in this business; perhaps . . . perhaps . . . And another thought struck him. The Rinland had been unbelievably lacking in anything of value; was it possible that for some reason Bemid had been used as a storing place for wealth? Was Madselin out to get possession of what was rightly hers, her heritage from her husband and from her mother? He had a feeling, quite inexplicable, that about this whole bit of business there was something more than he, or Sir Volfstan, knew. Something not concerned with rubies and emeralds.

"It remains," she was saying, "to set a time for this talk. To-morrow?"

"The day after," Sir Volfstan said. "I must be in Cressacre tomorrow."

That night she went to bed happy in the knowledge that Stigand was out of that dreadful hole and had been fed. Two nights from now, if he had anything to tell, he would be free, or in possession of the knowledge and the means to free himself. She fell asleep memorizing the instructions she had wrung out of Frieda. In the morning, refreshed by dreamless sleep and buoyed up by hope, she went about making her secret little preparations and well before dusk said to Hild, "I am going across to the church."

Hild said, "It will do no good. The Norman put his Norman god there. He thirsts for English blood."

"That is nonsense, Hild. There is one God, for English and Norman alike."

"So!" Hild said. "Did he look on English and Norman alike in the battle? And after?" Her voice changed. "But I have taken care of you. It will not be *your* blood."

"What are you talking about?"

"What I know. The god in the Norman's church has a deaf ear for *us*."

Madselin felt an impulse to say—But I am not going to the church to speak into God's ear; I can, I do, call into it all the time, anywhere, God help me to help Stigand; I go to the church too for a practical purpose. But since the moment when Stigand had lifted her down from the branch of the oak tree she had kept her own counsel, and she kept it now.

And so at last, here she was, riding alongside Rolf through a world which fog, combined with frost, had made into something like a fairy tale. All white and glittering, every bush, every branch encased in glass, not quite translucent. It was the seventh day of Christmas. "On the seventh day of Christmas, my true love sent to me . . ." She could no longer remember the exact words of the old singing game . . . seven maids a-milking? Seven swans a-swimming? No matter. She had put such childish things away, together with all thoughts of her true love, when she emerged from the dovecote. But as the horses, on their roughed shoes that made them safe on the frozen ground, picked their way along, her heart sang. On the seventh day of Christmas, I am coming, my love, to set you free.

By her side Rolf rode, disliking his destination. But he had chosen to come. He could have sent either or both the knights, or Giffard, or even the priest; but he had come himself because he felt, as he had felt for the last eighteen years, ever since he was sixteen, that whatever arose, he could deal with it better than most. In this whole business he was out of his depth, participating in something fundamentally distasteful to him, but if anything went wrong . . . he would be there.

They spoke little. Once he said, "It is very cold," and she said, "I am well wrapped." So she seemed, bulky under the fur-lined, fur-trimmed cloak. He said, presently, "Nothing may come of this." And she said, "We shall have tried." He followed his own thoughts for a while and then said, "Whatever comes of it, I plan changes. By June the worst will be over. And I have watched that fellow who went free."

"Yes," she said. "With him Emma and the children could starve but the pigs and fowls were fed and made marketable." She wished that he would ride without talking. *I am about to see Stigand.* She had hardly seen him since his marriage to Gundred, her marriage to Eitel. There had been so little time before the world was overset and she had deliberately avoided encounters.

She listened, without much attention, as Rolf, wrestling with the words, explained what he meant to do whatever the result of this venture. Every man to have his strip in the fields, his own animals and tools. She said, "Yes" and "You are wise" and "So things are done, I understand," but although their horses ran shoulder to shoulder, she riding one and he the other, they were as far apart as England and Byzantium, wherever Byzantium might be. A far place. And as she rode she thought—If Stigand had brought so much as a pearl from that far place . . . he would have given it to me in that little time, in those few happy, happy days. She had started to say to Frieda, "I know, because . . ." and then clipped the sentence short. But she knew that had Stigand brought emeralds and rubies from Byzantium, they would have hung about her neck and wrists, decked her fingers.

Sir Volfstan awaited them. Not himself, she noted almost instantly. Fussy, unconfident. The hall was empty, the table set with the stuff which hospitable people offered to those who arrived between ordinary mealtimes. There was the device which she had seen only in Winchester, a dish on long legs above a candle to keep the contents warm; small sausages and strips of meat and liver taken straight from the spit, placed in an almost red-hot dish. Little cakes. Apples. Wine.

"You have had a cold ride," Sir Volfstan said. "You will take some refreshment? Oh surely . . . Come to the fire then . . ." He would have taken her cloak, but she said, "I may need it." Finally he said, "I fear you have come for nothing, my lady. It is a bad day with him. His moods vary. He is very . . . surly." And all the time he wore such a dubious, sly look and moved things about on the table, and fingered his belt and pulled the lobe of his ear and seemed to wish to delay her, that she felt a mounting sense of something having gone wrong. And she knew that if it had, now at this last stage, she could not bear it.

"Where is he?"

"Through there," Sir Volfstan said, indicating a door.

"Then I will go in."

"Wait," Rolf said. "Is it safe?"

"Chained to the wall. You may see for yourself." He opened the door and looked with concentrated hatred at the man who had, he felt, won in this battle of wills; Rolf looked and was satisfied that the man was harmless, his hands pulled behind his back and manacled and attached by a chain to a staple in the wall. Madselin looked and saw something worse and more pitiable than anything she had imagined by day or dreamed of by night. In every imagined or dreamed-of scene a recognizable Stigand had centred, emaciated, filthy, but bearing a resemblance to the handsome young man she had known. Of him there was nothing left, except, astonishingly, some essence, nothing to do with shape or size or colour. It was possible to think at one and the same time—I should not have known him: and—I should have known him anywhere; from a hundred in like case I could have picked him out.

She had stipulated that he should be clean, and he was, even his head was shaven, the skull curiously knobbed and hollowed. She had bargained for his being reclad; he wore a new homespun tunic, short enough in skirt and sleeve to reveal stick-thin arms and legs with grossly swollen joints. He sat on the floor, his legs stuck out at unlikely angles, his body sagged forward against the pull of the chain.

She said, "Stigand," and he looked at her, without recognition, with a kind of dull terror. "It is Madselin. I am Madselin," she said. Newly brought from darkness, perhaps he did not see well. She moved forward, repeating his name and her own and then, overcome by what closer inspection revealed, said, "My poor love! What have they been doing to you? It is over now. All over . . ." She went down on her knees and put her arm around him. He cowered, growing smaller. He said, "No. No."

"It is Madselin. Come to help you. Stigand, you shall be free." He shuddered under her touch, an animal terror shaking the body even thinner than the old priest's. She withdrew her hand and squatted back on her heels, surveying the wrecked remnants of a man. The useful small tool hidden within her gown was sharp against her breast; the carefully memorized instructions as to how to reach the free men in the forest weighed, heavy and useless, in her mind. She remembered Sir Eustace's remark that the man could not walk a mile; she had attributed this inability to enfeeblement and never thought of legs made useless by the rack. She looked at the hands from which the nails had been torn—recently—and through the sick passion of pity she was still able to think—That was done yesterday; Sir Volfstan thought to forestall me! But over and above such a thought rode the certainty that Stigand could never free himself. And alongside that thought ran another— No man would have suffered so much in order to keep a secret. But since if he were ever to leave Bemid he must be carried out, she reverted, hopelessly, to the line that Sir Volfstan, on the other side of the door, imagined her to be taking.

There was still a link between this broken mind and the words "hidden" and "treasure." They evoked the same response as a touch. "No. No." And the shuddering anticipation of further pain. It was useless to say, "This is Madselin. Stigand, if you know anything, tell me and I swear you shall go free." Something, perhaps the shape of the phrase, aroused a memory and although she did not touch him again he began to scream, weak, pitiable screams like those of a hare going down, after a long coursing, under the hounds' teeth.

She stood up at last; no hurry, she had said that she must be allowed time. She went into the hall. It was difficult to look at the man who had done this to Stigand and retain composure, but she managed it and said, "Even with me, reticent. But we shall get there. Wine would help."

Sir Volfstan, pierced by the thought that never once had he thought of loosening the man's tongue with wine, poured a cup full to the brim. And while he did it she took an apple, red-skinned but wrinkled by winter, and the silver knife that lay beside the dish. She put the blade to the skin of the apple and said, casually, "Blunt. Silver takes no edge. Rolf, lend me your knife." His was always sharp.

Back in the little room she said, "Drink!" And although his own name and hers had seemed to mean nothing, to bring no assurance, and a loving touch had seemed to threaten only further torment, the rim of the cup, pushed against his mouth, had meaning. Possibly thirst had been one of his torments. He drank avidly, sucking and gulping in such a way that she could hardly keep pace in tilting the cup. When it was empty she set it on the floor. She peeled the apple, quartered it, cored it. He ate it, as he had drunk the wine, like an animal. To such a state, she thought, burying all hope, man's cruelty can reduce a man.

She tried once more, her name, his name, promises, persuasions, but in the end even her tough, tenacious mind accepted the hopelessness. So she did the one thing left to do, helped by her memory of seeing a wounded deer dispatched.

Nobody would have believed that in the wasted body there was so much blood. As it ran, spurting and splashing, she thought—Now I shall hang and Sir Volfstan will take vengeance on Rolf and on my child. Murder was no longer, as in the old days, a matter of paying wergild to the dead man's kin. Those who killed were strung up by the neck. But better that than to leave Stigand to the mercy of one who did not know the meaning of the word.

It was over now. Her strength deserted her, her will failed, her resourcefulness was expended. She knelt there and all the tears that she had not shed over the woes of the past year crowded into her eyes and fell, unchecked. She did not look round when the door opened.

Afterwards she marvelled at the way the thing was done; the instant perception; the cunning, the speed. At the time she was conscious of nothing but the fact that she was being roughly handled as Rolf put his arms, one on either side of her body, and braced himself for the most tremendous effort of his life. In what seemed a single gesture he broke the manacle, pulled one skeleton hand free and set it on the haft of the knife, and lifted her and turned to face Sir Volfstan who was in the doorway.

"You said he was safe!" he said, not angrily, but with a cold intensity of accusation more deadly than rage.

"But he was. Chained to the wall," Sir Volfstand said, his voice gone shrill. "What happened?"

"Look for yourself. He might have killed her. Let me pass."

He carried her into the hall and would have set her on a stool by the fire, but she stiffened her knees, her will reviving, she would not sit down under this roof. She stood, held upright by Rolf's arm, and wept and wept, helplessly.

Sir Volfstan, having taken his look, followed them to the fire. "I gave ten marks for him and what he knew. Ten marks."

There was a secret traffic in Englishmen who were supposed to know such secrets, or ply special skills, or even to wield influence over their own.

Rolf said, in his own peculiar fashion of ignoring the most recent remark and following his own train of thought, "What a thing for a woman to witness!"

"She was to blame. In part. She went near and put the knife within reach."

Inside the encircling arm her body drew itself together and the arm around her stiffened in support; it was akin to, a parody of, the response their bodies had made to one another—in bed. She said, still weeping, "Could I throw a cup of wine . . . to a man whose hands were chained?" She braced herself again. "I held him the cup. I began to eat the apple. He craved a piece . . . and then . . . Horrible. . . ."

"All a very great pity," Sir Volfstan said. "He was stunned at Senlac and his memory was imperfect, but given time . . ." For a moment he mourned his wasted ten marks and the wealth they had promised. And then he remembered that stout stone castle and the fact that its owner, negligible, contemptible by every standard of chivalry, went four times a year into the King's presence. He said, "I am sorry."

Rolf said, "You should be. And you should look to your gyves. His were rotten with rust."

CHAPTER NINE

Outside in the deceptive sunshine which so often followed a
night of frost and gave promise of spring and primroses, Rolf
said, "Can you ride? Or ride before me and I will lead your
horse."

"I can ride," she said. She was still crying in the same hopeless way as she had cried beside Stigand, letting the tears fall
into the blood and the peel and the core of the apple. Hopeless
then; and after just enough strength, resolutely mustered, to
tell a tale in support of Rolf's action; now hopeless again.

There, across the commonland, Father Alfleg's house stood,
empty, desolate; as though one old man and one old woman,
merely by being there, breathing, moving about, lighting a fire
and, when night fell, a rush-dip, had held the roof up. She
wept, amongst the multitudinous tears, a few for the old priest
and for Frieda, now bedridden. She wept for her mother, that
stern old woman who had thought—Like father, like son, and
brushed Stigand away, a known spendthrift and perhaps, like
his father, a womanizer. And she wept for Eitel whom her
mother had chosen and she had despised. She wept for herself
for whom, had things gone otherwise, life might have been so
different; and for William, with all his sorrows yet to come.
And suddenly, at that thought her flaccid breasts became tur-
gid, pressing against the useless little trowel, the candle, the
flint and the tinder, all she had meant to give to Stigand. . . .

Rolf said, suddenly breaking the silence, "You must have
loved him very much."

"I did. Long ago. When I was young."

"You were brave," he said.

"No. Desperate. And selfish. While he lived in such misery, I was in misery, too. I have often wished him dead. And now he is. And in Heaven, having served his Purgatory here."

"You gave him the *coup de grâce*. Nothing more. I have given it myself, many times. To men hurt beyond hope." It was a task relegated to such as he, skilled with their hands and not bound by any inconvenient rules concerning one fighting man's duty towards another.

"I have tried every other way," she said. "All I could think of. None served . . ." She cried harder, remembering her failures. Then, with some idea that this last deed needed some justification, she gulped out, between sobs, all she had tried to do.

Had Rolf been handier with words and less in the habit of examining them in order to be sure that they were worth saying, he would then have said—Why did you not turn to me? He had access to the King, and though he was too proud to ask anything for himself he would have asked William's intervention to spare her such misery. But before the words were spoken he had time to think that to say them would be cruel; she would reproach herself forever for not having chosen so simple and obvious a way.

He said awkwardly, "You did your best. It is over now. You must put it away." She thought dully—That should not be too hard; I put Stigand away when he married Gundred; and again when I believed him dead; and now I have, with my own hand, put him away forever.

"You are still young," Rolf said. "You have your child."

In her present weak state she knew a momentary temptation to make the ultimate confession; but what good would that do? And who could be sure? Hild believed what she wanted to believe and probably all babies at birth resembled old men, lacking teeth, lacking hair. And if William were in fact Eitel's son, it was only right that he should inherit what had been his father's. So she said nothing, but the thought came—I owe Rolf a son.

So! her mind said, already you are thinking of the future. Yes, she admitted; I must surely be the most indestructible woman God ever made. Out of the dovecote to keep my secret and outshine the bride; out of Bradwald, a homeless widow on Monday, and back, remarried and reinstalled on Thursday; crushed by each small failure in my attempts to help Stigand, and immediately planning something further. And now, with his blood on my skirt, my sleeves, my hands, thinking of the future.

She gave another sob, a dry, rending one, a prelude to the end of weeping, and her horse, uneasy from the moment she had mounted, started and tossed his head and stepped sideways. He was not used to carrying a rider who smelt of death and shuddered and seemed to have no hold upon the reins. Taken by surprise, she swayed in the saddle. Rolf reached out his hand and took her rein.

She said, "You hurt your hand." The little finger and the one next to it, and all the side of his palm, as far as the wrist, were puffy and purplish red.

"Nothing Giffard cannot mend," he said, shifting his hand a little to remove the hurt from sight.

"Mend? Did you break a bone?"

"Maybe. It will heal. I wronged Sir Volfstan. The fetters were strong."

"You were so prompt. To see at once; to act so quickly. You saved me from hanging." Gratitude and a kind of respect warmed her voice. It was almost her night-time voice.

He said in that dry, flat way which at times only just fell short of ironic humour, "I'm against having my wife hanged."

She thought—I have not been much of a wife to him lately and he broke his hand for me. Other thoughts crowded in by the way that thought had opened. The evening of their first meeting when he had seen that she was hungry, and had been anxious that she should be safe; the many times when he had comforted her, whimpering from a bad dream; his considerate behaviour when she was pregnant; his concern that she should be warm, getting into debt for the hangings. These and a hundred other instances of his care for her flocked into her mind, pointing to the inevitable conclusion. He loved her. He would never be ruled by her, he was incapable of making a pretty speech, but he loved her.

Deep within her, aroused by that thought, a curious excitement began to stir; something she had never known before. In part it was what she had felt when she had kissed and clung to Stigand, but then it had lived in her mind, her inexperienced body ignorant of what shape passion and tenderness could take; in part it was akin to the joy in bed which she had known with Rolf, but that had been purely of the flesh, her mind, in fact, set against him, holding aloof, slightly ashamed and wholly derisive. Now the two blended and she was dazzled by the wonder of it.

She put her hand, very gently, over his and said in her night-time voice, "I will make it up to you, Rolf. Fretting has made me poor company—but if he had been an animal, starved and ill-treated . . . That, and a fondness, long outgrown . . ."

It was the kind of talk which he was not equipped to deal with. But he moved his hand and between the thumb and the two sound fingers, took hers. The night-time touch.

Once the Abbess had said, acidulously, "I fear you have a frivolous mind, Madselin." And she may have been right, Madselin thought, riding into Bradwald, her hand in Rolf's. Only a frivolous woman could have done what I have done and now be making ready to live on and love again. . . .

3